PARIS, MODIGLIANI & ME

JACQUELINE KOLOSOV

LUMINIS BOOKS

LUMINIS BOOKS
Published by Luminis Books
1950 East Greyhound Pass, #18, PMB 280,
Carmel, Indiana, 46033, U.S.A.
Copyright © Jacqueline Kolosov, 2015

ISBN: 978-1-941311-91-2

Printed in the United States of America

10 9 8 7 6 5 4 3 2 1

LUMINIS BOOKS

Meaningful Books That Entertain

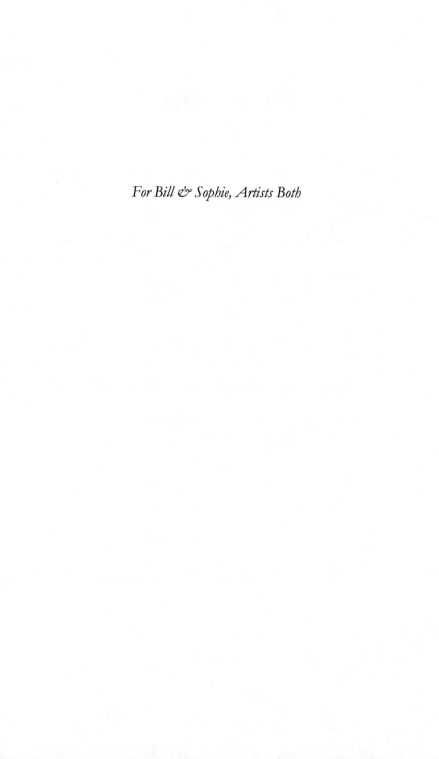

For Bill & Sophie, Artists Both

Advance Praise for *Paris, Modigliani & Me:*

"This story has at its center the most complex joys and struggles of life—love and family and vocation and identity—all set against the beauty of Parisian culture and art. It will carry readers right along with Julie for a taste of first romance and the sweet thrill of searching for both freedom and belonging."

—Kirsten Lunstrum, author of *Swimming with Strangers*

"Jacqueline Kolosov's *Paris, Modigliani & Me* is a delightful trip through the City of Light's art world and into the heart of a girl who is searching for family and love. I highly recommend it!"

—Mary Beth Miller, author of *Aimee* and *On the Head of a Pin*

Praise for *Along the Way:*

"*Along the Way* delivers on a dazzlingly unique premise — three best friends decide to walk the Camino de Santiago, a pilgrimage route that dates to the ninth century. Readers will feel that they're walking in the footsteps of Piper, Tessa and Dani as they experience romance, adventure and a touch of mystery. The combination of humor and heartfelt emotion adds to the appeal of this sparkling story."

—Suzanne Harper, author of *The Juliet Club* and *The Secret Life of Sparrow Delaney*

"Evocative, cinematic, and romantic, *Along the Way* will transport you, taking you on the journey of a lifetime that will test the bonds of three childhood friends."

—Megan Frazer, author of *Secrets of Truth and Beauty* and *Very, In Pieces*

Your real duty is to save your dream.

—Amedeo Modigliani

Part One

One

I HADN'T PLANNED on parting with my art supplies, but when I stood at check-in at United in Houston, the Hercule Poirot-look alike behind the counter told me the flight to Paris was oversold. "Your tackle box, large even for international carry-on, is just too big, mademoiselle. You'll need to check it." His smile was steely, the kind that would brook no argument. I had no choice but to brace myself against the faux wood and watch the tackle box carrying my charcoals, pastels, and sketch pad disappear through the airport vacuum.

Close to fourteen hours later, I stood before the carousel at Charles de Gaulle. Dressed in my grungy jeans and wrinkled handkerchief blouse, I fought the urge to duck into the Ladies to brush my teeth, fearing I'd miss the moment my tackle box appeared through an opening in the wall, this one resembling an oversized dog door. My heart leapt each time a new piece thumped out among the others: a battered red suitcase, faux alligator attaché case, iridescent purple duffel; but disappointment hit again and again, and my mouth felt increasingly muzzy.

If the airline had to lose something, why couldn't it have been my suitcase? Yes, I'd packed the butter soft sandals I'd splurged on and my favorite muslin dress. But even the olive green cloche I wore whenever it rained seemed replaceable when I considered trying to get through the summer without that drawing pad and the pastels I'd bought on my last trip to Utrecht's in Chicago.

My ex-boyfriend Danny, who'd traveled to more countries than I could count on both hands, would have known how to talk to the airlines so that they found my tackle box—fast. What was the word for 'fast' in French? I knew box—*boîte*—but tackle? Why was it none of the Fluency in Five Weeks CDs included the phrase for 'Please find my tackle box. I'm lost without it.'

"At last," a woman in stilettos said when the little opening spit out a leopard-print case.

"Let me get that for you," a bald man said, and set his Chihuahua down on the dirty linoleum.

Something about the dog's sad, brown eyes brought a sick feeling to my stomach, and that pathetically impersonal letter from the Art Institute came flooding back. 'We received an extraordinary number of outstanding applications this year, and I'm sorry to say—'

Bottom line: *You're not going to art school. Kiss your dreams goodbye.*

Tears nipped my eyes, but there was no way on earth I was going to start crying in an airport in Paris my first time overseas, especially not with Claire and Genevieve waiting for me just on the other side of Customs.

I licked my lips, raked my fingers through my snarled hair, and stared at a tattered poster of Tourist's Paris, a collage of the Eiffel Tower, le Arc de Triomphe, and other hotspots.

"Something tells me this belongs to you," the bald man said, placing my tackle box on the ground, his sad-eyed dog watching from the safe perch of his other arm.

"Oh," I said, overjoyed enough to hug him—thankfully I held back. "Thanks."

"*De rien*—think nothing of it." A glimmer came into his gray eyes. "Drink a lot of water and get some rest. Tomorrow Paris will look like Paris. This is the city of light, after all."

"JULIE!" CLAIRE CALLED out, on cue, waving vigorously as soon as I emerged through the maze of plexi-glass.

I waved back. The last time I saw Claire, she'd cut her auburn hair really short, giving her pixie face an angled look. The softer bob suited her better, made her jaw and sharp cheekbones stand out less.

When Mom and Claire were in high school, she'd been small enough for some boys to lock her in a tuba case on a dare. Even now Claire was so little that she and her daughter, Genevieve, who stood beside her in a purple polo shirt and matching cargo skirt—too hip to believe in a ten-year-old—stood nearly eye to eye.

"Hey," I said, as Claire lunged forwards and hugged me so close I breathed in the chamomile scent of her shampoo.

"You're looking good, Julie," Claire said, stepping back to study me. "The Texas sun has turned your hair to gold."

That was generous. My hair was actually the color of sand on an overcast day.

"I can't believe it's been two years since we last saw you."

"Actually," I said, "it's more like three. Mom and I came out to L.A. for that conference, remember? We went to Disneyland, rode the roller coasters too many times. Mom may have even thrown up."

"Oh, right, the air-conditioning broke on the way home," Claire said. "She had that tutti-frutti smoothie."

"I don't remember going to Disneyland with her," Genevieve said.

"Well, you did," said Claire. "You rode the roller coasters and everything."

"I have a photograph of us with Mickey Mouse," I said. "You're holding Mickey's hand."

"Is my dad in the picture?" Genevieve asked.

I shook my head 'no,' thinking about what Claire said when she invited me to Paris. "Genevieve misses her friends, her old school, home, and especially her father."

I'd only met Mark Goodman a handful of times. He had chestnut-colored hair like Genevieve's and the kind of good looks found in men who model underwear in glossy magazine ads, or star in silly sitcoms, which had been his dream, one that came true when he was forty-five. "Just in time," Mom said, "to cover up those first signs of gray, start lifting weights again, and get a tummy tuck."

Genevieve continued to stare, and I tried to think of something to say to her, the kind of breakthrough thing you see in the movies just before the music turns all syrupy, and the characters hug, and you know it's going to be okay, even though there was a car wreck or a bar fight between feuding girlfriends or some other major crisis in the last scene.

"Well," Claire said, reaching for the handle of my suitcase, "we should probably get moving."

"Right," I said.

Claire zigzagged through the crowded airport, Genevieve and I struggling to keep up. Everywhere I heard snatches of English and Japanese and Spanish, but most of the people spoke French (obviously), and all of the ads and signs were in French.

Soon we were crossing two electronic walkways, the railway station's long staircase (downhill, fortunately), and then yet another walkway—this one maybe two blocks long—before we could finally collapse into a trio of red vinyl seats on the train that would take us into the city. "How you holding up?" Claire asked.

"Alright," I said, as three guys about my age with Mohawks in violet, chartreuse, and pink sat down opposite us. Truth was, their hair made my head hurt, and I felt on the verge of total exhaustion.

The train pulled out of the station, and through the foggy window I saw only gray sky and a stretch of weedy ground filled with dull houses.

"Not the postcards people send home, is it?" Claire said.

"Not exactly," I said.

"Don't worry," Claire said. "You'll like our neighborhood. It's only ten minutes from the Seine. If it weren't for the *Invalides*, you could be at the Louvre in less than half an hour."

"Is that a hospital or something?"

Claire laughed. "Hardly. It's the building where Napoleon's buried. It takes up two whole city blocks so you have to walk all the way around it."

"It's the ugliest place in Paris, next to the Opera House," Genevieve added. "That place was built by Playmobile wanna-bes."

"Really?" I said.

I waited for her to say something more, but Genevieve just pressed her face to the window, and stared out at the passing landscape. What was worse, I wondered, to feel like the father you loved had betrayed you (which is how Genevieve must have felt) or to know next to nothing about him?

Until fifth grade, I used to tell people that my parents were divorced and my French father, Gustave Fermiere, lived in Paris. Fact was, I'd never even met him, knew only that he was French and an artist with whom my mom had fallen in love while studying in Paris eighteen years ago. At the end of her holiday, she came back to the States pregnant and alone. She moved back in with my grandmother who started working the evening shift so she could be home with me while Mom taught classes and studied for her doctorate in English at the University of Chicago.

My mother almost never spoke about my father; he was basically taboo; but coming to Paris had made me more determined than ever to try to find him, despite my fears. I mean, what if he said, 'You're whose daughter again?' And when I mentioned Mom, her time in Paris, the dates, he might frown and say, 'Sorry, I'm afraid I don't remember.'

But what if that wasn't how he responded? What if he was overjoyed or at least happy to see me? What if there was some explanation for his absence from my life these last seventeen years?

That chance, howsoever infinitesimal, meant I had to risk it.

The hour long train ride led to another ride on the Metro. At our station, more stairs led up from the fluorescent gloom until at last we were out in the fresh air.

"To your right," said Claire, pointing to a shimmering ribbon of blue-gold, "you can just see the Seine. We might go for a walk on the quay later. And," she said, with a lift in her voice, "if you take the Pont des Arts—the Artist's Bridge, you'll find yourself just opposite the courtyard of the Louvre."

"Fabulous," I said. In the last few weeks I'd practically memorized the Louvre's palatial floor plan and major holdings. It was a dream come true, for all in one place I could find paintings by Titian, David, Rembrandt, and Vermeer.

The magic of the city sank into my skin, and for the first few blocks I believed I could have stayed awake for hours, or more realistically, until we reached the apartment building. There were bakeries with unbelievable-looking pastries and croissants in the glistening windows; and a whole shop devoted to Madeleines, that butter cookie my mom ate by the tin every time she read Proust. Even the graffiti, splashed on the walls of centuries' old buildings, felt like magic.

A busy uphill street led to a quieter one paved with cobblestones, and Claire said, "Well, here we are."

I craned my neck to look up at the gorgeous old stone building, each of its windows bordered by a white box of pink and red geraniums.

"Our apartment is on the fifth floor," Claire explained as an old man in a tailored tweed suit tipped his hat on the way out of a wrought-iron door I knew I'd have to sketch.

Inside the staircase was steep, winding and narrow. "The elevator only holds one person, or one suitcase," Claire said. "We usually take the stairs."

I was hoping she'd let me ride up.

Instead she hoisted the suitcase and the tackle box inside, pushed the button to the fifth floor. By now, I felt like I had sand bags attached to my ankles, but Claire took the stairs two at a time, the pink treads of her sneakers slapping the wood.

Outside the apartment, Claire turned the key in the lock, and a small, bristly-haired black dog bounded into the hall. "Annie," Genevieve said.

The dog glanced at me and wagged her tail, then proceeded to lick Genevieve's face and hands as if she'd been gone for days and not hours.

"She looks just like Toto," I said, bending down to stroke her fur.

"She's a cairn terrier," Genevieve said proudly. "My dad's allergic to dogs, but Mom let me get Annie once we moved here."

"Well," I said, locking eyes with Claire, "it looks like you're the best of friends."

Genevieve beamed. "We are."

"Come on," Claire said, "let's go in."

The apartment was small, but it had high ceilings and long windows with old-fashioned iron panes. One of these windows opened onto a balcony that Claire and Genevieve had filled with pink and red geraniums and a variety of bushy ferns. In the distance, I could actually see the Eiffel Tower.

"I thought France was all about its food," I said, stunned by this kitchen the size of a walk-in closet. A closer look revealed that the faucet actually folded down so you could open the window above.

"It is," Claire said, "but apartments are ridiculously expensive. Most people can't afford a real kitchen. The take-out business here is booming. Imagine trying to put together a soufflé or something more complicated in this kind of space."

"Oh, I see." The picture of me whipping up a flan or mastering the art of French bread began to crumble.

"Genevieve," Claire said, "do you want to show Julie your room?"

"Okay," Genevieve said, motioning for me to follow.

With Annie at our heels, we walked down a narrow hallway off the living room.

"Mom's room is on the right," Genevieve said, and I looked in at a simply-made up bed and single dresser; behind them, floor-length windows through which the sun danced among a few dust motes.

"My room is across the hall from the bathroom," Genevieve said.

I ducked my head inside. There was a claw-footed tub that looked straight out of another century. The last time I'd seen a tub like this was in Oma's old house in the city; the very sight of it filled me with warmth.

When Genevieve opened the door to her bedroom, I expected a closet-sized room to match the closet-sized kitchen, but this room turned out to be big and airy with natural wooden floors and beautiful pale yellow wallpaper decorated with columns of pink flowers that reminded me of wind-blown peonies. A white desk sat in front of the window, its surface littered with what looked like cut-outs from *Teen Vogue, Elle*, and other magazines. More pictures—of hairstyles, cigarette slim pants, poodle skirts with a modern twist, and half a dozen different purses—were tacked to a huge, pink-edged bulletin board just above. So Claire hadn't been exaggerating when they'd said that Genevieve was majorly into fashion.

"It looks like she's inherited my grandmother's talents, wouldn't you say?" Claire said, joining us.

"Sorry?" I said.

"My grandmother, Genevieve's namesake, was a seamstress."

"She worked for Coco Chanel," Genevieve said casually, as if every ten-year-old had heard of Coco Chanel.

"Briefly," Claire said, "but yes, we have a photograph of the two of them in one of the old family albums."

Along the opposite wall, there were two beds. A wicker basket with a mint green pillow, which I took to be Annie's bed, stood between them. "This is where I sleep," Genevieve said, sitting down on and settling against the pillows. "That bed will be yours."

It was a trundle bed with a lumpy looking mattress. No matter: one look at the soft, white duvet and the mass of pillows, and the jet lag really kicked in.

"Why don't we let you get settled and have a nap?" Claire said, appearing in the doorway. "Afterwards we can have some lunch, take a walk to the Luxembourg Gardens, or if you're not up to that, there's Rodin's house which has an incredible sculpture garden. It's just down the street."

"*The* Rodin?" I said, for I'd copied his statue of the banished Adam and Eve at the Met.

"That's right. It's a ten minute walk."

Two

"MORNING," CLAIRE SAID, startling me as she came up from behind where I sat sketching the wrought iron balcony and the buildings beyond.

She was bundled into a big, white terrycloth robe imprinted with the logo of some hotel. Mom said Claire was fond of accidentally packing—she never said *stealing*—hotel goodies like fluffy towels, a glass alarm clock—when she checked out of boutique hotels.

"Hey," I said, curled into one of the cream-colored armchairs with my drawing pad, my tackle box open on the floor beside me, colored pencils everywhere.

She scanned the coffee table that held my second cup of hot cocoa and the remains of a second buttery croissant, proof of how quickly I'd made myself at home. "How long have you been up?"

"Since four," I said, reminded of how gross it had felt to wake in the same grungy jeans and dirty blouse—thirty six hours without a change of clothes or a bath, though at least I'd brushed my teeth just before exiting Customs. "What time is it anyway?"

"Just after seven, but don't worry, you'll sort the time change out soon enough. I remember my first trip to Paris. I kept waking up at two a.m. for the first four days, craving breakfast. I came with your mother, the year we graduated."

"Yeah, she told me." I almost added 'like a million times,' so often had I seen Mom's photographs outside Notre Dame, and heard the story about the triple scoops of ice cream at a fancy café followed by a foot-long baguette. ("We were starving and couldn't afford a real lunch.")

"I like what you've done with that drawing," Claire said, sitting down on the coffee table beside me, her hair brushing my cheek as she leaned in for a closer look. "Your choice of perspective—the way you've set the houses against the backdrop of the balcony design. The juxtaposition of patterns: rooftops against chimney pots, balcony against sky."

"Thanks. We worked a lot on perspective in that studio class I took last semester. Figure drawing mostly, a few experiments with oils."

"Your mom sent me one of them—a woman with an elongated neck. I felt sure I saw the influence of Modigliani."

"Yeah, I remain a major fan," I said, remembering not only my passion for Picasso's contemporary, but how sure I'd been back then that I'd have my work shown at some gallery by the time I was twenty-five.

But then I received that letter from the Art Institute; one read-through crumbled my vision of living in one of the dorms off Lake Shore Drive, buying my supplies at Utrecht's, and waiting tables at the Third Coast in between classes.

CLAIRE HAD SCRAMBLED up a plate of eggs and toasted a day-old baguette which she served with sweet butter and strawberry jam, before Genevieve padded into the room wearing a Betty Boop t-shirt that reached all the way to her knees, her small feet upholstered in the fluffiest, pinkest slippers I'd ever seen.

"Those are majorly cool," I said, a little blinded by their screaming pinkness.

"They're a big thing right now," Claire said.

"They're the kind of slippers Eloise would have worn," I added.

"Who?" Genevieve said.

"Don't tell me you don't know Eloise, the girl from the story book, the one who lives at the Plaza Hotel?"

Genevieve shrugged. "Sorry, no."

"Well," I said, "we'll have to find an English bookstore and fix that."

"Okay," Genevieve said, "as long as I can pick out another book."

"Great idea," Claire said. "Genevieve could stand to work on her reading."

"I do read, Mom."

"*Elle*," Claire said, "*Teen Vogue*."

"Give me a break. These are summer holidays, time to rest and all that," Genevieve said, tapping her feet together. "You know, they sell these slippers at Bon Marché. Maybe we should go and get Julie a pair."

"Bon Marché, huh, sweetheart?" Claire said. "Weren't we there on Friday?"

"So, it's a historic landmark Julie has to see."

"Uh huh," Claire said.

"Please," Genevieve said, spooning out a dollop of strawberry jam, which she ate straight from the jar, then went back for another.

"Very well."

"We're going to walk the Rue de Sevres, right?" Genevieve said.

"Yes."

"So we can stop at Monsieur Rimbaud's?"

"I suppose," Claire said. And to me: "Perhaps the most remarkable antique shop on a street of remarkable antique shops. There's a wooden doll's house Genevieve's had her eye on forever."

"I want to repaint the outside yellow," Genevieve said, "and green shutters. I want to put on green shutters."

From the way Claire was looking at Genevieve, I had this feeling she was describing her old house in L.A.

SOME TWO HOURS later, we found ourselves inside the antiques shop where turn-of-the-century dolls with porcelain faces and jointed teddy bears shared window space with footstools, gilt picture frames, and heaps of old jewelry. There was even a fat marmalade tabby drowsing on a small rug in the sun.

"Madame Goodman," said a white-haired man with a neatly curled mustache and the bushiest eyebrows I'd ever seen. "I've been expecting you and Genevieve. My dear girl," he said, nodding at her t-shirt and leggings, "it's good to see a girl who can wear chartreuse."

Genevieve made a theatrical curtsy.

"And who is this?" Monsieur Rimbaud asked, turning his pale blue eyes on me.

"Julie Hankla, my best friend's daughter," Claire said. "She's here to spend time with Genevieve during the summer holidays."

"Splendid, splendid. By the way," he offered Genevieve a toffee from the decanter, "someone inquired about the doll house just yesterday, but I told them it was sold."

"We never promised—" Claire began.

"You didn't have to," the old man said. "I've been in this business long enough to know when a particular piece is destined for somebody."

"It's still here then?" Genevieve asked.

"But of course," he said, stroking his mustache. "How could I give this house to anyone other than a girl whose great-grandmother worked for the legendary Coco, a girl who can wear clothes in the manner of a true Parisian, one who shares her name with the patron saint of Paris?"

"Really?" I said, though I thought he was laying it on a little thick. "There was actually a St. Genevieve?"

"*Oui*, while still a girl, she saved the city of Paris from Attila the Hun."

I wanted to hear more about this St. Genevieve, but Monsieur Rimbaud turned on his heel, and Genevieve skipped after him. We passed a pair of enormous armchairs upholstered in purple velvet, an umbrella stand shaped like a flamingo, and countless armoires, until we reached the back of the shop.

There, tucked away on a dusty shelf above an old-fashioned bicycle stood a two-story doll house with what looked like an authentic tin roof. Like all well-made things, this one had been made from wood. Up close it had a sweet, musty smell. The house had four rooms, each bearing a window of what looked like real glass. The paint in places was worn away, and the staircase, also of wood, needed mending, but there was no doubt it once was and could be beautiful again.

"It's a marvelous piece, but it will require some work. Since there is no furniture, I will make you a very good price." Monsieur Rimbaud talked as if selling the house was actually a gift. "Unless you would like to see some doll furniture? I have some exquisite pieces from a recent estate sale, true works of art."

Genevieve fixed her bright eyes on Claire.

"That sounds too expensive," Claire said.

"I could help Genevieve make some furniture," I volunteered.

Monsieur Rimbaud raised his enormous eyebrows and smiled at me. "You are a young person good with your hands, I see. Am I mistaken, or are those paint stains on your fingers?"

"It's paint." I held out my hands, spread the fingers wide.

"Julie is an artist," Claire said.

He continued to stroke the edges of his mustache and gazed at me thoughtfully. "Well then, you'll have to come back and see me sometime. While I was growing up in Montparnasse, many artists would come into my grandfather's café in the late afternoons and evenings."

"Where in Montparnasse?" I asked, as if I actually knew that neighborhood.

"Just around the corner from the Académie de la Palette," he added.

Claire leaned against an old table, clearly interested. "Who were the artists?"

"Brancusi, Soutine. That one, my grandfather said, had the worst manners. He used to come in and eat sausages with his fingers. And then there was the beautiful Sonia Delaunay, with her vibrant palette and her hypnotic laugh, sometimes even Picasso."

"Then Modigliani must have come, too," I added, reminded of the hours I'd spent studying his work at the Art Institute in that last year before we left Chicago.

"Yes, but not very often. That one preferred places where the wine was cheaper. Still, when he came, he'd sit at a table just off the street and sketch, no matter the weather. If someone admired his drawing, he'd give it to them. If someone wanted to pay him for it, well—" He shook his head.

"What?" I said. "What did he do?"

"He'd tear the picture up right before their eyes. Meanwhile, he had a wife and child at home. The wife, just a girl really, came to find him at the café sometimes. My grandfather was terribly sorry for her. They weren't well off. He should have taken the money."

"What about the doll's house?" Genevieve asked.

Monsieur Rimbaud's eyebrows waggled, two enormous caterpillars. "Do you want to take it with you now?"

"That's probably the best way," Claire said. "We could take a cab."

"No, no," said Monsieur Rimbaud. "My grandson is here. He will give the dollhouse and all of you a lift home."

It was clear, from Genevieve's bright eyes, she wouldn't mind if we now skipped the trip to Bon Marché and my happy, pink Eloise slippers.

"Paul Henri," Monsieur Rimbaud called.

I pictured someone older, but the grandson who emerged from the back was twenty at the most. He was very tall and thin, with pitch black hair that fell across his high forehead; and the kind of nose found in medieval portraits of men with names like Charlemagne or Richard the Lion-Hearted. His eyes were as blue as his grandfather's, and they seemed even bluer against his gray t-shirt and faded jeans.

"Paul Henri," the old man said. "He helps me out some Sundays."

"*Bon jour,*" Paul Henri said, taking us all in at a glance.

"I'm Claire Goodman," she said, holding out a hand. "And this is my daughter, Genevieve, and our friend, Julie."

His blue eyes met mine, and I felt myself blush.

"Julie is an aspiring artist," Monsieur Rimbaud said.

"Ah," Paul Henri said, as if his grandfather had just said I liked to eat raw eggs or collected gum ball machine jewelry.

"I had hoped Paul Henri would choose to study at the Académie de la Palette," said Mr. Rimbaud. "But he has other ideas."

I was dying to hear why someone would turn down the chance to study art in Paris, but Paul Henri lifted the doll house, and so I had no choice but to follow him and Monsieur Rimbaud out back where a vintage silver Renault was parked.

PAUL HENRI DROVE expertly through the crowded streets, weaving around slower cars, and managing to dodge a swerving cyclist. He must have pressed his palm to the horn six times in the three miles between the shop and Claire's apartment, getting out of the way of a huge truck that thrust itself into traffic and setting off horns from every car within earshot.

"It's like it came out of nowhere," Claire said anxiously, so I thought of that first day when I nearly stepped into traffic, and she pulled me back to the curb.

Once inside the apartment building, it took forever for the elevator to arrive. "These old-fashioned buildings," Paul Henri said, as if the elevator were alive.

At last its accordion doors rumbled open and a diminutive, gray-haired lady stepped out. In each of her arms she held a poodle: one white, the other ginger-colored. I expected them to bark, but they just gazed at us from the fragile perch of her arms.

"Bonjour, Madame Fourniac," Paul Henri said, tipping his head in her direction, as if this were the end of the nineteenth century instead of the start of the twenty-first.

"Paul Henri! So it is you," she laughed. "I did not see you there."

We may have been in Paris, but at that moment the city seemed small, the way our old Chicago neighborhood, Hyde Park, with its cooperative bookstore and its postage stamp park, could seem small. It had been more than five years since we'd left, but I still missed it.

"Be sure to have your grandfather call me when he gets in the Sevres plates," I heard Madame Fourniac say, thrilled at how much French I understood.

She left with her dogs, and for the next few minutes Paul Henri and Claire struggled to get the doll house inside the elevator. But it just wouldn't fit so that the doors would close.

"It will be safer if I take the stairs," Paul Henri said, then carried the doll house up all five flights without stopping, and without arriving at the top out of breath, which was more than I could say.

"Put it down here," Genevieve said excitedly, clearing the coffee table of its art books.

After he did, Paul Henri stepped over to the balcony window and looked out at the view. "I did not realize you could see le Tour Eiffel from here. Have you been up to the top yet?" he said, turning to me.

I shook my head, pictured the two of us peering out at the city together—was he going to offer to take me? But Paul Henri just continued to stare out into the distance, his profile calling attention to his aquiline nose.

"What will we make first?" Genevieve interrupted.

"The things dolls can't live without, of course," I said.

"A table and chairs then," Genevieve said, "and beds with blankets and real pillows."

"And a sink, and a claw-footed bathtub," I added. "We could make these out of modeling clay."

"And a chandelier," Genevieve said. "I want a chandelier with two crystal doves."

This had to be the chandelier in her old house. It was gorgeous, and when the light poured through, the blue-gold of the doves' wings cast patterns on the walls. What had become of it?

"There's a shop around the corner that sells glass animals," Paul Henri volunteered. "You might improvise—"

"Great idea," I said, hoping to learn more about him, and what about the Eiffel Tower? "Your grandfather said you live close by."

"On the Impasse des Deux Anges. It's about five long blocks from here."

"The Street of Angels?" I said, proud of my translation.

"The Impasse of Two Angels," he said, brusquely. "*Mine* is not a thru street."

"Right," I said, just as Claire came back with a tray of Cokes and Chex Mix—who would have guessed you could find Chex Mix in Paris.

The Eiffel Tour forgotten, talk now turned to L.A.

"I've always wanted to see that big 'Hollywood' sign on the side of a mountain," Paul Henri said.

"Really?" Claire said. "How come?"

"It's so American. But with all those earthquakes, don't people worry about the letters toppling on their homes?"

Claire shrugged. "The sign's made it through several quakes without budging."

"And you?" Paul Henri said to me. "Are you also from L.A.?"

"Chicago, but I live in Texas now," I said, my mouth mortifyingly full of Chex Mix.

"Such a big country," Paul Henri said. "My father was born in Montreal, but his parents moved to Detroit when he was small."

Paul Henri's cell phone rang, and soon he was talking so fast in French that I could not follow. "It's Grandpère," he said, clicking his phone shut.

"Is it serious?" Claire asked.

"A small emergency involving an incomplete set of Limoges china. The client is one of Grandpère's oldest—and his most particular. She needs seventy-five place settings for her daughter's wedding, and she's short nearly a dozen bowls and teacups."

Claire smiled. "You do take your work very seriously."

"I must. The business will be my own one day. Besides," he said, "my grandfather counts on me."

"Thank you for the Coke. Enjoy the doll house," he said to Genevieve. "My grandfather is an excellent salesman, but what he said to you was sincere. He believed the house was intended for you. Be happy with it."

Genevieve beamed.

To me, Paul Henri just nodded and said, "Enjoy your stay here."

Three

Dear Julie,

I just knew, as soon as Claire suggested it, the time in Paris would be positive. Travel, life in another place—both should help bring you a wider perspective.

Just remember, sweetie, Austin College needs an answer by early July. I know it's not what you hoped for, but it's a solid school. And think of how you're going to feel if you stay in Lubbock all next year. Sure, you can take a few art classes at the university; you can continue to work for Amber. But each and every one of your friends will be going away to college. Give this some serious thought now that you're in another country, and try to imagine what your next year will be like. Okay?

Oh, Danny stopped by with popovers (your recipe).

Love,
Mom

I shot back a quick email and made a definite point not to bring up Danny. Sure, he and Mom got on famously; she adored him and had been one reason why we'd stayed together so long; but who would have thought he'd show up after I left with popovers? I mean, he had his own mother to bake for. I should never have taught him how to make them, but at the time—one Saturday afternoon after we watched *Titanic* on TV—it had seemed like a good idea. (Thanks to my mom, I'd always been a sucker for period films.)

"Julie?"

Genevieve was standing in the hallway in her hot pink slippers, the bristle-coated Annie at her heels. "So you're up already."

"Since seven."

She grinned, came closer. "That means you'll pass."

I searched her face. "Huh?"

"The garbage trucks—on Tuesdays, they come by about six. They woke me up for like the first two months we lived here. Mom thought we might have to move, but I got used to it. If you slept through the garbage trucks, and the car alarms they always set off, you can sleep through anything."

"What else can I expect?"

"All night parties if France wins in soccer," she said, crossing her legs and kicking her hot pink feet, so that it looked like a pair of Dr. Seuss creatures were dancing. "There are always drunk teenagers shouting or sobbing on the days of major sporting events, and holidays. And Monsieur LeBoeuf."

"Who?" I said. "You're seriously telling me there is a person named Monsieur LeBoeuf? Doesn't that mean 'beef'?"

"Yeah, it does. He's that beautifully-dressed old man who's always tipping his hat to us whenever we see him."

"No way: what could he possibly do?"

Genevieve giggled. "When Monsieur LeBoeuf and his wife get into a fight, she locks him out of the apartment, and he stands on the street calling her name: 'Francoise, Francoise…' Sometimes, he serenades her with his guitar."

"Right," I said, wondering if Monsieur LeBoeuf was copying a classier version of Stanley Kowalski in *A Streetcar Named Desire*, the play of every high school drama teacher's choice.

"Anyway," Genevieve said, "this being our first day and all, I thought we could go to the bakery for breakfast."

"Why not?" I said. "And you haven't shown me the Luxembourg Gardens yet. Maybe we could go there afterwards?"

"Cool." She looked down at Annie. "You'd like that, huh?"

The dog wagged her tail.

Ten minutes later we stood on the street, the sky so bright everything stood out in bold outlines, from the creamy stone of our building to the cobblestones. The neighborhood glowed, and for the first time it really clicked why people were always going on about the light in Paris. It was incredible, as if a huge rain had just washed the city clean and launched the sun.

Little by little, Genevieve began telling me about her friends here. "There's Celeste and Nina, but Margaret's my best friend. Her mom works for a fashion designer, and she makes Margaret the coolest clothes, the kind of thing that makes the latest issue of *Paris Vogue* look ancient.

"One day," Genevieve continued, "Margaret's mom said she'd help me mock up my own design. It's going to be a sort of laid back version of John Galliano."

"Who?"

She stopped in the middle of the sidewalk, and a boy in leather shorts nearly knocked into her. "I can't believe you haven't heard of him. I mean, he's only one of the most amazing designers around. He dresses Madonna, and he made Giselle Bündchen's wedding dress."

"Giselle who?"

"The Brazilian model who married that quarterback; honestly, Julie, I thought you'd be more with it."

"I'll try," I said, trying to imagine what Genevieve would be like at seventeen.

We walked on, past the huge outlet store that carried designer clothes in unpopular sizes, and right beside it, a cooperative garden where Parisians could buy a plot of ground to farm. Most were filled with vegetables and herbs, but I spotted one devoted entirely to hollyhocks, bright, happy flowers that Oma had loved.

A man waved to us from an old-fashioned black bicycle with big white tires, and then we took a couple of funny turns that it would take a while to learn by heart before the candy cane-striped awning of the bakery–or *patisserie*—on the Rue Clare stood before us. "Come on, girl," Genevieve said to Annie.

"You mean she's coming in, too?" I said.

"Paris isn't like the States," Genevieve said. "Dogs are welcome pretty much anywhere so long as they're well-behaved, and Annie here is the best."

At the sound of her name, Annie wagged her tail and followed us inside where we bought two fist-sized brioche and a *pain au chocolat*.

"Oh-my-god, will you look who's here. Genevieve!" someone called out as we were leaving.

Genevieve looked up, frowned. "Oh, hi Pilar."

Dressed in a white mini-skirt and a tacky tank top sporting a rhinestone kitten, the chocolate-eyed Pilar looked a lot older than ten, and she was with a boy who looked closer to my age.

"Clay Ranger," he said, tipping his baseball cap my way.

"You're American?" I said.

"From Boston." With his carrot-colored hair and smattering of freckles, he looked like one of those Norman Rockwell guys in a cute, old-fashioned way.

"Clay's dad's the assistant headmaster at my school," Genevieve said.

"And my father's the headmaster," Pilar said, her pert little chin held high.

The wind snatched the napkin from Pilar's hand, and Clay dashed after it, his sneakers tapping on the pavement.

"Cleats?" I said when he joined us again.

"Cycling shoes," he explained. "I'm training for the Dordogne race next month."

"But you're not biking now, are you?" I said.

Clay flushed a shade just a little redder than his hair. "Let's just say I'm a little obsessive and leave it at that. The cleats," he tapped his heels against the pavement, "you might say the cleats reassure me."

Like my tackle box, I realized, reminded of that panicked feeling at Charles de Gaulle.

I would have liked to talk to Clay, but Pilar was giving Genevieve's denim dress the once over in that universally mean way of certain girls. "Well," I said, an idea coming to me on the spot, "we'd better get going, or we'll be late."

For just a minute, Genevieve looked at me blankly. "We will?"

I laughed, nudged her. "Our haircuts, remember? The stylist on—"

"Rue de Bac," Genevieve said, suppressing a huge grin.

"You actually know someone there?" Pilar said.

"Paul Henri," I said, spitting out the first French name that came to mind. "I can't believe you haven't heard of him: a friend of a friend, if you know what I mean. He's very exclusive."

"Oh yeah," she said at last. "I've heard of him."

The carrot-haired Clay grinned and said, "Have fun!"

Once we broke away from them, Genevieve grabbed my hand, and Annie began to yap merrily. "That was so great. Did you see Pilar's face? She totally believed you."

"Yeah," I said, "she did." In a way I felt as if, in astonishing Pilar, I wasn't just bonding with Genevieve, I was also managing to get some small revenge on the girls I'd met like her over the years.

Genevieve and I laughed most of the way to the Luxembourg Gardens, Annie quick on our heels and occasionally bounding ahead, tugging Genevieve along with her. We stopped to look in shop windows, pressing our noses to the glass to get a better look at hats or jewelry or shoes. At a hat shop—'a milliner's,' Genevieve corrected me—I fell in love with a bell-like creation made out of white velvet.

"You want to go in?" Genevieve asked.

I stared longingly at the hat, pictured myself wearing it at some café while I sat and sketched.

But the shop—with it silk shantung curtains and winking, crystal chandelier—was obviously way out of my price range. "In another lifetime," I said.

"Okay, well, maybe we'll come back when they have a sale."

"Maybe," I replied, but I knew that even then I could never afford it.

Not far from the garden, we bought bubble gum and penny taffy from a street vendor, paused to gawk at row upon row of handmade scarves that a coffee-skinned woman with a face like an Egyptian statue had laid out along the street. Standing before her, I tried to memorize her features so I could sketch her later.

"Vous voudrais les foulards?" she asked, standing behind her display, her own clothes so colorful and flowing, especially the waterfall layers of her skirt, they looked as if they'd been made from a hundred scarves.

"Very much," I replied, torn between a turquoise length of crinkly silk and a watercolor-delicate floral.

In the end, I bought the silk.

Genevieve chose something silvery and soft and on special for two Euros. As soon as the woman cut the price tag, Genevieve twirled it around her neck. "Aren't you going to wear yours?"

"Of course," I said, feeling instantly more Parisian as I put it on.

"That color makes your eyes pop," Genevieve said.

"Does it?" I said—without a doubt, Genevieve was going to be a force in the fashion world.

"See those golden gates." Genevieve pointed to an elaborately fenced garden at the end of the Rue des Fleurs. "That's it."

I grabbed her hand, suddenly feeling about ten years old myself. "Let's run!"

In the Luxembourg, sunlight filtered through the chestnut trees' leaves and dappled the pebble path. It was like stepping into an Impressionist painting. If someone had given me a parasol and a ruffled bonnet, I could have been Berthe Morisot's daughter, Julie Manet, out for inspiration, drawing pad in hand. I could have been Berthe Morisot herself; or better yet, Mary Cassatt, the only American woman to work among the French Impressionists, and someone whose paintings I'd been looking at on the walls of the Art Institute since just about forever.

Children's laughter lilted through the air, a girl on a bicycle pedaled past, dinging her bell, and happiness surged through me, washing away the email residue from my mom.

"The carousel is over there on the other side of the tennis courts," Genevieve said, before bending down to let Annie finish off her cone.

I expected a merry-go-round like the ones in the summer carnivals at home, gaudy confections with lots of lights and too many colors. But this was something straight out of the nineteenth century. There were horses and camels, even a unicorn and a sort of pelican with outlandish wings. The children riding the animals each held a little rod—or wand, and as they passed the carousel master, they tried to reach for the bronze ring in his outstretched hand.

"Ever seen anyone catch it?" I asked Genevieve.

She shook her head, entranced, and I was really surprised—was this wide-eyed little girl the same Genevieve who earmarked pages in *Vogue*?

"Do you want to ride the carousel?" I asked when the children climbed down, and the carousel master, whose broad grin revealed two missing front teeth, called to those waiting in line.

"Do I!"

We bought a ticket, and then she hooked her legs over a fantastic bird with rainbow-colored wings and gold-tipped plumage. Every time she neared the carousel master's ring, she held out her rod, and as she reached, I found myself wishing she would catch it!

My mom, who often taught novels like *Emma* and *Jane Eyre*, novels that focused on a child growing up (*Bildungsroman* being the official word), talked about how much it mattered to really have a childhood.

"It might seem like a long time," Mom told her students at the start of each term, "but if you take a longer view, twelve, fifteen years is just a fraction of a person's life. And those years have to be full enough to sustain a person through the tough times. It's childhood one draws upon. The stories we'll read will help us understand that. *And* the stories we live," she always added.

Once more I thought about my absent father, and then a strange fear, something like panic, seized hold of me, as up through the depths returned that terrible time Missy Millhouse, a girl I thought was my close friend, told everyone in my fourth grade class that I didn't have a father.

"Is it true?" Bruce Schwartz asked when I came into the classroom to find all seventeen kids staring at me.

"What?" I asked, shocked by the meanness in his voice.

"That you never met your dad?"

The seventeen pairs of eyes pressed even closer, and even though no one else said a thing, I felt sick, and desperate. Never ever would I come back. I couldn't bear it—those awful staring eyes. I spent the lunch hour locked in a stall in the girls' bathroom, and the rest of the day I could barely speak.

That night, I told my mom I was sick. I wound up staying in bed for two days before a friend's mother phoned with the truth. "You had me terribly worried," my mom said, squeezing my wrists a little too tightly.

Mom loaded me up with B vitamins to help calm me (a health phase she went through), and I went back to school. The kids looked at me strangely, but no one mentioned my father again. I couldn't explain it, but I understood, then, that I would just have to live with the fact that I didn't have a father or any clear reason why he hadn't wanted to be a part of my life.

The carousel went round and round, and Genevieve tipped her head back and laughed, her dark braids flying out behind her. I took out my drawing pad and began to sketch, trying to tame the emotions surging through me. I held the pencil steady, quickly marking out Genevieve's small figure, the lines of the carousel, the scene in the background.

AFTERWARDS, WE COLLAPSED into some lounge chairs beside the boat pond. God knows how long I slept, for the sun glowed tangerine by the time I awoke, the concerns about my father pushed to the furthest reaches of my mind. Meanwhile, Genevieve continued to sleep beside me. The number of people sailing boats had dwindled to a handful while the number of ducks were out in droves. Cigar-shaped chimney swifts were zipping up and down in search of insects.

Soon I was drawing Genevieve, my pencil sashaying across the paper, light and quick. I began with her cat-bright green eyes, trying to capture the lush dark of her lashes and the faint crescent of freckles just beneath her left eye. Only now did I notice the tiny scar beneath Genevieve's lip. When I asked her about it much later, she told me a friend's brother had pushed her into the coffee table when she was four—"six stitches." That was the magical thing about drawing, the way it enabled me to really see something, or someone, for the first time. Once I finished, I turned to the faces around me. I drew a woman and a little boy sitting nearby. I didn't know enough to say if she was his mother or his nanny, but the fact that I was sketching a subject that had attracted artists since just about forever gave me a special feeling of connection.

Something about the set of the little boy's shoulders told me all I needed to know about his passion for the boat pond. The way the woman kept brushing a stray lock of hair off her face suggested that her mind was on something else or maybe she just wanted to be on their way. When they got up to leave, she caught my eye and smiled.

I finished the sketch as best I could and searched for my next subject.

"Lovers," I said aloud when I spotted them. "What could be more Parisian than that?"

The frizzy-haired woman in a nearby chair looked up from her book to stare. Had she heard me? Had she understood? I couldn't see the man's face, for he was obscured by the woman sitting on his lap, her back to me. Her auburn hair was the kind one sees in shampoo ads. All I saw of him were his hands. Even at this distance, I could tell his fingers were long.

Pretty soon I was filling in the background: the urns overflowing with geraniums and petunias along the staircase leading to the tea shop, a potted palm—yes, the Luxembourg Gardens was full of tropical plants and trees; a bicycle leaning against the wall.

Then the woman stood up.

And that's when I saw him. Paul Henri.

Genevieve's heart-shaped sunglasses were resting on her belly. I grabbed them.

What I didn't count on was Genevieve waking at precisely that moment. "*Bonjour*," she cried out as Annie yapped noisily. "Look, Julie," she said, so loudly everyone within twenty feet could hear her. "It's Paul Henri!"

'Please don't let them come over here,' I prayed.

Of course they stood and started towards us.

"I thought I recognized you," Paul Henri said, his expression more a smirk than a smile.

"I'm Marie France," the girl at his side said, her eyes the violet blue of early morning, as she extended a hand graced by a single, perfect pearl ring. A gift from Paul Henri?

"Julie," I said, still hiding behind the heart-shaped sunglasses.

"How are you enjoying the doll house?" Paul Henri asked Genevieve.

"I love it," she rushed on to tell him about our plans to look for a craft store before we walked back to the apartment.

"There's a lovely place just two blocks from here," Marie France said, then sketched a rough plan on my drawing pad.

"Marie France's parents run an old hotel nearby," Paul Henri added. "She probably knows every shop and restaurant in this district."

"He exaggerates." Marie France began rummaging through her perfect little handbag for what looked like a business card. "Still, if you need any help, call me." A wide smile. "Anytime."

Four

"Julie, right?" I looked up from the display of books just outside of Shakespeare & Company. It was the ultra-fit guy with the carrot hair from a few days ago, the one who'd been with Pilar; at his feet a trio of tiny apple-headed Chihuahuas with bulging eyes, none of which could have weighed more than four pounds. One wagged its tail.

"Clay," he said, tip-tapping over in his cycling shoes. "Clay Ranger."

"And your friends?" I pointed to the bright-eyed dogs.

"Meet Piñata." He pointed to the fattest of the three, a boisterous-looking dog with a shiny black coat. "And these are her daughters: Chloe and Esmeralda."

"Those are pretty wild names," I said.

"Chloe was named for Chagall's daughter," Clay said. "My mother is all about Chagall, and now that my sister and I are older, she's all about Chihuahuas."

"And Esmeralda?" I asked, as an old gentleman dressed entirely in seersucker grinned at the dogs.

"My mother's favorite girl's name. She grew up watching *Bewitched* reruns."

I twitched my nose.

Clay laughed. "You're not serious? You know *Bewitched*, too?"

"What can I say? My mom was a fan, too."

"Cool. Point: Dad wouldn't let her name my sister Esmeralda, so—"

"What's your sister's name?"

"Mickey."

"As in the mouse?"

"As in the actor," Clay said, nudging the ground with the toe of his shoe. "Mom had a thing for Mickey Rooney that year."

"You mean that short guy? Wasn't he in some movie about a horse?"

"*The Black Stallion.*"

"Your mom sounds like a trip," I said.

"She is that," Clay said, toeing the ground, "if you mean a trip to Mars or Bolivia or Chihuahua, Mexico. She's totally obsessed with these dogs and has started breeding them."

"Here in Paris?" I asked, picturing one of the old apartments filled with these dogs. They were known to be barkers—what did the neighbors say?

Clay nodded. "Piñata's sister just had a litter. Interested?"

I shook my head. "I'm only here for the summer."

"Yeah, well, no worries. My mom is what you'd call 'enterprising.' She'll find good homes for all six of them before they're weaned. People think the British are bad, but in my opinion the French have them beaten hands down. They're obsessed, and the more foreign the breed the better." My laughter seemed to egg him on. "I'm not kidding," he continued. "Have you seen all the retrievers and labs in this city? I would have thought the French would have more national pride. Even the English bulldogs are more popular than the French."

"We are talking about dogs, right?" I was beginning to like Clay Ranger, despite his habit of wearing cycling shoes as casually as other people wore flip flops.

"Yeah, dogs," Clay said, with a smile.

"So," I said, taking in the dimple on his left cheek. "Do you come here a lot?"

"Depends."

"Julie, look what I found!" Genevieve, who I last saw sitting Indian style in the fashion section, now stood in the doorway, squinting in the late afternoon light.

She took one look at Clay, and her wide-open expression vanished. I'm sure she thought Pilar was with him. When she didn't see her nemesis anywhere, her small shoulders relaxed, and she hurried over.

"It's a book of Coco Chanel's designs," she said, as Annie and the Chihuahuas sniffed each other.

"Coco who?" Clay asked.

"*Coco Chanel*," Genevieve said, "just about the most famous designer ever. My great-grandmother worked for her." She fixed her bright eyes on me. "Do you think there might be a picture of her in here? A caption?"

I laughed, squeezed her small shoulder. "There's only one way to find out."

After Genevieve hurried off to look further into the book, Clay and I talked for a while. He was easy to be around, laid back and funny without being full of himself like too many guys I'd known. If it weren't for the cycling thing, I might have been interested, for he was pretty cute, and I liked the way his t-shirt highlighted his muscles, though athletes had never exactly been my type. Danny's idea of sports had been designing a computerized version of lacrosse. And then there was the fact that I was hoping to meet a French guy—I was in France after all; and Clay, well, he was about as American as you get.

"I live on the other side of that bridge," he said, pointing to a part of the city now obscured by Notre Dame. "I cycle most mornings, but maybe we could meet on the Isle de la Cité some afternoon? Even take a trip to the Louvre? I have a leg up on the floor plan—"

"Why not. Do you bike in Paris?" I was trying to picture the concentration a person would need to dodge traffic and pedestrians on the congested streets.

"I have a route that gets me out of the city as quickly as possible," he said, "via Montmartre and then on into Belleville and the suburbs."

"You ride far then?"

"Fifty kilometers some days, usually more like thirty. The race I'm entering is seventy, but it's in the Dordogne. I'm counting on the landscape to get me through the last ten."

I flashed back to the Irish mathematician with zero body fat and hungry eyes who was always running around our neighborhood back in Lubbock. Morning and evening. And even when the temperature dropped below thirty, he wore shorts.

"Seriously," I said. "Would you tell me why you started biking?"

"Well if you must know, Lacy Shields," Clay said.

"A girl friend?"

"Ex-girlfriend. We went out for three years, talked about going to the same college. Then," he swallowed hard, "she fell in love with someone else."

"I'm afraid I saw that one coming," I said.

"No, you didn't." Once again, he nudged the ground with his cycling shoe.

"You mean—?"

He nodded. "It's bad enough being dumped for another guy—but to be dumped for a girl."

"Oh god, I'm really sorry." I bit my lip, realizing how rude I was, practically smiling.

"Yeah, it was pretty rugged there for a while. The best thing that happened was my dad taking the job in Paris. The move's given me some much-needed distance and the chance to really bike."

"Distance I can understand, but biking? Isn't Paris sort of dangerous?"

"Not if you compare it to Boston where we used to live," Clay said. "Picture big American cars on colonial streets and lots of impatient drivers. Here at least, most of the cars are compacts."

By the time Genevieve rejoined me, outraged that the biography had left out her great-grandmother, Clay was asking for my number and I was slipping his into my pocket. "Soon?" he said.

"Soonest."

"I like that." He grinned, and again that dimple appeared. "By the way, that famous stylist did an incredible job." The glint in his hazel eyes told me he'd been on to us all along.

"WANT TO STOP by the gallery on our way home?" I asked, once we left the wide quay along the Seine and began navigating the denser maze of streets that make up Saint Germain des Prés.

"You bet I do," Genevieve said, turning towards the melody of a guitar lilting out of one of the geranium-bordered windows.

Not far from the café Les Deux Magots where writers like Ernest Hemingway once gathered to drink, eat, and talk about art, stood the famous three-hundred-year-old cathedral of Saint Germain, its soot-stained stone proof of the pollution, despite the blue skies and nearby horse chestnut trees, their leaves a collage of shimmering chartreuse.

Today the cathedral grounds were covered with dozens of booths manned by whiskery-old men and reed thin women and men dressed in eternally hip black. A closer look revealed a wine seller's stall. He caught my eye, waved, called us over.

"Well?" Genevieve asked, a mischievous glint in her eye.

"No way." I could just imagine what Claire would say if I took Genevieve to a wine tasting. I looked back with a pang at the wine seller. With his high-bridged nose and red beret, his leathery face and crooked smile, he would have made an incredible study of Paris street life.

Two blocks later, we rounded the corner and breathed in the faint smell of fish at an outdoor restaurant where dozens of well-dressed people basked in the sunshine slanting off the red café tables. Most were drinking wine or beer and eating the raw oysters for which the restaurant was famous. More than a few were smoking and sipping coffee. Paris, I realized, was a city where lung cancer seemed not to have registered.

On a little street called the Rue de Confiance, the Street of Belief, right beside an old-fashioned toy store with a display of marionettes in the window, stood the gallery, L'Espace Stein, with its Jerusalem blue door and gold lettering. I originally thought Claire worked for a French art dealer, but Raphael Stein or 'Rafi' as he asked me to call him, was from Jerusalem—why I knew the precise color of the door.

The gallery showcased art by Jewish artists. One small, early painting by Picasso depicted a pair of owls in a tree. I loved its magical simplicity: black sky, a slice of silvery moon, and two owls nesting in the leaves. There were several pastels by Marc Chagall, including one in which a rouge-colored, winged horse flew over the moon. In another, a pair of lovers danced; at their feet, a carpet of stars and above their heads, a grinning moon.

Alongside small treasures like these, L'Espace Stein specialized in the contemporary work of Israeli artists. One piece incorporated yellow silk, the husks of seed pods, and other found objects. I could have looked at it for hours. Entitled *Autumn* or *L'Automne* in French, its harvest colors and textures captured the season's beauty, while suggesting the starkness of the winter that lay ahead.

The gallery walls had been painted a tranquil cream, and the floors were of natural wood, but alongside the Bach and Saté piano sonatas lilting through the minimalist speakers, the Israeli news station played continually on the television screen above Rafi's desk, which was always in a state of chaos. ("Rafi's strategy," Claire joked once. "That way, he's the only one who knows where the important papers are.")

"Bonjour, mademoiselles," Rafi called, as we stepped inside.

"Bonjour," I said.

Beside me, Genevieve chirped, "Hi."

Rafi was in his fifties, and except for his messy desk, everything about him—from his small, gold-rimmed glasses to his very expensive suits—was precise; everything, that is, except his peppery shock of Albert Einstein hair. "Claire darling," he called to the back. "Your girls are here."

While Genevieve showed Rafi her book about Chanel, I stood near the doorway and studied a new piece. It was a painting of a street scene in the rain, a jumble of brightly-colored umbrellas beneath which the faces of people carrying armfuls of flowers and other pretty purchases glowed. I liked it okay. It was hard not to when it was so pretty, but I couldn't help feel it was too much like the work of the Impressionists. Hadn't swirling ice cream colors and fuzzy outlines all been done before?

Rafi said paintings like this one sell. And even though I wanted to say—but does that make it good art?—I was clued into reality enough to understand that a gallery in Paris had to pay the steep rents to stay afloat. So there were more than a few pretty paintings on the walls in sherbet colors, and more than a few sexy sculptures of nude women, as well as one or two sexy men.

But there were difficult works, too. A driftwood sculpture of a starving horse stood in a plexi-glass stall. I hadn't had a chance to ask about its history, but every time I looked at it I felt hollow inside—windy—and I thought of the wild mustangs I'd seen in Colorado once, creatures that had lost their grazing land and were so gaunt their ribs protruded when they breathed.

On the opposite wall hung two small gouache paintings by the artist Charlotte Salomon who had fled during the Nazi occupation of Berlin. The paintings, Rafi told me, were from a series called *Life? Or Theater?*

"It's like the woman in the paintings is living on the verge of fantasy," I said, when I first saw her swirling figures.

"More like a nightmare," Rafi said. "While Charlotte was living in the south of France during the occupation, in hiding from the Nazis, she painted this parallel life. The focus kept her from going crazy, for she knew it was only a matter of time until they found her."

I stood for a long time before her painting of a woman and a child in a bed, an ordinary scene, except for the angel waiting just outside the window. "What happened to her?"

"She died in Auschwitz," Rafi said, then went on to tell me that before she was deported, she entrusted the paintings to an American who had been helping her. "Otherwise it's doubtful her work would have survived."

The piece that always hit me the hardest was a huge canvas by a German artist named Anselm Kiefer that ran the length of one wall. Its colors ranged from eggplant to charcoal and then black, and in it the artist had embedded straw which he'd set aflame.

"In remembrance of the Holocaust," Rafi explained. "He burned through the suffering to make something new, while leaving the traces visible for all to see. In Hebrew, we have a word for such memory: *zakhor.*"

"HEY THERE," CLAIRE said, coming into the main gallery, her auburn hair tucked behind her ears, her eggshell-blouse and lemon skirt in harmony with the ivory walls and unstained wooden floors. "Good to see you. Tell me, what have you been up to?"

"We went for a walk around Notre Dame," I said, breathing in a perfume that smelled faintly of roses.

"You all set for supper?" Claire asked, smoothing Genevieve's dark hair with her fingertips.

"I'm going to make new potatoes and a quiche," I said.

"With mushrooms," Genevieve added. "Julie knows the names of all the weird-looking ones."

"Sounds delicious: I sure wish I could join you," Claire said. "There's still so much to do before tomorrow's benefit. I'll probably have to stay until nine at least."

"We'll take good care of each other," I said.

"Oh Julie, there's something I have to tell you," Claire said. "I've been so preoccupied with tomorrow—I should have told you right away."

I looked from her to Rafi, who had just clicked off the phone and was pouring himself an Orangina.

"Yes?" I said. Secretly, I was hoping they would ask me to help out at the benefit to raise money for the homeless of Paris, many of whom I'd seen sleeping beneath the aqueducts along the Seine. Unlikely, of course, since the benefit would run late into the night: who would watch Genevieve?

"Rafi's contact in Nice has located a Modigliani."

My heart fluttered butterfly-fast. "You're serious?"

"Yes," Claire said.

"It's better not to raise our hopes just yet," Rafi added. "Other galleries are equally interested, and several of them have far more resources than us. A Modigliani in and of itself exceptional. But this is a Modigliani for which there is no record."

"Let me get this straight," I said. "You're saying no one knew about this painting before?"

"That's what it comes down to," Rafi said. "The portrait resembles two others, but it seems to have been part of a late collector's estate. The person was most reclusive, which is why there's been no talk of it until now—"

"And the subject?" I asked.

"Jeanne Hébuterne," he said.

"Modigliani's muse," I said.

Rafi's black eyes flickered behind his glasses.

"Julie's been looking at Modiglianis since she was Genevieve's age," Claire said.

"At the Art Institute of Chicago," I added. "I spent a lot of time there before moving to Texas."

"Just a minute, I have a photograph of the painting here," Rafi said, and began rummaging in the pile on his desk. "Ah yes," he said, and handed it to me.

The photograph had cropped the painting just below the woman's throat, but that didn't take away from its power. The woman's dark gaze was both direct and mysterious, and her mouth curved into a small smile that suggested she was about to say something smart or funny. Could this really be Jeanne? From the little I'd read about Modigliani, Jeanne had not been strong. At least she was no longer strong by the time his friends came to make the death mask of his face. A few weeks later, nine months pregnant and unable to take care of their eighteen-month-old daughter, Jeanne jumped out the fifth story window on the night of his death.

Even though Jeanne's situation had been way more desperate than my mother's, her archly Catholic parents disowning her once she fell in love with the Jewish Modigliani, I couldn't imagine how my mother would have managed without Oma's support when she returned to the States pregnant with me. My grandmother once told me that one of the professors for whom my mom worked, a man in his fifties, tried to get the university to discontinue her scholarship. He called her into his office and told her to stay at home and out of sight until after the baby was born. When she refused, he fired her. If she hadn't gotten her degree—if she'd had to drop out of school to take care of me, or at least to support me—what then? At the very least, wouldn't she have grown to resent me, the child for whom she'd had to give up so much?

"Well, Julie," Rafi said, laying a hand on my arm. "You seem deep in thought."

I looked back at Rafi, relieved he couldn't read my thoughts.

"He painted her eyes—the iris, even the pupil."

"True," he said. "How curious."

"At the end of his life, Modigliani painted the shape of the eye, but he didn't include the iris. Instead, he washed the almond shape through with a wash of blue so that it looked as if his sitter was dreaming. Was Modigliani asking Jeanne to look beyond herself, beyond their love? And what about my father: what parting words had he left my mother with?

ABOUT THREE A.M. I awoke to a sapphire-blue sky and a crescent moon shining through the curtains. In the distance the hum of a passing car was followed by a series of beeps. I'd had a strange dream that I couldn't clearly remember, except that my father was in it, or some version of him that my subconscious had made up. In the dream, he looked like the twenty-something man in the very few pictures my mom had held onto; and he was standing in the courtyard of some museum, the Louvre, I think, waving and smiling as I came towards him. But before I could reach him, before we could exchange words, I woke up.

Lying there, I thought about what my mom had said about my father wanting nothing to do with her after she became pregnant with me. He wasn't ready for a baby, he said. A baby would only get in the way of his ambitions as an artist, force him to compromise his focus.

I was never dumb enough to think my parents would seek each other out again, like those Disney movies no one could possibly believe in past the age of seven; but more than once I convinced myself that Gustave Fermiere would have second thoughts about not being a part of my life. Every Christmas, I used to say, he'll finally write. He'll invite me on a holiday. He'll send me a stuffed bear, a box of charcoal pencils.

Instead, in seventeen years, nothing, not even a postcard or anonymous Valentine. Did he ever think about me? Wonder what I looked like? Or whether I was good at math? Or loved art like he did?

Careful not to wake Genevieve, I switched on the bedside lamp, found my charcoals and a drawing pad. I told myself I would free draw myself back to sleep, something I often did when I was troubled. But all the sketches I came up with captured the tilt of a man's head, partly hidden beneath a fedora, or in the shadows of a tree. In one, a man was walking away.

I didn't need a psychic or an analyst to figure out what my sub-conscious was telling me. It was time to tap that stranger on the shoulder so that he turned around. Time, a voice said, to go out and find my father.

Five

THE NEXT DAY Genevieve and I stepped inside Monsieur Rimbaud's antique shop after the two-hour pause that followed lunch, a time when the curtains were drawn in the apartment windows and nearly every shop, except a department store like Bon Marché, closed so that the city became almost quiet.

"*Bon jour, mademoiselles.* I felt sure St. Genevieve's namesake and you," he pointed a long finger at me, "the artist, would have come to see me long before now."

I didn't dare admit, even to myself, that I had been avoiding the antiques shop after that mortifying experience with Paul Henri at the Luxembourg.

"We've come to find some dolls for my house," Genevieve explained, after describing the renovations and additions we'd made—fabric wallpaper, a table and chairs, the postage stamp pictures in their cardboard frames, the palm-sized beds with the neatly sewn quilts and pillows. "Come October," she added, "I can scavenge acorns for tiny bowls."

"Ah, I knew you were the right person to care for that house," Monsieur Rimbaud said. "Its original owner was about your age when she acquired it."

"How do you know?" Genevieve's green eyes opened wide.

"That little girl was a school friend's mother."

"They didn't keep the house in the family?" I said. "It's an heirloom, a *souvenir,*" I added, pleased with my French.

"Not all families cherish their pasts, *cherie,*" he said. "And perhaps, for this I should be grateful. Otherwise," he sighed, tapped his fingers along the counter, "I would not have my shop."

He turned back to Genevieve. "Since your last visit, I found something I believe you should have."

Genevieve hurried after him, and even the button eyes of the jointed teddy bears and the faded faces of several portraits seemed to look on as he retrieved a carefully wrapped object from one of his desk drawers. "Have a look," he said, handing her the gift.

Beneath the layers of tissue paper, she brought forth a small, wooden box just the right size for a doll house; its surface was decorated with wreaths of tiny red flowers like the poppies in the Luxembourg Gardens.

"It's a music box," he explained, then turned the box upside down, revealing a winding knob like the one on wristwatches. "I thought your doll family might enjoy a little music."

"*Merci!*" Genevieve said, pressing the box to her ear as a melody began to play.

"Somewhere over the rainbow…" Monsieur Rimbaud hummed.

"That's from *The Wizard of Oz*," I said, reminded of the afternoons and evenings I'd spent watching that movie over and over again, half in love with Scarecrow and wishing for my own field of poppies, despite my terror at those creepy winged monkeys.

"*Oui*—Judy Garland's voice," he said, his own turning dreamy as he closed his eyes. "I sat in the cinema a dozen times just to hear her sing."

"But why did you think the music box was for me?" Genevieve asked, looking up at him.

Monsieur Rimbaud smiled, a bit wistfully. "Let's just say that like Judy Garland—like Dorothy—you seem to be a girl for whom home matters a great deal."

Genevieve gazed back at him as if he'd seen straight into her heart, and I wondered if he was one of those people with extraordinary intuitive powers, for what could he know about Genevieve's history? Or maybe, the cynic in me said, it was just a good guess.

Afterwards Monsieur Rimbaud made tea which he poured into antique Limoges cups edged with violets, and we spent the next hour sitting at a small, ornately carved table—"from the end of the eighteenth century—the Rococo period." Sunlight slanted across the faded Oriental rug as a chorus of silver church bells rang in the distance. Monsieur Rimbaud showed us doll after doll, from early cloth dolls to exquisite nineteenth century creations with porcelain faces that had been painted with all the care of fine works of art.

"The firm that made these dolls was called Jumeau," Monsieur Rimbaud explained. "In their day, there was no one better. A doll like this is a rare find. There were at most a hundred like her produced at that time. No factory-produced faces, *merci mon Dieu.*"

How could Monsieur Rimbaud possibly think Genevieve could afford such a thing? The doll's golden hair had been spun from mohair, her detailed features painted by hand.

"Not only are her clothes of burgundy silk," he explained, "but the style is very much like what a lady of the 1870s would have worn, from the wired bonnet to the cut of her dress."

"That teensy waist looks suffocating," I said.

"Corsets," Genevieve said, always the fashion authority.

"Every well born lady's best friend and enemy," said Monsieur Rimbaud. "My dear mother insisted on wearing one well into her eighties."

Of all the dolls he showed us, the one I liked the most had been made in 1918, and it didn't take me long to realize that was just two years before Modigliani's death. "Except for the boots which are replicas, everything about her is original," he said, placing the doll on the table before us.

The auburn-haired doll wore a black velvet dress with a lace collar, and her boots were of real leather with two buttons for snaps. While studying the doll, I remembered the photograph in the biography on Claire's bookshelf of Jeanne wearing a loose dress that seemed a world away from black velvet and lace. For nearly all of the years she spent with Modigliani, they had to count the cost of everything if he was to pay for his materials, especially oil paints. Certain colors, like alizarin crimson and verdigris, were beyond expensive. The only way he could have used them would have been by giving up other things like clothes and fuel and food. Sometimes they must have had only days-old bread and the ends of sausage or a rind of cheese to eat.

"Penny for your thoughts," Monsieur Rimbaud said, startling me with this old-fashioned American expression, one of Oma's favorites.

"Yes, well," I hesitated, "I was thinking about something I read about Modigliani and Jeanne Hébuterne."

"Ah yes, of course." He shook his head. "In my old age, I seem to becoming more forgetful. I read about the painting in Marika Teretre's column."

"Who?" I said.

"*Je suis étonné*—I'm surprised," he said. "I thought a girl with paint stains on her hands would have discovered Marika by now. She writes about art for *Le Cité*." He stroked his mustache, his caterpillar eyebrows joining in a 'v.'

"Marika has ears everywhere," he continued, once we followed him back to his desk, and he placed the paper before me. "You can find her column every Tuesday and Friday. Here, see for yourself."

With the help of Monsieur Rimbaud, I translated:

L'Espace Stein, 13 Rue de Confiance, has acquired a hitherto unrecorded painting of small size by the modern master, Amedeo Modigliani. As one would expect, it is a portrait. The subject is a young woman with a disarming gaze and long, dark hair who is most likely Jeanne Hébuterne, the tragic muse who devoted herself to him. According to the gallery owner, Raphael Stein, the portrait is a variation of another work in Modigliani's oeuvre now held in a private collection.

'The tragic muse,' the columnist called Jeanne, the words bringing back what Monsieur Rimbaud said about his grandfather's café, the fact that Jeanne's shoes were always patched, and she, pale and frightened looking.

"Such a mysterious thing, that love story," Monsieur Rimbaud said. "The poor young woman gave up everything to be with Modigliani."

I LEFT EMPTY-HANDED, but along with the music box Genevieve carried two small but perfectly made cloth dolls—a properly dressed man with a mustache a lot like Monsieur Rimbaud's and a woman in an eyelet dress—carefully wrapped in brown paper. They had to be worth a small fortune, but Monsieur Rimbaud insisted on giving them to her. "I cannot imagine anyone else taking proper care of them," he said.

Genevieve practically galloped down the streets after that until we saw the sign for Shakespeare & Co., and beyond it, the Seine, its water rippled with silver in the late afternoon light.

We were early, but Clay was already there, his muscular shoulders and arms highlighted by a clingy red shirt; his cycling-strong legs encased in black shorts, the lycra kind. His carrot hair fell over his eyes as he browsed the half-priced bins outside, as un-self-conscious in this stand-out gear as if he were wearing bleached out jeans and a faded t-shirt.

"Don't tell me," I said, striding up to him, "you just finished a bike ride."

"Forty kilometers," he said, his mouth breaking into a happy-to-see-you-grin. "I started out by cycling up to Sacre Coeur. My calves are killing me."

"I bet," I said, for Sacre Coeur stood on the highest point in Paris. "So, where are the Chihuahuas?"

"At the groomer."

"Um, they have short coats. How much grooming do they need?"

He shrugged. "They get bathed, and the groomer cuts their toenails after muzzling them."

"You're kidding?"

"I'm not. They're ferocious about anyone touching their feet. Afterwards he makes it up to them with treats, and he puts bows on the girls. My mom is very particular about the bows."

I tried to picture Clay taking 'the girls' for a walk post-salon. If this were West Texas and not Paris, he'd have never gotten away with it, especially not in those shorts, muscular legs or not.

"Like I said, they're Mom's children."

"Look," Genevieve said, hurrying the dolls into Clay's arms.

"For me?" he said, holding the dolls stiffly.

"Monsieur Rimbaud, the antique dealer, gave them to me, but I knew you'd want to see them."

"I sure do. They're beautiful," Clay said, turning the dolls over in his freckled hands and examining them with more care than I imagined. The gentleness in his face just then warmed me from the inside out, and I wondered what it would feel like to touch his skin.

"What are you going to name them?" he asked Genevieve.

She frowned. "I'll have to think about that."

"How about Coco?" he asked.

I smiled, and our eyes met. It wasn't many guys who'd remember something like that.

"Perfect," Genevieve said. "And maybe this one will be Valentino."

"Not Isaac?" Clay asked.

"Huh?"

"As in Mizrahi," Clay said.

"And how do you know that?" I asked.

"My mom owns stock at Target, and he's got a line there."

"Seriously?" I bit my lip, determined not to laugh.

"What?" He stared. "What's so funny?"

"I'm sorry, it's just that I can't believe you know that."

"I'm not naming my doll Isaac," Genevieve said practically.

"What's the problem?" Clay said. "Too biblical?"

"Can't you figure it out?" Genevieve said. "Mizrahi is just a temporary fad."

Clay pressed a hand to his heart and said, "My mother will be crushed. She takes her investments very seriously."

We stood there a while longer until I pointed to the book in his hands. "What are you reading?"

"A biography of Jean Aerts."

"I'm supposed to know who he is, right?" I said.

"I would say so." Clay sighed dramatically. "I mean, if we're going to hang out, I expect you to catch up on the world of cycling. Remember: I know Coco Chanel."

"Gotcha," I said, "I'm a quick study. So tell us, who is Jean Aerts?"

"A brilliant cyclist from Belgium and a major player in the Tour de France in the 1930s, winning six of the race's ten stages."

The look on Clay's face told me not to even think about telling him I couldn't name a Tour de France cyclist from 2008, much less the Thirties.

"If he'd had a titanium bike," Clay added, "he would have been unbeatable."

"Yeah, well, he sounds pretty impressive."

"He is. Now," he said, "I'm going to pay for this. Do you want to look around, or should we get going? There's bound to be a line at the Louvre."

"I want to see if they have a book about Modigliani and Jeanne," I said, then made my way to the register.

"If we do," the girl said, "you'll find it in the section called Bohemian Paris."

I looked up at the endless aisles, the ceiling-high bookshelves that smelled woodsy and reminded me of libraries. "Where's that?"

"Here," she said, "follow me."

This girl wore powder blue, rhinestone-studded Catwoman eyeglasses, the kind Marilyn Monroe wore when she wanted to look both gorgeous and smart. With her platinum hair and mascara-laden eyes, she reminded me a little of Marilyn; as did her retro clothes, the pencil-narrow capris and crisp cotton blouse. The admiring way Genevieve gazed at her told me she approved.

Clay claimed a spot on the couch, among the bookstore cats, and for a moment I thought about curling up beside him, wondered what he would do, how he would react. But the girl with the Catwoman glasses was waiting, so Genevieve and I trailed her to the back, where she climbed a stepladder and then stood squinting at what must have been a dozen dusty books.

"You're in luck," she said, bending down to hand the book to me. *A Private Portrait: The Story of Amedeo Modigliani and Jeanne Hébuterne, Modigliani's Faithful Wife.*

"I thought they weren't married?" Genevieve said.

"Not legally, no," I said, then went on to say that because Modigliani was Jewish and Jeanne, Roman Catholic, they hadn't been allowed to marry.

"But my parents were from different religions," Genevieve said.

"Things were different ninety years ago." I turned to the same faded photograph of Jeanne from the biography on Claire's shelf, the one in which she stands before a sunlit doorway in that drapey caftan; on the wall behind her, what looked like dozens of sketches of people in casual poses. Her own work, I felt sure; she, too, had been an artist.

"So," the girl's eyes glinted behind her glasses as she sat down on a nearby stool. "Is this what you're looking for?"

"It sure is, but thirty Euros?" I said.

"It's a first edition," the girl said, crossing her legs, the center seam on her capris iron-pressed perfect.

"It's still more than I have."

"If you're short on cash, we can place the book on hold for forty-eight hours."

The odds of someone coming in and asking for a book like this one were highly doubtful, but a needle of uncertainty said I shouldn't let it out of my sight. "Any other options?"

She pointed to the drawing pad poking out of my backpack. "You an artist?"

"She is," Genevieve said right away. "If she draws you, will you give her the book?"

The girl laughed, and the glasses slid down her nose. "That would be against store policy, but I have another idea."

I leaned closer. "Go on—"

"We're going to have a little party here on Saturday in honor of a visiting writer. You might do portraits of the guests—"

"I don't do caricatures," I said, reminded of those ridiculous sketches in which a person's ears or her smile or her breasts were absurdly huge.

"You wouldn't be expected to," the girl said, "just some informal portraits—Conté crayon, charcoal."

"You draw, too?" I asked.

"Hardly, but the visiting writer is also an artist so I've learned a thing or two," she said, already flipping through the pages of my sketchpad.

"Find what you need?" Clay said, ambling over, the biggest tabby I'd ever seen—the creature must have weighed thirty pounds—purring like a rusty motor in his arms.

Genevieve shushed him, and I mouthed, 'Hold on.'

"Nice work," the girl said, holding out a well-manicured hand.

I was about to say 'thank you' when she saw Clay and said, "My compliments: Maurice is usually stand-offish around men."

"What can I say," Clay grinned. "I have a way with animals."

"I'm Henrietta," she said, then turned to me. "If you can be here at six o'clock on Saturday and will stay and draw portraits during the party, you can take the book now—" the rhinestones in her glasses sparkled—"on good faith."

The tabby's eyes were half-closed now, and his purr, a growly rumble.

"There's just one thing," I told her. "My French is abysmal."

"Julie," Clay said, "this is an English-speaking bookstore."

Six

At six twenty-five on Saturday, Genevieve and I jogged up the metro steps, the three long blocks to Shakespeare & Co. still ahead of us. "Hurry," I called to her.

"I'm trying," she said, clomping along in retro clogs I'd never have dared to run in, having sprained my ankle in clogs with half the heel when I was twelve.

Clay was already waiting outside dressed in a charcoal sweater and perfectly worn jeans. I was hugely grateful that he wasn't wearing anything with lycra, though one look at his feet proved that he was still wearing cleats.

"What took you guys so long anyway?" he asked.

"Let's just say we had some fashion issues," I said, nodding at Genevieve.

"This is the only shirt that goes with these pants," Genevieve said, "and it wasn't dry in time."

"Well, it was worth the wait," Clay said to her. "You look gorgeous. Who would have thought that yellow-green could be so wearable."

"The color is chartreuse," Genevieve said crisply.

"My apologies," Clay said, with a theatrical bow.

"And me?" I said, though my peasant blouse and jeans couldn't compete with Genevieve's chic top and skinny jeans.

"Smashing," Clay said, what had to be a blush stealing over his cheeks. It must have been contagious because heat crept to my own face.

"Is something going on here?" Genevieve said, glancing from Clay to me.

"What are you talking about? I'm just nervous, that's all."

Genevieve nodded, but she continued to watch Clay and me closely.

"Well then," Clay added, turning back to Genevieve, "let's get in there so our artist can pay for that book."

We found the bookstore overflowing with guests, half of them wearing jeans, the other half in black or beige or the new "it" color: silver. At least Genevieve said silver was "it."

When I finally spotted Henrietta, dressed in a daisy-sprinkled dress reminiscent of the late Princess Diana, I almost didn't recognize her. Gone were the Catwoman glasses and the mascara-heavy eyes of the other day. Tonight, with her platinum hair swept into a high ponytail, she could have been standing in an English country garden.

"Oh good," she said, kissing me on the cheek. "I was beginning to get worried. I've only been the manager for a month, and this is a major event."

"Right," I said, repeating 'Don't be nervous' again and again.

Henrietta handed Clay and me cocktails—champagne and cranberry juice. "And for you?" she asked Genevieve, who looked up at me hopefully.

"Just juice," I said quickly.

The party was being held in honor of a visiting American writer named Josh Chaplin who'd written a novel about Paris's art scene. I spotted him over in a corner mobbed by people. He wore Levis and a t-shirt, and his too-long, sandy hair kept falling into his eyes.

"He's going to do a reading later," Henrietta told us, a little breathlessly, flushing as Josh waved her over.

"Get the feeling Henrietta likes this guy?" Clay asked.

"Looks like it's mutual," I said, for just then Josh Chaplin kissed her, a really romantic kiss in which their hips cinched into place; it was a kiss worthy of the most romantic movies—when would someone kiss me like that?

Clay stepped a bit closer, so I could smell the sweat on his skin and the clean scent of Ivory soap. "Um, Julie, someone's here to see you."

"You're the little lady doing portraits?"

I whirled around to find a gristle-bearded guy who immediately sat down in the faded corduroy armchair opposite me. "That's me," I said, faking a smile.

"I'm Waco," he said. "I want to send this picture back to my girlfriend, ex-girlfriend that is, so could you make me taller?"

"I'll try," I said, "but you're sitting down."

All the time he was posing, Waco made a point of drawling on about how he now lived in a penthouse overlooking the Seine—"I'm earning my architecture degree"—but he was originally from Texas. "I come from a long line of cattle people," he said.

I couldn't help but picture Waco standing at the front of a line of people with cows' heads. Given his posh address, it was more than likely his family helped supply the nation's McDonald's with cheap, hormone-injected beef. I'd never been hard core about meat consumption, but it bothered me, in a big way, the way cows and other animals were destined to become two dollar burgers complete with soda and a plastic toy.

After Waco told us that he planned on winning his ex-girlfriend back with a building named after her, Clay said, "Does anyone ever call you Wacko by mistake?"

"No," the Texan said with total seriousness. "Why?"

"Just wondering," Clay said.

I could have hugged him, except the tabby was in his arms, eyes closed, purring like a locomotive. I had to admit: this

Maurice creature looked pretty cozy. And I wanted to ask Clay if he'd doused himself with Eau de Catnip before coming over.

After playing the faithful assistant for three sitters, including Kiki, whose tangerine-streaked blonde hair reminded me of a Creamsicle, and whose boyfriend went by the name of Suki and claimed to have invented a new musical instrument—"a cross between a didgeridoo and something even less pronounceable— Clay said, "I skipped dinner. You mind if I get something to eat?"

"I'm hungry, too," Genevieve said, tugging at Clay's sleeve.

"Dig in," I told them both.

"Should I bring you something?" Clay asked me.

"A few of those chocolate-covered strawberries would be most appreciated."

A woman who could have been Morticia Adams's little sister sat down next. Black hair, black nails, black lips, black dress and shoes; and the whitest skin I'd ever seen. I felt cold just looking at her, though at least she simplified the color scheme.

"So you're the artist," Josh Chaplain said after she slunk off.

"And you're the writer," I said, glancing over at the couch where Genevieve and Clay, and his heaping plate of food, were seated; and beside Clay, Maurice, who looked more than a little eager to climb back onto his lap.

Josh grinned, held out a hand. "Good to meet you, Artist."

"And you, too, Writer. So tell me about the book."

"I spent a year working at a bookshop on the Left Bank that sells artists' supplies. I thought I would write the next great American novel about living the bohemian life in Paris while working there. Instead, I found myself broke with writer's block."

"So what changed?" I asked, shading in his enviably high cheekbones.

"After worrying myself sick for a few weeks, convinced I could only stay on in Paris if I moved into the local hostel and survived on Ramen, I finally clued into the fact that my subject was right in front of me. All day, local artists would come in to the shop to buy their supplies. Others would come into browse books. I studied them more closely and began taking notes, writing up informal sketches during the downtime. Next thing I knew, I had my subject. What I didn't know: I would write about six versions before getting it right."

"But you didn't have to move into the hostel and eat Ramen?"

"No, I didn't."

"Well then, cheers. You must have done pretty well for yourself. This place is packed."

"All Henrietta's doing. She set this up."

"Kudos to her," I said, taking note of the honey in his voice. "So tell me, how did you two meet?"

"Believe it or not, I've known Henrietta since kindergarten."

I pictured the two of them kissing on the playground. "You're kidding."

"No. I used to pull her ponytails. I couldn't help myself. Her hair was strawberry blonde and curly. Whenever she saw me coming, she'd run, but to her credit she never told our teacher."

"So, did it get better after that?" I said, for this did not sound like an auspicious beginning.

"By the fifth grade, we were buddies. We liked the same books and bands. I played hockey. She figure skated. We used to drink hot cocoa on the bench outside the ice rink. But her family moved just before junior year of high school, and we lost touch. Fast forward twelve years, and here I am in Paris, and I run into her on the street."

"But you didn't pull her hair?"

He grinned. "I did actually. The next thing I know, we're eating ice creams on the Isle de la Cité."

"Sounds like you two were meant to be."

"I have that feeling too," Josh said. "I had a serious girlfriend when I came here, but she high-tailed it to Morocco in search of camels and equanimity. Funny, I go halfway across the world, and I find the girl-next-door."

I glanced over at Clay near the food, traced the outline of his broad shoulders. You couldn't get more boy-next-door than him, a voice inside me said.

But boy-next-door, I reminded myself, was not what I was looking for in Paris. And besides, he and I were just friends, weren't we?

"Josh!" Henrietta called from the other side of the store.

"That's my cue," Josh said. "I think I'd better get ready for my reading."

"I salvaged six chocolate-covered strawberries," Clay said, bowing as he handed me my plate.

"I see two strawberries here," I said, traces of chocolate edging his lips.

"My metabolism asks your forgiveness."

"Granted."

A lanky girl in a clingy turquoise dress came over, her dress so tight she had to sort of shuffle. "Anyone else in line?" she asked.

"You just missed the rush," Clay said, stepping aside. "She's all yours."

I smiled at her, but secretly I was disappointed. I would have liked to draw Clay.

He zipped up his jacket. "You're not leaving yet?" I said.

Clay tip-tapped his cleats. "Afraid so: I came for moral support, but you've got this down. Besides, I'm getting up early; I've got fifty kilometers planned."

"Soon?" I said.

"Soonest," he said, and bent to kiss my forehead. The touch of his lips was warm, nice.

"Hey," the lanky girl said, struggling to cross one leg over the other in her tight dress—what would Genevieve say? "I don't want to break this up, but I'm waiting."

"Right," I said, as Clay waved goodbye.

JOSH TURNED OUT to be a natural in front of the crowd, full of anecdotes and asides; but during the book signing, I left to check out the shelves devoted to contemporary art. I scanned the titles devoted to all the big names: Lucy Frankenthaler, Mark Rothko, Robert Motherwell. On an out-of-the-way shelf, I found *The New Younger Painters of France*.

I opened it, and there between Lucie de Falaise and Justine Fontaine, I found him. Gustave Fermiere must not have been promising enough to warrant a whole page and a big photograph, unlike some of the others. But at least there was a long paragraph, and a slightly-out-of-focus picture that proved he was the man with whom Mom had fallen in love:

Born in Paris, in 1961, Gustave Fermiere was trained in drawing and in art restoration. He began his career refinishing the frescoes and art in the city's churches and other sacred places. His most well-known painting to date, Self-Portrait on Notre Dame, *shows the artist as gargoyle, crouching along one of the cathedral's steeples, his posture more despondent than menacing. It was painted in 1990, just before his breakdown. Since then, Fermiere has lived a retired life in the countryside outside of Aix, where he keeps a small farm and continues to restore church frescoes in the area. He has not exhibited since the early 1990s.*

I copied the paragraph word for word in my sketchbook, trembling as I wrote down the year: 1990. I was born in 1988, and two years later he had the breakdown. Was it possible that he felt so terrible about abandoning my mother, and me, that he became 'despondent,' as this bio claimed? Or was there another reason?

Alongside the photograph, there was a single blurred reproduction of his work, just a little bit bigger than a postage stamp. It was that famous self-portrait. Hopeless was the word that came to mind when I took in the gargoyle's slouched shoulders, the miserable face. What had brought him so low? And how was he now?

The book's copyright was 1997, nearly eight years ago. A lot could have changed since then. Gustave Fermiere could have made a comeback. He could have left the country. He could even be dead. Only one thing was certain: he hadn't contacted me.

"There you are," a voice called.

I slammed the book shut. Of all people, it was Marie France dressed from head to toe in a flowy dress of many shades of blue, her red-gold hair cascading down her back. Did that mean Paul Henri was here, too? Had she noticed anything in my expression? Had there been anything to notice? "Oh, hi," I said, concealing the cover with my hands. "I didn't expect to see you here."

Her lips curved into a half smile. "Why not? It's not only you Americans who like your fiction. Besides, I could say the same for you. What are you doing here anyway?"

"Weird story," I said, grateful she couldn't hear my pounding heart, the words about my father reverberating through my brain. "I came in looking for a book about Modigliani's life."

"And?" she said.

"I couldn't afford it. Henrietta, the manager, saw my drawing pad, one thing led to another, and—"

"Synchronicity," Marie France said, pushing her Pre-Raphaelite hair out of her face and blinking her morning glory eyes. "You like Modigliani, then?"

"Major understatement."

"Well then, I should show you Modigliani's last studio."

"Really? You know it?" I said, still dizzy from what I'd read about Gustave Fermiere.

"It's upstairs from a restaurant run by an old friend of my parents, Madame Marthurin."

"I didn't even think it still existed."

"*Mon Dieu*, not only does it exist, there are stories about it."

"What kind of stories?" I asked, realizing only now that it was creeping towards ten. I had to go and find Genevieve and get her back to the apartment, for at this rate it would be eleven before we were home.

"According to Madame Marthurin's late grandmother, another painter rented it after Modigliani died, but he couldn't work there, found it very difficult to concentrate."

"How come?"

"I don't have the complete picture, as you say. I do know it is a place with—how do you say in English?—a place with a heavy presence."

Seven

"A telephone call? For me?" I said, then sat up in bed and blinked at Genevieve, who stood there looking as serious as the picture on her t-shirt: Charlie Chaplin in *The Kid*.

"It's Marie France." She handed me the phone, flopped face down on her bed, and lay there, very still.

"Hello," I said, unable to look away from Genevieve—what was wrong? Had something happened?

"Madame Marthurin just called," Marie France said.

"Who?" I said, a muzzy image of gargoyles resurfacing from a dream.

"Remember last night? I told you: her restaurant is below the old studio of Modigliani."

"Oh yes, of course," I said, troubled by the fact that the latest issue of *Paris Chic* still lay in its wrapping beside Genevieve.

"She's short one waitress today," Marie France continued. "I offered to help out. I thought you might like to come along. I could show you the studio."

"Oh no," I said, noticing that Genevieve's eyes were red; she'd been crying.

"What?"—Marie France.

"I mean, I'd love that. Just tell me when, and where."

"Let's meet at the Closerie des Lilas. Say noon?"

"I think I've heard of that."

"*Mais bien sûr*—but of course. It used to be a great gathering place for artists going all the way back to Monet and Renoir.

Such a shame it's not the place it once was," Marie France sighed. "But thankfully there are still echoes."

I wrote down the address of the café on the Boulevard Saint Michel, close to where it intersected Montparnasse.

"What's going on?" I asked Genevieve, touching her shoulder, after I hung up the phone.

She turned to face me. Tears glinted there. "Just before Marie France called, I talked to my dad."

"And?" I said, sitting down beside her on the bed. Usually talking to her dad cheered her up, re-established a connection frayed by the Atlantic Ocean and the length of the United States.

"*And* Margot is going to have a baby."

"Okay," I said, feeling as if I'd joined her on the downward plunge of a rollercoaster.

"When?"

"December twenty-eighth: it's bad enough Margot's daughters get to live with them," she said, pulling at a loose thread on her quilt. "Now he's going to have another kid, Margot's. What about me? I barely see him anymore."

I'd seen the silver-framed picture of Margot's two golden-haired daughters: Sierra, age fourteen, and Montana, age eleven, dressed in picnic-bright colors, bookended by their golden-haired actress mother (she played a secondary role on a popular sitcom) and Genevieve's dad. Genevieve kept the picture on her shelf, but she kept it face down.

'Think, Julie,' I told myself. 'Think fast,' for Genevieve was looking at me the way dogs looked at you at animal shelters. I knew this. I'd volunteered for one.

"I always thought it would be nice to be a big sister," I said finally, thinking back to the years spent envying friends who built forts in shared bedrooms, sang and griped through family vacations, pets, chicken pox. "I would have had someone I could share my experiences with, someone I could boss around."

What I didn't tell Genevieve was that some nights I lay in bed wondering if I had a French-speaking half-sister out there who shared my long, thin nose, the same nose I recognized in Gustave Fermiere's photograph. Or my charcoal-dark eyes. And what about my crazy passion for sharp cheese (I'd been the only four-year-old at Hyde Park Montessori who craved goat cheese) and olives and anything tangy and acidic? Mom couldn't stand food like that. And I always sobbed through movies, while Mom never shed a tear, not even during *Titanic* or that all-time tearjerker, *Bambi*. To this day I couldn't understand why the fawn's mother had to die.

"I don't want to be a big sister," Genevieve said, "unless the baby is Dad's and Mom's."

"I hate to say it, Gen, but that's not going to happen."

"I know," she said, a tear welling up in each eye. "That's what makes this so awful."

"At least you'll see your dad in August," I said hurriedly. "Think about it: a whole week together on the beach. Maybe it'll be the kind of thing you two could do every year."

Genevieve managed a small smile. "That'd be nice."

I breathed deeply, relieved, until Genevieve said, "What about your dad?"

I stiffened, reminded of the passage about him that I'd copied down so carefully, the way my mind had been turning over the words, wondering what to do with them. No wonder I'd dreamt of gargoyles.

"Julie?"

"I heard you," I said. "I'm not sure what you're asking."

"Is it true that you never met him?"

"That's right."

"So," her voice quieted, "do you ever think about finding him?"

I studied Genevieve's face, wondered if she could somehow read my mind, or had spied me reading the book at the party.

"Well?" she said again.

"I used to," I said, then to make up for the partial lie I told her about the miserable Christmas I tried to send a letter to him only to discover, at the post office, I needed more than a name. I needed an address. "Later my mom found the card in my desk drawer and asked me about it. 'I just can't believe he doesn't want to know I'm out there,' I told her. Mom's face closed down, and she turned pale and silent, and I knew my words had re-opened old wounds. So I didn't mention him again, at least not for a long, long time."

"I'm sorry," Genevieve said. "That must've been terrible."

"Yeah, it was."

I almost told her about last night, wondered about including her in my plans to find him, but she was so young, my responsibility. I couldn't risk that.

It was then Claire appeared in the doorway, her hair tied up in a messy ponytail, her mouth a taut frown. "Who was that on the phone?"

"Marie France, a friend of Paul Henri's," I said. "We met her again at the party. She knows where Modigliani's studio is."

"Is that right?" She relaxed a little against the doorframe. "I knew it was somewhere in Montparnasse, but I never thought to look where."

"Would it be okay if I went and took Genevieve along?" I asked.

"Why don't you take the day for yourself? Truth is," Claire's own voice sounded tired, "Genevieve and I could use some mother-daughter time."

ACCORDING TO MY guidebook, the Closerie des Lilas, which translated to "The Pleasure Garden of the Lilacs," was originally surrounded by lilac bushes. Now the only flowers in sight were the white roses on the tables, the edges of their petals already browning in the sun.

Montparnasse may have been home to artists of Modigliani's day. Today, instead of poets and painters knocking elbows as they talked art over drinks, a ruddy-faced German family plotted a tour of the sites along the high traffic Boulevard Hausmann, while another group, this one speaking a language I did not recognize, seemed totally obsessed with their complicated photo and video equipment.

"Listen, Morris," a bleached blonde at the next table said. She wore an expensive-looking sweater set and pearls. "It says here that the Closerie first became famous because it's on the way to Fountainebleau."

"The palace? Geez," he said, "that's an hour's drive from here—in good traffic."

I turned back to my lemonade, trying hard not to feel depressed by how far downhill this artist's café had come.

"Julie!" Marie France was striding towards me. Even dressed in the typical waitressing uniform of white blouse and black jeans, her phenomenal hair pulled back in a high ponytail, her makeup kept to lip gloss, she stood out.

"I'm sorry I'm late—I had to help my mother at the hotel," she said breathlessly. "I hope you haven't been waiting long."

"No, it's alright."

The hawk-nosed waiter with the to-die-for-blue eyes who had taken his time coming over to my table, immediately brought over a glass of iced tea and placed it before her.

"Bonjour, Marie France," he said, then rambled on in rapid, hard-to-decipher French, as she laughed, and rambled back.

"You know so many people," I said, once he left. "Paris is a city with millions of people."

"Once you've been here for as long as my family has, Paris seems more like a series of, how do you say—enclaves? You see, my parents' hotel has been in our family for generations. We've been in the same house since my great-grandparents moved here from Normandy. Maman's school friend still lives just down the street."

It was hard to imagine what it would be like to grow up in a house with that kind of family history. Yes, there was Oma's white row house with its wraparound front porch where I used to sit for hours; the bathroom with its claw-footed tub, the poppy wallpaper peeling at the edges; and the tiny room tucked into the eaves where I first slept. The house, with its slanting attic and its wonderful garden which bloomed with hollyhocks and roses, had been like a close friend.

But my mom took the job in Texas after Oma died, and within the year the house had sold. Since coming to Lubbock, we'd moved two times before finally settling into our current home. These days, my roots felt about as deep as the tumbleweeds the winds picked up and propelled across the dusty west Texas landscape.

"I spoke to Paul Henri before I came over," Marie France said. "I told him I was going to show you the studio."

"Really?" I said, unsure of how I'd handle it if he joined us. "Is he going to come, too?"

"No, no. He's not a great fan of Modigliani."

"Why?" I asked, relieved, but also surprised that the impeccable Paul Henri would not appreciate Modigliani's strong, classic lines.

"He wouldn't want me to say so, but Modigliani's history makes him uncomfortable. You see," Marie France said, her violet eyes darkening as she stirred sugar into her tea, "Paul Henri's father drinks too much."

"Oh," I said, the edges in Paul Henri's personality beginning to make a little more sense.

"Paul Henri's father can be very pleasant, of course, generous and full of stories; but he's had many disappointments. There are days when he's very difficult to be around. Bitter and angry, you know?" She touched her hair, visibly nervous to be telling me this—so why was she telling me this? It's not like I was prying.

"Paul Henri is very fortunate to have his grandfather."

Was this why Monsieur Rimbaud left out Paul Henri's father when he talked? Was he some sort of dark horse? Did we actually have a little something in common?

"How did you and Paul Henri meet?" I asked after a while.

"Oh," she laughed, "a silly story. Paul Henri's mother is a candy maker. My parents ordered some of her chocolates for the hotel—"

"—And Paul Henri delivered them." I pictured him stepping into the lobby of her parents' hotel and seeing Marie France.

"*Exactement.*" Marie France closed her eyes, lifted her face to the sun. "It's so nice here. I could sit here all afternoon. Oh well." She sighed. "Madame Marthurin expects me within the hour."

"But you don't work at the restaurant every day?" I said.

"No, no. Still, I have plenty of other jobs to do."

That first time I saw her and Paul Henri in the park, I assumed Marie France was the sort of person who had it all. Because her eyes were like morning glories and her hair was a Pre-Raphaelite painter's fantasy come true, and because she was with Paul Henri.

"What do you do?" I asked.

"Most mornings during the summer, I serve breakfast at my family's hotel," she said. "My brother, Jean, recently moved back to Paris with his daughter, and I'm helping to look after her. My niece is great, but sometimes I just want to be lazy. How about you? What will you do after you leave Paris?"

"I don't know yet," I said, then told her a little bit about what happened with the Art Institute, my mom's expectations for me at the second-rate Austin College; the reasons I came to Paris.

"All those choices—*les posibilités*." She sighed, closed her eyes. "I'd love to have the chance to go to university in a year. I wouldn't be so choosy."

Resentment nipped at the edges of her words, and for the first time I saw the dark circles beneath her eyes. "What would you study at university," I asked, "if you got the chance?"

"Chemistry."

The word brought back smelly, complicated experiments, memorizing the periodic table, Mr. Feinstein's close classroom with its smells of chemicals and disinfectant. "I've never been any good at that," I confessed.

"Ah well, I've been enamored of it ever since I read about Marie Curie in the fourth grade. When I have the time, I read on my own, but there comes a point when the subject gets too complicated to figure out without a teacher."

In the distance, church bells announced the hour.

"So late already?" Marie France said, and stood. "Sitting here is very nice, but if you want to have a look at the studio, we must be on our way."

Eight

MARIE FRANCE WALKED so fast I could barely keep up, one reason I couldn't exactly say how we got from the Boulevard Saint Michel to the Rue de la Grande Chaumière in maybe ten minutes.

"Well," she said, looking up at a rather ordinary building of tarnished stone, its battered wooden door spruced up with red paint. "This is it."

If it weren't for the brick-sized plaque bearing Modigliani's name, nothing would have told me this five story building with the geranium-filled flower boxes in the windows and fading lace curtains was anything more than a neatly kept house.

Inside we were greeted by the warm smells of herbs, butter, and something rich and onion-y. The restaurant had been paneled in dark wood, and there was a great mirror behind the bar like the one in that marvelous painting by Manet; and in the dining room's center, an ornate chandelier free from even a speck of dust.

Right away, a woman who could only be Madame Marthurin glanced up from the bar. She had faded blonde hair, dramatic brows, down-turning eyes the color of melted chocolate and a high, wide forehead. If I had to guess, I'd say she was at least seventy, but something about the way she moved and the flowing pink dress she wore beneath her apron (of which I was sure Genevieve would approve), suggested she had once been as beautiful as Marie France. In some ways, she still was, beautiful that is.

"So," Madame Marthurin said, wiping her hands in her apron, and looking me up and down. "Marie France tells me you're an artist. I would have known right away."

"Honest?" I said, flushing with happiness.

"*Oui—l'expression* in your face, yes, you have that look about you."

"*Merci,*" I said. Madame Marthurin had the practical, efficient air of someone used to taking very good care of others. "Marie France told me your restaurant has quite an amazing history."

The older woman's face opened like a flower. "You wish to hear about it then?"

"Very much," I said.

"Here, have a look." She pointed to the nearby wall where these the war years were immortalized in faded black and white photographs of men and women eating, singing, playing guitar.

She touched my shoulder, smiled. "During the war, my grandparents used to prepare daily meals for many of the people who lived in the neighborhood. They prided themselves on good food at a good price: for a pocketful of centimes, one could sit down to soup, a vegetable, sometimes—sugar being rationed, you know—even dessert. And always, there was a good glass of wine." Madame Marthurin's smile widened, revealing a gap between her top front teeth.

I searched the faces for Modigliani's and quickly found him standing just to the left of a group, his thick, black hair wild, his eyes as intense as ebony stars. Even if his clothes did look shabby, the knees of his trousers completely worn through, he wore them with incredible style: the collar of his shirt turned up with disheveled flair; his pants, loose and slightly marked with paint. No wonder he became a symbol for the Bohemian way of life in Paris.

"Are there any photographs here of Jeanne Hébuterne?" I asked, standing so close to Madame Marthurin that I breathed in her sweat and the earthy smells of the restaurant.

"You are interested in her?" she said, her voice snagging on the words.

When I nodded, she pointed out a waiflike figure surrounded by others, everyone in costume including Jeanne, who was dressed as Harlequin. I leaned closer, straining to make out her features in the faded photograph, unable to shake the feeling that even in the midst of so much company, she seemed alone.

"My grandmother always said that one loved Modigliani far too much," Madame Marthurin continued sadly, "the way one should only love *Dieu*."

"God," Marie France translated.

The meaning of the word, but especially Madame Marthurin's voice, windy and sad, made me shiver.

"No man is worthy of such devotion," said Madame Marthurin, "especially if he does not treat a woman well."

I didn't have to read between the lines to know that Madame Marthurin did not believe that Modigliani had treated Jeanne well. Knowing what I did, how could I possibly argue?

Only after Madame Marthurin made me a very good cappuccino, with delicious chocolate shavings, served in a pristine white cup and saucer, did she give Marie France the key to the studio.

"It's not upstairs?" I said, as Marie France motioned to the back door.

"Oh no," she said, then led me outside and across a small, paved courtyard with a few big plane trees and a tidy garden of roses and a sweet-smelling bed of herbs and lettuces. In a corner stood a fountain, its stone basin tinted with moss. A butterfly perched on the faucet.

"The fountain's not used much anymore, but this is where Modigliani and Jeanne would have fetched water," Marie France explained. She motioned to the building on the other side of the courtyard. "The studio is on the top floor."

I stared up at the wall of windows reflecting the afternoon light, struck by what a fascinating picture it would make: the angles of the building, the texture of the stone, the play of light and shadow.

"Come on," she said, motioning for me to follow.

Once Marie France led me up four flights of winding stairs to the top floor, where I struggled to catch my breath, did I begin to understand what life here must have been like.

"Everyone thinks garret life is so romantic," Marie France said. "*Fou*—crazy. Imagine carrying a liter of milk and a sack of groceries up all these stairs, or a child, or," she sighed, "a drunk Modigliani."

Even though a small window, rather like a porthole, was open, the hallway had that musty, sealed-up smell associated with abandoned places. I don't know what I expected to find on the other side: an easel and some old brushes, paint stains still along the floor, perhaps even a faded photograph.

But when the door opened, the wood floors were immaculately clean, as were the floor-to-ceiling windows. What sign was there that Modigliani and Jeanne had even been here?

The bright colors Modigliani had used on the walls, too, had been painted over with a camouflaging white. Where the roof slanted at an angle, there was a built in book-shelf that someone had filled with pottery, most of it chipped.

As if she sensed my disappointment, Marie France took me by the hand and led me to the far end of the studio. "This will interest you," she said, and turned the knob of a door that led to what once must have been a kitchen or a pantry.

On the other side of the door, someone had painted a portrait of a woman with a long neck and red-gold hair. She wore a deep pink tunic and around her neck, a necklace of silver beads. She was smiling, a dreamy smile, her face tilted at that indefinable Modigliani angle.

"Is this a Modigliani?" I asked, thinking the woman could be Jeanne, though the color of her tunic—its rosy shade— somehow didn't remind me of his palette which tended more towards dark colors and earth tones.

"*Non.* If it was, it would be in a museum, or a gallery," Marie France said.

"Whose work then?" I asked, becoming aware of the soothing coos of pigeons on the windowsills beyond. Modigliani and Jeanne would have listened to these same sounds nearly one hundred years ago.

"Some people say it was the work of an artist who lived here later," Marie France said, "someone who hoped to conjure Modigliani's spirit—or at least his talent."

"That's a bizarre theory," I said, unable to look away from the eyes of the woman in the portrait.

"That's not the only one," Marie France said.

"What do you mean?"

"Madame Marthurin's grandmother swore the painter was Jeanne."

"Jeanne? But the style is so like Modigliani's," I said.

"Put two and two together. Jeanne was always here. She knew his style intimately—"

"And she had artistic training," I heard myself say, for Jeanne had met Modigliani at art school.

"Not so hard to imagine now, is it? He was given to drink and drugs. There were days when his health was poor. There must have been unfinished canvases, or work in which he had lost faith. They had bills to pay, food to buy, a child." She shrugged. "Jeanne had time, and she certainly felt hunger gnawing at her belly, especially once she became pregnant a second time. Why not consider Jeanne the artist?"

I continued to study the portrait. The woman's mysterious smile gave nothing away.

"Other art historians have said as much," Marie France said after a while, "and then there are the stories passed down from Madame Marthurin's grandmother."

"What stories?" I asked, reminded of that moment downstairs when I asked about Jeanne, the focused way Madame Marthurin looked at me.

"She claimed Jeanne was always drawing in a notebook. Many views from these windows, a few sketches of her child, women very much in the style of Modigliani." Marie France gazed out the windows at the courtyard's trees below. "And then there was the terrible picture they found after her death."

"A picture?" I said. "Tell me—"

A voice—Madame Marthurin's—called Marie France's name from below.

"I'm coming!" Marie France replied in French.

"But the picture," I said, grasping her forearm.

"After Jeanne's death," Marie France said in a softer voice, "her best friends brought her body to the studio. They found a picture, a self-portrait. It's terrible, that portrait."

"You've seen it then?"

"Once." Marie France's voice dropped an octave. "There was a small show about Modigliani's relationships at the Musée Modern last spring, and the portrait was tucked away in a corner. I went with Madame Marthurin. Neither one of us could look at it for long. We never spoke about it afterwards."

"Marie France!" The voice called again, closer now.

Some awful curiosity in me needed to know what it was like, but there came the sound of footsteps, and then Madame Marthurin stood in the doorway.

"I'm sorry, *cherie*," she said, looking even older in the bright light of the studio. "My Sunday regulars have come from church. A dozen people are waiting to be fed. I need you to serve the salads and the roast chicken."

"I'm coming now," Marie France said, then turned to me. "You can stay up here for a little while longer if you like."

"No, no," I said, unable to imagine myself staying in the studio by myself, with the woman painted on the other side of the door, and the fragment of the story Marie France had just shared.

DOWN BELOW, THE restaurant, quiet less than an hour ago, now bustled with customers, nearly all of them dressed in their Sunday best, which generally meant crisp white blouses and dark skirts for the women and equally classic styles for the men, many of whom had hung up their fedoras on a hat rack. The tables were all filled. Additional people had gathered around an upright piano I somehow missed when I first came in—so much for what Madame Marthurin said about my expression.

The other waiter, a middle-aged man with heavily pomaded black hair and a mustache so thin it looked as if it had been stenciled on, looked relieved when Marie France entered. Immediately he began to call to her, very rapidly, pointing to the many tables, his round eyes like sharp, black buttons.

"Is that Monsieur Marthurin?" I asked.

"No, no. Sadly, he died years ago. That's Georges, the headwaiter. He's a real perfectionist and likes to run me off my feet," Marie France said, a little wearily, before joining him.

I began to gather up my things.

"You're not to leave just yet," Madame Marthurin said.

"But you're so busy," I said, taking in the number of people in the increasingly crowded dining room.

"I cannot send you home hungry. Besides," she said, giving me that gap-toothed grin, "my *potage aux legumes* is known throughout the district. You must have a bowl."

Her smile, but also the comfort of the room with its wonderful blend of earthy smells—bread, butter, cheese—made me say 'yes.'

Minutes later she placed a steaming bowl before me, and along with it, a baguette with butter, and a glass of lemonade. "*Bon appetit.*"

Seated at a small table beside the window, I dipped my bread in the heavenly soup, which tasted of fresh sorrel and carrots with the slightest hint of onion. Face flushed with sweat, Marie France hurried in and out of the kitchen, carrying her tray perfectly steady despite the many dishes piled onto its surface. Still thinking about the portrait on the back of the studio door, and what Marie France had said about Jeanne, I hoped to snag her attention, at least for a minute.

But the people kept coming, bringing with them the street sounds and the heat.

A man entered, carrying a cello case. Our eyes met, and the shadows in his gaze, offset by his pale skin and pitch black hair, brought to mind one of Modigliani's own late portraits of a gypsy musician. It was almost like déjà vu, and given the warmth in the restaurant, the room seemed to swirl around me.

When the door opened once more, I locked eyes with a guy at least half a foot taller than me whose shadow of a beard, dreadlocks of gold-brown hair, and agile movements held me fast. He was everything that guys in Lubbock, Texas were not, and I knew at once that he was someone I had fantasized about meeting when I first thought about coming to Paris.

"Luc," Madame Marthurin called in French. "Shame on you! Had you come any later, Marie France would have had to run to the baker's, and you know how much I need her help today."

"You worry too much, *grandmère*. I'm here now," he said, kissing her on both cheeks.

I took in the bags in his arms, each one bearing at least a dozen loaves of bread.

"Who is he?" I asked Marie France when she breezed by to refill my water glass.

"Ah, Luc," Marie France said, wiping her brow with a napkin. "Madame Marthurin's grandson, and he's brought the bread."

He lay down the bread and began trading jokes with another patron. His eyes were the yellow-gold of topaz, a tiger's eyes or a panther's.

No one would have called him handsome, but he was compelling. I found it hard to look away. "What's he like?" I asked, seeing in him his grandmother's dramatic eyebrows, her high wide brow.

Marie France hesitated, her voice a low whisper. "A liar when it suits his purposes, someone it's difficult to rely on, but a charmer, too, you know?"

From the way he was looking at us, he knew we were talking about him. And he liked it. I wondered if the French had an expression like 'black sheep.' If so, Luc was the real thing. There was the way he smiled, the deep echo of his laugh, and the loose-hipped way he stood at the bar and poured himself a glass of red wine, as he talked easily with the other diners. Nearly all of them seemed to know him by name, and from the way they smiled and laughed it was all too obvious they adored him.

"Does he live here?" I said, as he picked an old lady up in his arms and whirled her around as if they were dancing.

"Luc grew up here," Marie France said. "That woman is Madame Touchette. She told me that when he was a little boy, she used to chase him from her garden almost every morning in August—he liked to steal her cherries. The old man with the blue fedora, the one drinking all that wine, is Monsieur Poussin. He taught Luc how to ride a bike."

"Marie France!" Madame Marthurin's cheeks were red, and she was waving from the kitchen doorway.

"I'm sorry, Julie," she said and quickly remade her hair into a high ponytail. "I'd love to stay and chat, but I have to work."

I finished my soup and stole glances at Luc, telling myself he would make an incredible character study; I sensed he was looking at me, too.

What did Marie France mean when she said Luc grew up here? Did his mother work at the restaurant, too? Did they live near the studio?

When I stood to go, he turned and smiled once more, raising his hand to his forehead as if he might salute me. I half-hoped Madame Marthurin or Marie France would introduce me, but both of them were too busy serving the customers. As for the other waiter, Georges, he just scowled at Luc as he walked past.

Nine

WALKING HOME, NOT just the mysterious portrait, but Luc's parting wave stayed with me. I'd catch my reflection in the glass of a passing bus or a distant window, and I'd see those topaz eyes behind me, feel the presence of that smile. This was part of the reason why I lost my way twice while trying to find my way along the winding streets of the diplomatic district between Montparnasse and the Invalide.

The other was that I couldn't tell one high, white building from another. Besides, outside many doorways soldiers stood guard, their belts weighted by guns. Nearing them, I always walked faster, forgot where I was, so that I had to retrace my steps.

"You must have had quite the adventure," Claire said when I finally turned up. "I felt sure you'd beat us home."

"I wandered around for a while," I said, pouring a glass of mineral water. The last thing I wanted to do was admit I'd had to backtrack between Rue St. Dominique and Boulevard St. Germain, especially since I'd been in Paris now for nearly three weeks.

"That's one of my favorite things about living in Paris—the wandering." She smiled. "How was the studio?"

"Not what I expected," I said, then described the winding stairwell, the brightness of the windows, the rooms' emptiness, the painting of the woman on the door.

"If it was authentic, that door would be worth a fortune," Claire said. "It certainly wouldn't be hidden away like that."

"What if Jeanne Hébuterne painted it?" I said.

She peered at me through her glasses, wide-eyed. "An astonishing thought: whatever gave you that idea?"

"Madame Marthurin's grandmother said Jeanne was always drawing."

"Yes, that's what they say, but I find it hard to believe the painting's hers."

"Why?" I said. "If the painting was hers, there would be proof that she'd continued to work at what she loved."

"A beautiful idea, Julie, but I don't think it's possible."

"Well, I do."

She sighed. "Just think about it. If it was hers, it would be in a collection somewhere."

"I suppose so. But there's always the chance."

"I'll give you that."

I would have loved to debate this further, but from Claire's expression, I could tell she had something else on her mind.

"So," she began, "Genevieve told you Margot's going to have a baby?"

"She did…"

"Yeah," I said, unsure of how Claire felt about this news.

"Well, I hadn't planned to tell you this, but it feels important now," she said, joining me on the couch.

I pressed my hands beneath my hips to keep from fidgeting. "Okay."

"Before Mark and I split up, we talked about having another child. I wanted Genevieve to have a brother or a sister, and she knew we were trying. She was really excited." Claire pursed her lips together tightly, as if something was fighting to get out, something she could not share. "With Mark's news, crazy, irrational as it sounds, I feel as if we've doubly let her down."

I nodded, the memory of the day I opened the paper-thin envelope from the Art Institute returning, and with it, questions about my own future. If I didn't go to art school, what then? Austin College,' Mom was quick to reply, but the idea felt lukewarm, like drinking coffee that's sat on a table for too long.

My gaze travelled along the walls which were covered with Claire's art. "Your photographs," I said. "Why did you stop taking them?"

"I met Mark, and he was struggling to make it as an actor. For a while it was a shared adventure, but after a while I started to miss things like vacations and air conditioning and cars that didn't break down on the freeway," Claire said with a nervous laugh. "And then I got pregnant, and suddenly it wasn't even a question anymore. When a friend told me about a public relations job at the Los Angeles County Museum of Art, I applied.

I glanced at my favorite of her still lifes: the ragdolls on a shelf leaning against each other. They were like two children tired out from a day of play, their heads pressed together, sharing secrets, dreams. Behind them, the interplay of light and shadow suggested the quick flight of time. "But don't you miss it?"

"Of course I miss it," she said, turning towards the photographs. "Each still life was a meditation for me. I became absolutely focused."

This I understood.

"But they belong to another part of my life, and I am happy with what I'm doing now. It's satisfying," she said, looking directly at me. "Maybe, when Genevieve's older, I'll go back to them."

"I hope so."

"Thanks. Look, I know you're at a crossroads," Claire said. "It's why you're here, right? And I won't lie to you. Being an artist is incredibly difficult. You've got to keep believing in yourself. Always putting yourself out there through what you create—keeping that fire, that faith in your art—front and center. It takes a lot of energy."

"But wouldn't it take a lot more energy to convince myself that I could come to love anything else nearly as much?"

"Yes, it would," Claire said. "Your mom might not like me to say this, but I wouldn't be in such a hurry to go to Austin College. You have other options. You have time—and a hell of a lot of talent."

"You believe that?" I looked out the window at the twinkling lights of the Eiffel Tower, the colors ranging from deep purple to gold, thousands and thousands of little wishes, little dreams.

"I would never say so if I didn't mean it."

"Thanks, Claire."

I sat there, silent, glowing, never having expected Claire to say anything like this.

After all, she was my mother's oldest friend.

"One more thing I've been meaning to tell you," Claire said. "All of this change, well, it's been overwhelming for Genevieve, for both of us. I haven't said so until now, but she's more cheerful since you arrived."

I smiled, a red balloon of joy lifting me up and up. I squeezed Claire's hand.

"Hey." Genevieve's voice.

I glanced up. She wore her fuzzy pink slippers—we still hadn't made it to Bon Marché for mine—and a giant t-shirt cinched with a wide pink belt. Annie followed close behind.

"Hey, darling," Claire said. "Hungry?"

"Sort of." Genevieve sounded as if she'd left part of herself in her dreams.

"I'll take that as a 'yes,'" Claire said. "Dinner's almost ready. Light the candle, will you?"

IT WAS A knock-your-socks-off evening, the sky purple-rose; the three quarters moon, opalescent in a sky now darkened to an amethyst shirred by wispy blue clouds. After supper, we linked arms and walked along the Seine all the way to the *Pont des Arts*, the Artist's Bridge where that long ago picture of Gustave Fermiere and my mother had been taken.

"Oh great," Claire said. "The exhibition from Somalia is still here. I was hoping to catch it."

"Honest? An exhibition on a bridge?" I said.

Claire grinned. "Welcome to Paris."

All along the bridge, poster-sized photographs shone beneath the lights. Many of the faces depicted there were beautiful, in particular one portrait of a girl who looked about my age, her smooth skin like milk chocolate, her eyes the color of dark stones. She wore a batik-scarf for a skirt, and her bare chest was adorned with maybe two dozen colorfully beaded necklaces.

The bridge itself was a kaleidoscope of color, the dozens of people lounging, playing guitar, selling wares, or picnicking. Some had spread out blankets. Wherever you turned, people were sharing meals composed of anything from pizza and salad and brownies to exotic saffron-gold rice and fish served along with egg rolls and ripe fruit. An Asian girl had threaded her black hair through with electric blue. Another girl with a halo of fire engine curls wore a series of flowing peasant skirts, dozens of bangles around her wrists and ankles. One guy had tied a red bandana around his forehead, and his dog, a fluffy, brindle creature, wore a red bandana around its neck, too.

When it came to clothes, my mom looked like an ad for J. Crew on casual days, Ann Taylor or Talbots when she dressed up. It was hard to picture her pleated trousers and crisp shirts fitting into this scene. In that long ago picture taken with my father, she looked different, not bohemian by a long shot, but more relaxed. How much there was that I didn't know about her—about the person she had been that summer she spent with Gustave Fermiere.

"Look!" Genevieve called, when I joined them.

Before us lay the amusement park at *Pont du Carousel.*

"Let's go for a ride on the Ferris wheel," Genevieve said, and seized Claire's hand. "Please, Mommy."

"At this hour? Really, honey, it's late. Besides," Claire said, glancing at me, "Julie looks cold."

"No, it sounds like fun," I said, seduced by Genevieve's excitement, even though I'd had an uneasy relationship with heights for as long as I could remember.

Genevieve was small enough to squeeze between us in the compartment, and soon the carnival man was buckling us into the seat. Minutes later, the music box bells began playing, the Ferris wheel began to move, and we were gazing down at the rooftop of the Louvre with the iridescent pyramid leading to its new entrance.

Beyond lay the formal grounds of the *Jardin du Tuileries,* where the trees and bushes had been sculpted into geometric shapes. At the very center, the serene white bodies of the ducks and swans in the octagon pool floated like tiny ghosts. It was all so gorgeous I kept telling myself I could get used to this.

Until the dizziness started, then turned into pressure, as if someone was pressing down on my stomach and lungs. I tried to distract myself by imagining how I'd paint the scene before me. Watercolors or gouache accented by pastels would capture the dreamy, dizzy look of rooftops dotted with chimney pots, sequined lights, and a network of roads thronged with cars, buses and the odd bicycle. But oils would give the view particular vibrancy and dimension, especially if I applied the paint in thick layers using a palette knife. Oils or watercolors? I said, my stomach plummeting.

"I could almost be eleven years old again, spinning around up here with your mother," Claire said to me, as we climbed higher and higher, my stomach now crowding my spleen.

The carnival music swooped us up in its electric, candy-coated rhythms. The Ferris wheel came to a stop, suspending us high above the earth, so that our little compartment creaked back and forth in the breeze. A bitter, acidic taste filled my mouth, and I spiraled back to that July evening I was eight and fell through the monkey bars of a jungle gym. Mom had been playing tennis on a nearby court, and one of the other kids ran to tell her that I couldn't get up. Actually, my legs weren't the problem. It was my left arm. I'd landed on it.

I still remembered the cold feel of the ice on my wrist in the emergency room as Mom filled out the paperwork. "Excuse me, ma'am," the nurse called, "but you left off the father's name."

"No," Mom said. "I didn't leave it off."

The nurse nodded and turned away, but in her face I knew I saw disapproval. It was an expression I'd become a little too familiar with by this time, having seen it at Teacher-Parent Conferences and sometimes at the reception desk at my pediatrician's office. Sure there were single parents in our world, but even kids with divorced parents, or a parent who had died, knew who their mothers and fathers were.

I thought of what Marie France had told me about her own family life. She slept in her mother's room, which I pictured as intimately small with long windows and solid, old furniture—generations old. How connected she felt to Paris, how sure of the person she was.

I couldn't imagine feeling that kind of belonging anywhere.

Oma's love had almost made up for not having a father, but now she was gone, and all I had left were her stories, the memory of how much she had loved me, and a few of her things with which I'd never part. If I'd known then, how little time we had, I would have asked her more questions. I would have tried to understand her life more.

After Oma died, I drew pictures of her, moments from our history together. The one I loved the most showed her walking in the garden she kept in her small yard, a miniature version of the one her family had kept in Hungary. She told me often that she brought the seeds over with her. Even when I knew her, she tended to carry seeds in her pockets—or acorns. "Possibility," she called them. In the picture, I surrounded Oma with flowers and vegetables. I kept the drawing in a silver frame on my desk, and when the goldenrod and Queen Ann's lace were in bloom, I placed a vase beneath the picture because she was so fond of wildflowers. "They have spirit," she always said.

My conversation with Claire flashed through me, and it was suddenly crystal clear. How could I possibly go to Austin? It would be like giving up, surrendering the person I had always been. The fact that Mom had even asked this of me was all wrong.

Breathe, I told myself. Breathe.

When the Ferris wheel resumed its movement, the cabin we were in swung forwards. I looked up at the sky, trying to find my balance there, but the stars at that moment seemed like so many thousand shards of glass: fragile, beautiful, and impossibly far away.

LATE THAT NIGHT, I woke up, my t-shirt drenched with sweat, the sheets tangled around me. Behind my eyes pulsed the memory of a day, maybe twelve years ago, when I rode my bike without training wheels for the first time. It was an overcast morning in early spring—I knew this because the crocuses were out. Mom released my bicycle from her hands, and I peddled away from her, a bit unsteadily at first, thrilled, and more than a little scared, but riding on my own, without my mom's help—

And I did not fall.

Genevieve's nightlight glowed beside her bed. I stood, changed my shirt, slowly figuring out that the dream about the bike wasn't just coincidence, but proof I knew what I had to do. My subconscious had been working on it all night.

While Genevieve's breath came butterfly-soft, I climbed out of bed and went down the hall, Annie trailing behind me, the pitter patter of her feet reassuring me.

At the computer, I sat down and typed up a letter to Austin College, thanking them for the opportunity. "Grateful as I am," I wrote, "I have decided to pursue another path."

Afterwards, I pasted the letter to Austin into an email for my mother. 'I know how much you want me to go, but I just can't do this,' I typed, my fingers quickly keying the words. 'Coming to Paris has only made me surer of what I've always believed: I'm an artist. I don't know yet what that's going to mean for next year, but I can't start a program I don't believe in. My heart—it just isn't in it. Sorry to disappoint you, but that's where I am. Love, *Julie*.'

Ten

I CLICKED ON the internet in the morning, but there was no word from my mom. Of course, eight a.m. Paris time meant one o'clock in the morning in Texas. Possibly she hadn't yet seen the email. Or maybe she was too stunned to reply. Just before I signed off, bikerman@parislights.com popped up on the screen. *Clay.*

Hi there, Julie,

Round two of the big bike race in the Dordogne is on Saturday, so I thought I'd check in before I head south later this week. Are you free today? Would you (and Genevieve) want to get together? Ice cream on the Isle de la Cité? There's a flea market happening near the Hôtel de Ville that we can check out afterwards. Genevieve would love it. No worries if you can't make it, though I can't say I won't be disappointed…

Clay's freckles and his contagious smile surfaced, and I felt a little bit lighter. "Well?" I asked Genevieve when she padded into the living room wearing her fluffy slippers and I showed her Clay's email. "What do you say?"

"Sure," she said, and plopped down on the sofa. "Maybe we can find some things there for my doll house, dishes and stuff."

I studied the house that was coming together so beautifully under our care. Instead of using clay, we'd fashioned a chandelier out of white paper—origami-style. Old matchboxes, we'd transformed into a chest of drawers and several tiny suitcases. A wooden thimble draped with a dollop of lace served as a table.

"Now," Genevieve said, "what should I wear?"

EVEN THOUGH WE stopped to take our own version of a bird bath in garden fountains along the way, by the time we arrived at the Isle de la Cité, the gritty heat clung to our skin and hair. Clay was already waiting for us, freshly-scrubbed, probably having showered after an infinitely long, super early ride. Two of the Chihuahuas were with him. "Chloe and Esmeralda, remember?" he said.

"Oh right," I said, as the Chihuahuas and Annie checked out each other's butts. "You think other species are as up front about introductions as dogs."

"Monkeys pick lice and bugs out of each other's fur," Genevieve volunteered.

"Thanks for the totally gross insight," I said.

"You asked," Clay said. He was wearing shorts that day, and the sheen of his muscular legs proved it: he shaved.

"So tell me," I said, encouraged by the upfront-ness of the dogs, "why do cyclists shave their legs?"

"Yeah," Genevieve asked, as we entered the ice cream shop, instantly engulfed by chilly sweetness. "Is it like those men who get pedicures? Metro-sexuals, Margaret's mother calls them."

"Metro-what?" Clay was now bougainvillea-red.

"Metro-sexuals," Genevieve said. "Monsieur Deleuze, my history teacher, is definitely a metro-sexual. He gets facials every other week and went wild when our class gave him a gift certificate to the Simone Spa for his birthday."

"That's not me at all," Clay said. "I shave my legs to protect them if I wipe out in gravel. Imagine taking a bandage off a *hairy* leg."

"It hurts to even think about that," I said.

"Been there, and believe me it's murder," Clay said, pointing to a wicked scar straddling his left knee.

"What'll you have?" the server asked, enunciating his English with exaggeration, as if we were a trio of tourists.

Clay ordered for all of us in fluent French. For Genevieve, raspberry swirl; for himself, chocolate; and for me, something fruity and full of pineapples and coconut.

"Delicious," I said. "How did you know?"

"You look like a tropical island sort of girl," he said.

"Is that a compliment?"

"You bet it is. Your hair has that sun-kissed look, and there's a glow to your skin that reminds me of warm breezes, salty ocean air—"

I hadn't expected such, well, such poetry. "Thanks," I said, hoping the sun's glare blocked out my blush.

"What about me?" Genevieve interrupted, licking her raspberry swirl.

"Anyone who can wear five different shades of pink—"

"Six," Genevieve corrected.

"Six then," Clay said. "Point is, if you can coordinate that much pink, you and only you should live on raspberry swirl."

"Does that mean I can have another scoop?"

"Why not," Clay said, then turned to me. "I mean, if you're okay with it?"

"Sure," I said, still reveling in the idea of my chlorinated hair described as 'sun-kissed ' from someone other than Claire.

Afterwards we strolled around the island, looking up at Notre Dame, especially its gargoyles, which inevitably got me thinking about my father. Why would he picture himself as such a creature? What demons had he been fighting off? And what was I going to do about taking steps to find him? And the much bigger question: what if he didn't want to be found?

"The word 'gargoyle' comes from the French, *gargouille*," Clay explained, chocolate ice cream dripping onto his t-shirt. (He, too, opted for a second cone.) "It's the word for 'throat.' Most gargoyles spout water," he said. "*Gargouille* has its root in the Latin *gurgulio* as in 'gurgle'—"

"I feel like we're walking around with an Encyclopedia," Genevieve said after Clay went into the gory background surrounding Robespierre's capture during the French Revolution.

"Yeah," I teased, though the truth was I rather liked it, if only because it kept me from dwelling on my own thoughts. "First the gargoyles, now this."

"Cut me some slack," he said as we neared the labyrinth of flea market stalls that had sprouted up like a makeshift village outside the Hôtel de Ville. "My dad's a historian. Can you begin to imagine what outings around here are like for me?"

"A lifetime of field trips sans school bus?"

"You got it."

"Seriously, I'm sorry."

"I'll take all the sympathy I can get on that front. But you have to admit, this is probably the most amazing city hall you've seen," Clay said, staring up at its gleaming white façade, its endless rows of symmetrical windows, and its high, silvery-gray roof.

"No argument here," I said, then opened my drawing pad, and did a quick sketch, confident I could remember enough to fill in the details later.

"You sure have range," Clay said, glancing over my shoulder.

"It's just a quick sketch—"

"Fine, be modest, but I watched you work at the bookstore that night. You had, what, twenty minutes with a sitter, and you managed to capture a personality. And now you've got the bones of the building down as well. How can you work so quickly?"

"Practice," I said, never having realized he'd been paying such close attention. Pretty soon, I was telling him about what happened with Austin College, my decision not to go.

Clay nodded. "When your body knows something, you have to listen. Now that you've put the decision behind you, you can focus on what's next. Be open."

"You think so?" I said, struck by what good advice this was.

"I'm positive. Think about what happened at the bookstore. You walk in looking for a biography, and suddenly you're being asked to sketch portraits at a party."

The relaxed way Clay thought about his future calmed me down. "I never thought about it that way," I said.

"Well, you should," he said, so close we were almost touching noses.

"Look, Julie, over here!" Genevieve called from a brightly-decorated stall protected by a candy-cane-striped canopy.

While Clay studied a tray of antique pens, I joined Genevieve before an array of bins containing every kind of toy imaginable: tin soldiers dressed in blue and red uniforms, elaborately designed wind-up toys, ancient stuffed animals by the German firm Steiff, dolls with porcelain faces, even a bin containing dozens of jack- in-the-boxes.

The woman behind the bins wore a baggy, woolen cardigan. Her blonde hair spilled out of a bun that reminded me of an unraveling skein of yarn. "*Vous voudrais quelque chose, mademoiselle?*" she asked.

I smiled at her noncommittally, until I spotted the pom pom animals including a dachshund and what had to be a poodle. I dug further in search of a Chihuahua but should have realized they were far too skinny to be made out of fluff.

Genevieve was intensely interested in a bin containing doll-sized potted plants and tiny trees. "I thought we could make a garden for the doll house," she said, excitedly.

"Great idea," I said, admiring a thimble-sized flowerpot filled with the tiniest yellow and white daisies.

Before long Clay sauntered over, holding out his new pen. "Van Gogh green."

"Don't tell me," I said. "You're a collector."

"*Oui*," he said with a flourish. "Since my father gave me my first Cross rollerball."

"And how old were you?"

"Ten."

"That explains a lot."

We faced off, me, grinning, Clay, mock-furious, until Genevieve seized my arm. "Come on, you guys. Stop wasting time."

We ducked by at least four stalls selling hippy jewelry, passed a stall selling crepes. The fragrance that wafted our way, a heavenly blend of butter and syrup and something inexplicable I had to chalk up to atmosphere, brought all three of us to a complete stop. "What do you say?" Clay asked, the three of us transfixed by a crepe bubbling on the griddle.

"Yes!" Genevieve said, and I followed.

Though our stomachs still churned with the ultra-rich ice cream, we shared a crepe filled with blackberries and whipped cream, then went back for another.

Clay put a dollop of whip cream on the Chihuahuas' noses, and they tried their hardest—without success—to lick it off. "You shouldn't tease them," I said, biting the inside of my mouth to keep from breaking into hysterical laughter. But hey, I was the role model here, at least as far as Genevieve was concerned.

"Come on, Julie," Genevieve said, as Esmeralda used her paws to swipe at the whip cream. "This is totally hilarious." Soon, Annie, too, had whip cream on her nose.

"Yeah," Clay said and grinned.

Deeper into the labyrinth, we paused to admire or gawk at various items for sale, the most outlandish being a hot pink divan resting on a gold platform. "What do you think?" I asked Genevieve, wishing I could drape myself across its pinkness. The scowling vendor dressed in a mismatched array of plaids made that impossible.

"It would go well with my slippers," Genevieve said.

"But I think this is more you," Clay said, and pointed to a table designed to look like one of those fairy tale mushrooms in *Hansel and Gretel*, and would have been just right in a backyard or a bedroom.

"You think so?" I said.

"I do," he said, splotches of pink—was he blushing?—appearing on each of his cheeks. "It's creative, magical, the word 'enchanted' comes to mind."

'You think I'm enchanted then?' I almost asked, but before I could, Genevieve shouted, "It's perfect for a tea party."

"A Mad Hatter's tea party," Clay said.

I just stood there, mulling over the possibility that Clay thought I was 'enchanted'—was that like 'enchanting'? I pulled out my drawing pad to make a quick sketch, but the scowling vendor shooed us away.

"*Interdit!*" he called.

"You'd think he'd lighten up a little," Genevieve said.

"Where do you suppose he gets that stuff?" Clay asked, looking back once more.

"Hollywood?" I suggested. "An Austin Powers yard sale?"

"Oh my god," Genevieve cried, and made a dash for a collection of vintage clothes—mostly pretty junk. For Genevieve, this stockpile of old hats, scarves, macramé handbags, belts, blouses, and skirts—from a tartan plaid to a go-go pink mini—was heaven.

"What do you think of this?" she asked, stepping out of the makeshift dressing room in a man's batik-print shirt that hit her knees. "Only three Euros. Wouldn't it be amazing with a belt or a ribbon?"

"You bet. Buy it," I said, captivated by a pair of totally unpractical pink silk gloves at an even more unpractical price—was Genevieve's infatuation with clothes contagious?

"Hey," Genevieve said, rummaging through a stack of old bathing suits, until she pulled forth a glittery gold one piece with a little fringe for a skirt. She explained that this was an original Nettie Rosenstein and went for $500 in the States. "This one is marked at thirty Euros."

"Nettie who?" Clay and I said together.

"Only the person who came up with the first 'little black dress,'" Genevieve said.

"You do know your stuff," Clay said approvingly, a statement that had Genevieve glowing for the next half hour.

"Lend me the money?" Genevieve stared mournfully at me.

"Sorry, but I haven't got it."

She fixed her gaze on Clay.

"If only I'd won the Chartres Race, I would hand it over in a heartbeat."

Having been forced to leave the bathing suit behind—really, it was six sizes too big—Genevieve pouted for a while after that. Nonetheless, it had turned into a good day, the kind of day I could never have imagined when I sat at the computer writing to Austin, and then my mother.

"You okay to walk home in those?" Clay said, eyeing the strappy violet vinyl sandals I found in a bargain bin. (Only the French could create cheap chic that was both uncomfortable and irresistible.)

"I'll live," I said, staring down at my chipped toenail polish. "We should meet up again soon."

"Name the day," Clay said. "I'm back from the Dordogne on Wednesday."

For just a moment, I tried to picture that ex-girlfriend of his, Lacy-what's-her-name. What had she looked like? And had biking really enabled him to forget her? And what about what he'd said about me: 'enchanted'?

"So, about the race," Genevieve asked. "Is it going to be televised?"

"Nah." Clay toed the ground with his shoe. "This is just for amateurs."

"Well, good luck anyway," Genevieve said, seizing hold of his arm, and tugging him down to kiss his cheek.

"Oh, one more thing," he said to me, after Genevieve released him. "Think I could have that sketch of the Hôtel de Ville?"

"It's nothing special," I said, a warmth beginning deep in my belly.

"Well then, you won't mind parting with it. You did say I'm obsessive about history," he grinned. "The Hôtel is about as historical as you get."

"I see your point," I said, carefully freeing it from my drawing pad.

"Merci," he said, rolling up the drawing up with real care.

We stood there looking at each other, and as I shifted my weight from one foot to the other, I sensed that Clay was doing the same thing also.

"Come on, Julie," Genevieve said, tugging at my hand.

"Yeah," Clay said. "It is getting late."

"Let me know where you hang the drawing," I said.

"Will do."

As he and the Chihuahuas faded into the Paris sunlight, his cleats tip-tapping against the pavement, I wondered what might have happened if Genevieve hadn't been there.

Eleven

Julie,

I can't deny the fact that I'm disappointed by your decision. That said, it doesn't come as a huge surprise. I knew you were dragging your feet, and I have to trust you to know what you need and want.

The big question is what will you do come fall. You told me the gallery is going to acquire a Modigliani. If you focused on arts administration, you could stay in the field—and paint. I'm still hoping that's the decision you'll come to, maybe not now, but in time.

Just think about it. And try, honey, to picture where you want to be in ten years.

Love,
Mom

In ten years? Was she serious? I hadn't even reached my second decade. I could barely think two years down the road, much less five or ten. Well, what had I expected, an 'I'm behind you all the way'? That would have been delusional. Mom had spent ten years in school between college and her PhD. At least, I told myself, she said she trusts me. That had to be a step in the right direction.

Like Clay said, the door was open now. I just had to listen for the possibilities. Question was: where did Gustave Fermiere fit into this picture? If he did fit in at all.

Twelve

AFTER A SERIES of delays, the first dealing with shipment problems, the second dealing with customs, the Modigliani finally arrived at the gallery. "Magnificent, isn't it?" Rafi said, the hazel flecks shining in his dark eyes, as he gulped Orangina straight from the liter-sized bottle.

"*Sans doute*," I said, studying the woman who cradled a baby in her arms, its tiny face peeking out from beneath a bundle of blankets. "But you never said there was a child in the painting."

"Because part of the magic of art is always the element of surprise," he said. "There are no portraits of Jeanne with their child, so that makes this portrait especially unique."

'And valuable,' I could hear him thinking.

"You said this portrait resembles two others," I said. "Is there a child in those paintings as well?"

"No, the woman is the same, but the child appears only here. Odd," he said, studying the painting more closely.

"What is it?" Claire asked, joining us, and behind her, Genevieve.

"The child has a slightly different feel than the rest of the portrait."

I stepped closer. "You're right," I said. I'd had enough experience working with oils to see that the child seemed to have been laid on top of the original design. "I think she was added later. Even something about the brushstrokes feels different."

"You may have something there," Rafi said.

"Imagine," Claire said, "finishing a portrait and then altering the composition. There must be a story here."

"What happened to her?" I asked, tuning into the way Modigliani had used just a hint of blue from the dress to accentuate the woman's cheekbones, and to give definition to the shape of her eyes. The child's white blanket, too, contained echoes of blue and gold.

Rafi looked at me through the glint of his glasses. "To Jeanne?"

"No, I know Jeanne's story. What happened to the child?" All the biography said was that Modigliani's friend, a golden-haired Polish aristocrat named Lunia, who was a little in love with Modigliani herself, often cared for the baby when Jeanne could not. The more desperate their living situation became, the less of a mother Jeanne was able to be.

"Modigliani's sister or perhaps it was his mother who adopted her," Rafi said. "The daughter, originally Jeanne but later Giovanna once she moved to Italy, became an artist also. She visited Israel once after the Second World War. There was a retrospective of her father's work, and my mother met her. She wrote a book about her father—"

"Really? What is it about?"

"It's a study of his work," Rafi said.

"Was she happy?" Genevieve asked.

Rafi looked at Genevieve, frowned. "Sorry?"

Rafi, who focused entirely on art, had obviously not clued in to the fact that Genevieve was fretting about her own father's absence.

Claire put her arm around her daughter's shoulder. "I think so, honey."

"Well," Rafi said, clapping his hands, "this new development should draw even more attention to the painting. Imagine—a portrait of mother and child, of Jeanne and their child."

Isn't that a little mercenary? I felt like saying.

"MY DEAR GIRL, if what you say is true, Monsieur Stein is only doing what art dealers have done for centuries," Monsieur Rimbaud said when Genevieve and I stopped at his shop afterwards and I told him what had happened.

"But is it ethical?" I said.

"*Cherie*, this is Paris, the city with nearly as many art galleries as *boulangeries*. Any art dealer worth his salt, or the plaque beside the door, needs to make his investment worthwhile."

"Maybe," I said, picturing a scale: on one side, Rafi; on the other, a container with the Morton salt girl holding an umbrella. What I said to Clay the other day came back—*When I draw, I know who I am.* I didn't want that focus mixed up with sales.

"Consider the aspiring artists your Monsieur Stein represents, all the artists whose paintings sell for a few hundred Euros. No art dealer could showcase their work without resources, especially here in Paris. My business may not be art," he said, measuring out precise spoonfuls of a black, aromatic tea, "but there are parallels. Always I must remember the financial side, even though it is my love of old things that keeps me in this world."

"I sense a serious conversation—"

That voice. I turned to see Paul Henri enter the shop. Dressed in crisp, black jeans and a gray t-shirt, his dark hair brushed away from his face to spotlight those incredible blue eyes, he looked even better than the last time. Or just more Parisian. That all-too-familiar and all-too-mortifying scarlet flush crept up my neck and across my cheeks.

"You seem different today," Paul Henri said.

"Doesn't she?" Monsieur Rimbaud said. "I'd say our Julie is becoming more Parisian by the day."

"You think so?" Paul Henri didn't exactly sound convinced.

"The scarf, the crown of braids: are these not reminiscent of early Catherine Deneuve?" Monsieur Rimbaud said.

"We bought the scarf near the Luxembourg Gardens," Genevieve said. "I helped her pick it out. It makes her eyes pop."

"Pop?" Paul Henri said. "Isn't it balloons that pop?"

"An American expression," I added. I should have realized he was never going to give me a compliment by his own free will.

"Tea, my dears," Monsieur Rimbaud said, placing four beautiful cups on a tray.

"Marie France said she took you to the studio," Paul Henri said to me.

"Did she?" Monsieur Rimbaud said, pouring us each a cup. "Such a lovely girl, that Marie France."

"Tell me, Julie," he said, fixing his radiant old face on me, "what was your impression of the studio?"

I thought of the emptiness of the rooms, the way the shadows clung despite the light coming through the windows. "Honestly, it made me sad. Are there many visitors?"

Monsieur Rimbaud shook his head. "The stairway is too steep, too narrow. The courtyard makes the studio hard to access."

"What about renovation?"

Paul Henri arched an eyebrow and turned to his grandfather.

"What?" I said, fearing I'd put my foot in it. Maybe this went again some ancient code that Paul Henri and everyone else but me knew about.

"You must have seen the old-fashioned cappuccino maker behind the bar," Monsieur Rimbaud said, raising his teacup to his lips. "The antique photos on the walls."

"Yes of course."

"Well then?" Paul Henri now fixed his blue eyes on me. What was this some kind of test?

"Madame Marthurin likes her life the way it is," Monsieur Rimbaud said.

"Oh," I said, relaxing a little as I remembered her gap-toothed smile, her pride in the photographs of the restaurant's history along the walls, her exceptional cup of cappuccino, the customers she'd known for years. Maybe some of those people, or their ancestors, had been coming into the restaurant in Madame Marthurin's grandmother's day.

"Marie France said that when the pipes in the restaurant get clogged, Madame Marthurin thinks nothing of fetching water from the fountain in the courtyard," Paul Henri said. "Once, this went on for days until one of the waiters told her the health officials could close the place down."

"That sounds like Marta," Monsieur Rimbaud said, chuckling.

"You know her well then?" I asked.

"Since I was twelve, and she, eleven, my older brother was terribly in love with her. He must have spent a small fortune on flowers—"

"And?" I couldn't resist asking, still waiting to find that love story with a happy ending.

Monsieur Rimbaud sighed. "As so often happens in this life, she did not have eyes for him, and a year later she married Jacques Marthurin, and for three decades they were as happy as any couple can expect to be."

"What about her grandson?" I could feel the heat rising to my cheeks. "If it were up to him, would he renovate the studio?"

"Luc?" Paul Henri's voice, at that moment, not to mention the tension in his neck and shoulders, brought to mind a cat with its back hairs standing on end. "You met him? He was there?"

"Yeah, why?" There was no denying I found this new edge in Paul Henri's voice satisfying. It went all the way back to that first day in Claire's apartment, the way he emphasized *impasse*, as if it applied to me—and him.

"Luc is a thief," Paul Henri said. "If you have any sense, you'll stay away from him."

"An exaggeration," Monsieur Rimbaud said to me. "These two had an unfortunate falling out a few years back."

"Don't whitewash the situation, Grandpère," Paul Henri said. "Isn't that the American expression? You know, as well as I, Luc hopes to inherit the restaurant. He'll turn it into something like a night club or a—"

"Studio," Monsieur Rimbaud said, smiling once more.

"He's an artist?" I asked, astonishment but something else, too—hope?—tugging at the corners of my voice.

Paul Henri seemed to hear it, too. "A kitsch artist," he said.

Monsieur Rimbaud shook his head. "Ignore him, *cherie*. My grandson exaggerates."

"What else can you call someone who makes so-called art out of hubcaps, fenders, old headlights?"

"Inventive," I volunteered, reveling in Paul Henri's scowl.

"She has a point," Monsieur Rimbaud said.

"Grandpère, you know that fool spends entire days scouring the junk heaps in the city."

"Luc is talented, and he transforms the car fenders and broken radios he finds there," Monsieur Rimbaud said. "You know that, and you used to admire his resourcefulness."

If I weren't so interested in Luc myself, I would have sat back and watched Paul Henri work himself into what Oma would have called 'a state.' It was like the green-eyed monster had taken over his body or something.

"Marie France said he grew up at the restaurant," I said.

"In an apartment above the restaurant," Paul Henri said.

He was about to say something else, but his grandfather cut him off. "Luc's mother was an actress here in Paris."

"She isn't alive then?" I asked.

"*Non.* Losing her the way they did: it was a terrible thing for Madame Marthurin and Luc. The boy was maybe seven when she died. The whole thing was terrible, terrible."

"And his father?" Yes, I knew I was prying; but I just couldn't help myself.

"He left for Morocco years ago," he said, for the first time speaking almost severely. "It was up to Madame Marthurin to see to Luc's upbringing. My old friend may run a good restaurant, but she hasn't much money. Luc's had to be inventive."

This time Paul Henri didn't argue.

Now I really wanted to hear more, but the door to the shop opened, and a dazzling older woman with a platinum bob entered, swathed in what looked like a velvet wrap.

"Ah, Madame Finisterre," Monsieur Rimbaud said, and immediately joined her with a bow.

"Who's that?" I asked.

"A very committed patron," Paul Henri said under his breath, as his grandfather guided the woman over to a display of nineteenth century Limoges china.

"Did you see her blouse? It has to be vintage," Genevieve said, looking up from a book of old-fashioned photographs.

"Madame Finisterre once worked in the atelier of Chanel," Paul Henri said.

"No way." Genevieve slammed the book shut, and she hurried after Monsieur Rimbaud and his fashionable client.

"Listen," Paul Henri said in a friendlier way than I'd heard before. "I have an appointment in the Marais tomorrow, but on Saturday afternoon I'm supposed to run an errand for my grandfather in the neighborhood around Père Lachaise."

I just stood there staring. Was he actually inviting me, the American with the capital A, to do something? What would it be like to spend a day, alone, with Paul Henri? Did I actually want to?

"The famous cemetery," he said. "Haven't you heard of it?"

"Yeah, sure," I said.

"Chopin, Heloise and Abelard, the singer Edith Piaf—my god, they're all buried there. And Modigliani, too, is there in the Jewish section, and alongside him, Jeanne. So, if you're interested, you could come along. The errand should only take a few hours. I have to pick up a few pieces for the shop at a monthly flea market."

"Is Marie France going to go, too?"

He shook his head. "She has to look after her niece this weekend. Well?" he said, leaning against an antique armoire. "What do you say?"

"Sure," I said, determined not to reveal a shred of interest.

"Where should we meet? Do you want to come here?"

"Come to the gallery." I said, deciding to meet him on my turf this time.

Thirteen

"I CONGRATULATE YOU, Monsieur Stein. This is quite a coup," said Marisol Becerra, the art historian whom Rafi had brought in to evaluate the portrait. A commanding woman with olive skin and coppery hair cropped just beneath her chin, Madame Becerra liked to slice through the air with her index finger to get her point across, as if it were a fast-moving metronome.

That Saturday, she was literally holding court in the center of the gallery before an audience that included Rafi and Claire, but also half a dozen interested collectors, among them a glamorous old woman with an upturned swirl of sterling silver hair. The woman's name was Isadora Dupont, and she was both fabulously wealthy and known to have been a great beauty in her day. According to Rafi, Madame Dupont's grandmother had posed for Modigliani.

"The introduction of this portrait will solidify the reputation and the future preservation of many of Modigliani's lesser works," Madame Becerra continued in a voice that reminded me of Spanish guitar pared down to a single chord.

'Reputation and future preservation,' I learned within the first few minutes, were favorite expressions of Madame Becerra's.

"How so?" asked the chic journalist in a red pantsuit (which Genevieve swore was vintage Halston) who was invited to attend.

"The portrait changes our perspective on his other work," Madame Becerra said, "not just the images of Jeanne, but his portraits of all women, especially mothers."

"*C'est possible*," Madame Dupont said, the smoke from her cigarette wafting dangerously close to Madame Becerra. Rafi may not have allowed smoking in the gallery, but he wasn't about to stop this influential potential buyer from lighting up.

"Nevertheless, Madame," she said, continuing to smoke, "you will have to say a great deal more before you convince me that this portrait sheds new light on our understanding of Modigliani."

Madame Becerra raised a perfectly plucked eyebrow, obviously astonished that anyone would doubt her—she taught at the Sorbonne, I learned, and had lectured worldwide. "Is that so?"

"Oui. You cannot deny that he was in love with the Madonnas in the churches," Madame Dupont continued, narrowing her gaze through the smoke. "It's no wonder he would paint the woman he loved in such a manner. Too bad he did not revere Jeanne in life as he did in art."

"The art historian is not concerned with the artist's private life which is often *mélodramatique*," Madame Becerra said, enunciating each word sharply. "It is the work that matters, the images that survive. The life, well," she said, frowning a little, "the work ultimately cuts free of that."

I imagined Jeanne's climb up the long stairway to the studio and what Marie France had said about Jeanne helping a drunken Modigliani up those stairs. And of course, somewhere beneath my reaction lay all that my mother had said about my father not wanting a child who would, she'd told me, interfere with his work.

"I disagree," I heard myself say.

Madame Becerra turned her sharp eyes in my direction. "You?" she said. "And who are you to disagree?"

Everyone was looking at me, waiting, even the journalist in red.

"Julie, my name is Julie Hankla, and I'm an artist myself," I said, strangely unafraid.

"This city is full of artists. Tell us: what are your grounds for disagreement?"

"Simple: how can a person fully appreciate the value of the painting without knowing the story behind it?"

"Well?" Madame Dupont said to the art historian. "It seems this *jeune fille* has an important question in need of an answer. You're the expert."

"Jeanne was a powerful presence in Modigliani's life and in his art," Madame Becerra conceded. "But art's power lies in the fact that it separates itself—becomes disentangled from the messiness of living."

How could that be? I thought, reminded of the un-tethered way I'd felt when I first came to Lubbock. Oma had died less than a year earlier, and our new house had seemed too new, too sterile, without any connection to the life I had known, the person I had been. Without understanding why at first, I began sketching Oma doing one of the things she loved best: curling up in an armchair and knitting. Except I placed her in our new house. And I felt better afterwards. Art was connected to life. Otherwise, what was the point?

But Rafi was scowling at me, and Claire mouthed the words 'Not now.'

And then I spotted Paul Henri taking in the whole scene with a little too much amused interest, or so it appeared to me.

So much for meeting him on my own ground.

"You're not really going to the cemetery with him?" Genevieve asked earlier as I stood before the mirror, trying not to let her see how obsessed I was about choosing just the right outfit, settling at last on my white jeans and apricot blouse.

"Of course, I am."

"But that's so creepy," Genevieve said. "Walking around gravestones all day…"

"No, it's not," I said, hooking a gold loop through my ear. "There's a lot of history there."

Paul Henri lingered at the back until the discussion died down enough for the group to move to a table where Claire had set up glasses, several bottles of chilled wine, and a plate of bread and cheeses. He helped himself to a snack, but it wasn't until we left the gallery that he told me about the letters. "They concern Jeanne Hébuterne," he said with a reserve I found unbelievable, even for him. "I thought you'd want to see them."

I came to a dead stop in the middle of the busy Rue Jacob, a few irritated Parisians streaming around me. "Of course I do, but why did you wait until now? Why didn't you tell me right away?"

"Think about it. An art historian who clearly loves the spotlight—isn't that the English phrase?—was in the gallery," Paul Henri said, the trace of a smile tugging at the edges of his lips. "It was not the place to cause a scene, not until we're sure what to do with the letters; not until we're sure they're authentic."

"How did you find them?"

"I was browsing a book fair near Notre Dame," Paul Henri said. "Several of the vendors there specialize in artists' books. I found them in an old book of Modigliani prints. I thought you'd want to have it."

"Really?" I said, never imagining Paul Henri would think to buy a book for me. "You found it for me?"

"Why not?" He said, casual.

"Thanks," I said quickly, afraid if he said more, he'd spoil the moment, or just shatter my illusion that he actually gave two figs about me when I was out of sight.

"The book's at the shop," he said, smiling his beautiful, crooked smile, "waiting for you."

"And the letters?"

"They were pressed inside."

"IT'S A STRANGE coincidence," Monsieur Rimbaud said, as we stood before one of the letters, which he had placed on the table before us. It was written on onion-skin paper, the ink so faded it was barely legible.

Marie France's *serendipity* came to mind. "What does the letter say?" I asked, reading the name of the writer: Germaine Labaye, Jeanne's best friend.

"It's addressed to one of Jeanne's old school friends," Monsieur Rimbaud said.

"Chana Sadkine—"

"I remember her name from the biography," I said, squinting at the loopy handwriting which, being faded and in French, proved well beyond me. "Please," I said, seizing Monsieur Rimbaud's wrist. "Read it to me."

August 8, 1918

Dear Chana,

I feel more hopeful about Jeanne than I've had reason to since she told me of the second pregnancy. She's painting again, you see, and although she continues to work in his style, her colors are bolder, more brilliant. If you were here, you would say they're the colors of the marguerites she used to weave through her hair on those afternoons when the three of us wandered the open markets; or the colors of the picture postcards she collected—'my harvest of images,' she called them, remember? The colors of the water and the sky she was always gushing on about on those schoolgirl holidays beside the seashore. How long ago it all seems, and how much all of our lives, but especially hers, have changed. The painting seems to be a celebration of life. I want to do all I can to see that this happiness continues, though I know that is out of my hands. Her happiness is so deeply tied to his, especially now that she is the mother of his child. How I wish there wasn't a second child coming when managing the first has been so difficult. At least he's to have a London show, and so it seems he will now have the success he so desperately needs—and deserves.

No, I cannot care for Modigliani as she does, not when I see how much this love has cost her. It's an impossible predicament, really, for if he could love her as he loves his art, they might be happy. But I have seen his passionate experiments with color and line, the animation in his voice and body when he speaks about a particular master—I know he doesn't have a choice, and so she, and their children, will always be confined to the shadows. Our only hope—that he makes a great success and can provide for them properly.

Yours,
Germaine

I thought immediately of the painting on the back of the studio door. "The colors of that portrait at the studio," I said to Monsieur Rimbaud. "They're so bright, so exuberant. So Jeanne was the artist—"

"A likely conclusion," Monsieur Rimbaud said quietly, "but the letter will have to be authenticated."

"Grandpère, we made a mistake," Paul Henri said, looking up from another letter, to which he held a magnifying glass, so faded was the ink. "This is not the only letter that mentions Jeanne.

"Here," he said. "This one is also signed Germaine Labaye, and it's dated mid-November, nearly four months later."

November 15, 1918

Chana—

Jeanne has ceased working with the bright colors, ceased painting at all. (There is no longer any money for it.) The reason? There will be no London show. Such a terrible disappointment after his hopes—and hers—were soaring. There was talk of buying a little house, finding a nurse for the children. But no longer.

Fame is such an elusive thing. He says he doesn't live for it, but what human being does not want to be recognized for the work he's done? And, despite his bohemian ways, he is an Italian and a proud one at that, not to mention a man who must provide for four soon. Why didn't they take precautions? He's begun drinking again. And his health is worse. Zborowski continues to support them, but with a second child on the way, a struggling art dealer's help is simply not enough.

At my urging—oh I was foolish—Jeanne came with me to her parents to ask for help. How certain I was they would not turn her away. Their own daughter. I was wrong. A woman's purpose is as a wife and mother, they told her. Or a nun. Or a salesgirl in a shop. Or an artist. But what business does a woman have in bringing children into this world without being properly married?

They closed the door in her face, Chana. How foolish I was to think it could have turned out otherwise.

I fear for her, and for the little girl. Only two years old, and already her life is so full of chaos and fear. What will become of her?

Yours,
Germaine

The words of the letter stuck in my throat; I felt sick inside, nauseous. The three of us sat in silence, as if the presence of Jeanne were here in this room with us.

"But who did the book belong to?" I asked at last.

"There's no inscription," Monsieur Rimbaud said. "I imagine it must have been Chana Sadkine's. All of the letters here were written to her—"

"—Except this one," Paul Henri interrupted, holding up another sheet of paper, this one crisper, the ink brighter. "Chana Sadkine herself wrote this letter," he said, scanning the print, "to her daughter."

September 1, 1952

Dearest Marguerite,

I hope you will keep this book close on the crossing to New York. It has always given me great pleasure to think of you pursuing a career in art, something I never would have had the courage to do. Yes, it was much more difficult in my day for a young woman to think of herself as an artist. Even for the most talented and the most egotistical man, it could be difficult—but for a woman it was nearly unheard of, especially if she thought of any kind of family life.

If I am honest with myself—and with you—I will say mine was never a great talent. I painted because it gave me pleasure. When I had to give it up, I found pleasure in many other things, especially in raising you.

You mentioned seeing the paintings by Modigliani at the retrospective in Milan last year. His work dazzled me, too. Even when he would give away a sketch in exchange for a liter of wine, I knew he had genius. I hope, then, these images provide you with some inspiration.

All I ask is that you do not allow the legend of Modigliani to confuse you. His life, as I said, was extraordinarily difficult. And his muse, my dear friend Jeanne, was the greatest casualty of his reckless, tragic life. She, too, had talent—though hers was not genius—if one understands genius to be a drive so strong it allows nothing else—neither love nor health—to come first. It was Jeanne's greatest gift and her worst failing that she believed so absolutely in Modigliani.

That was her genius, and it cost my dear friend her life.

And then there is the daughter, Giovanna. The poor girl grew up without either mother or father. When I met her in Paris all those years later, she was so desperate for some clues to help her understand her parents. Her grandmother had spoken to her about her father, of course, and there were the examples of his art. But her maternal grandparents wanted nothing to do with her, and so Giovanna's knowledge of her mother remained a street full of shadows.

For you, darling Marguerite, I do not want genius, for it does not mean a happy life. And you, with your daisy-light laughter, were meant for happiness.

Maman

"So the book belonged to Chana Sadkine's daughter, Marguerite," I said, a heaviness weighing me down as I thought about Modigliani, Jeanne, and their daughter.

"It would seem so," Monsieur Rimbaud said, still scanning the letter.

"I can't believe she would have given it away," I said, "especially when it is filled with letters such as these—"

"Grandpère," Paul Henri said. "Come here."

I looked over his shoulder. On the shop's computer, he'd typed in the name 'Marguerite Sadkine,' whose birth date read: 1931 and her death: 2007.

"Ah," Monsieur Rimbaud said, his blue eyes calm, his expression philosophical.

Even if I didn't know much about used books and antiques and flea markets, it wasn't hard to assemble a story from these pieces. Chana Sadkine's daughter must have returned to Paris from New York at some point, the book still in her possession, proof she had cherished it, and her mother's letters. When she died, whoever went through her things must have done so haphazardly. Otherwise, that person would have found these letters and realized their value and that of the book.

"Well?" Paul Henri said. "What next?"

"I'll call an old friend to see about authenticating the letters," Monsieur Rimbaud said. "It'll take several days, as he isn't in Paris anymore. Until then," he looked at me, "I think it's best we keep the discovery of these letters amongst ourselves, *c'est clair?*"

Fourteen

WHAT THE LETTERS might mean—how they might impact what we knew of the painting—swam through my head. I was desperate to reach Père Lachaise, for there I would have some time to think. But first we had to make the trip to the flea market or *marché aux puces*. The noise and commotion took my breath away. This flea market was at least twice the size of the one I'd visited with Clay and Genevieve. "It's one of the largest and the oldest anywhere in Europe," Paul Henri explained, steering us around a group of old ladies chatting beside a table of cloisonné china.

The flea market near the Hôtel de Ville had been a higgledy-piggledy array of wonderful items. This highly organized place was much more Paul Henri, the hundreds of brightly-colored stalls stretching out in rows all around us by category: textiles, furniture, porcelain, jewelry. The paths between them were thronged with people. Several pushed bicycles or baby carriages, making it a challenge not to bump into someone.

"What I especially like about browsing the *brocante*—second-hand goods—is you never know what you might find," he said, his voice brimming with excitement.

"Like the book about Modigliani?" I said, which I'd had to leave with Monsieur Rimbaud for now, though everything inside me was dying to hold onto it.

"Exactly."

Paul Henri quickened his pace, confident and happier than I'd seen him before, as we made our way through the crowd.

"Mostly I hunt for porcelain," he said, surveying a booth devoted to just that. "Grandpère has given me carte blanche when it comes to purchasing Limoges vases, children's tea sets, porcelain figurines, silver-edged mirrors. Certain patterns like this one," he continued, picking up a plate adorned with a border of violets, "are always in demand."

"But you put the plate down."

"It's a fake," he said under his breath.

I felt sure the vendor, a squat man with a toad-like face, heard him. "How do you know?"

He shrugged. *"Expérience.* Grandpère started me doing these hunts when I was ten. It's nothing specific that tips me off, but genuine Limoges, well, it has a radiance that one lacks."

It was Paul Henri's skill, similar to that of the painter who knows just where to brush in a speck of light on an otherwise dark canvas, that prompted him to select, from a table of bibelots, a tiny statue of an elephant carved out of some gray stone, his first purchase in over an hour of looking. "What's it made of?" I asked.

"Smoky gray quartz. Not an original Fabergé but an incredible copy," he said after paying the vendor, this one a woman with a knot of yarn-gold hair.

"Fabergé?" I said, as we made our way over to a stall selling all sorts of vintage clothes and accessories, the kind of thing that would have put Genevieve in seventh heaven.

"Mon Dieu, you need an education!"

'And you need to get a grip on your ego,' I would have said, except that I was curious. "So educate me," I said smugly.

"Very well. Fabergé was a Russian jeweler who worked for the czar well into the Russian Revolution. The poor man was still making beautiful objects such as this one while the czar was held prisoner in some Siberian village. Such was his faith in the old order returning to power."

"Or his delusion."

"A matter of perspective, Julie," Paul Henri said, then stopped to survey a rack of hats. "What do you think of this one?" he said, holding out a pale blue hat shaped like a bell.

"Very elegant," I said, reminded of that white velvet hat in the expensive shop.

"This particular style is called a cloche."

"I know," I said. "I happen to have one."

"*Bon.* Try it on, will you?"

"Okay," I said, pleased, as I took the hat from his hands, turned towards the mirror. The cloche fit me, and I admired my reflection in the glass. The way the brim shadowed my eyes gave me a mysterious, older look like those actresses in the old movies. "Well?" I said, turning to Paul Henri.

"Pretty," he said, "but I'm afraid not."

"What do you mean? It's gorgeous."

"You exaggerate," he said, turning back to the others. "The hat is nice enough, but Marie France has much more hair than you. It would not fit."

"Oh right," I said. How could I have been so naïve as to think he was considering it for me?

We kept browsing, but it was pretty clear after about ten minutes that nothing here was going to work for him. I wanted to buy the cloche, but I wasn't about to do so in front of Paul Henri. I did, however, find a brooch shaped like a bumble bee for me and a very small pair of chartreuse gloves that would be too, too perfect on Genevieve.

"Hungry?" Paul Henri said after I paid for them.

"A little," I said. Having eaten a brioche ages ago, I was starved.

"Well then," he said, "let's eat."

"But the food is in the other direction."

"We're not going to eat there," he said, as if I'd suggested McDonald's. "Come on."

I followed him to a bench a little away from the crowd, shaded by an enormous horse chestnut tree.

"You packed this?" I said, as Paul Henri produced a wicker box from his backpack.

"The food here is over-priced," he said, handing me a sandwich from the wicker box, then pouring us each a portion of white wine from a small bottle.

From a distance, we must have made a picture-perfect couple: a stunning French guy of the Merchant Ivory Films variety and a sort of pretty American girl sharing a picnic lunch. Of course I would have looked even better with the hat, or at least more the part.

"This is a great sandwich," I said. "What's in it?"

"Brie and apples, the tartness of the apple mellowed by the cheese."

"You sound like a food columnist," I said, for he did have the fussy nature of a gourmet chef. "How often do you come here?"

"At least once a month. Grandpère began bringing me years ago. He always believed my mother would come into the business to help him—"

"But she didn't?" I said, reminded of what Marie France said about his parents.

"Old things do not interest her," he said, topping off our wine. "No, Maman's passion has always been chocolate. All my life I have woken up to the smells of cocoa and other essences."

"Sounds heavenly," I said.

"Don't romanticize," he said, and sipped his wine.

"So you're going to run the shop?"

"Yes. Grandpère has given me leave to establish a vintage photography collection. I have a Man Ray and several by Ansel Adams."

"So there's an American artist you actually like!"

"Don't be ridiculous, Julie," he said. "I am not anti-American. You take everything I say in such an extreme way."

"Do I?" I said, glad I'd managed to strike a nerve.

"*Oui!*"

Paul Henri's love of photography didn't surprise me, not when he clearly loved cataloguing objects, identifying them. A camera did that better than anything else.

I took a bite out of my sandwich and tried to imagine what Paul Henri's darkroom would be like, instantly picturing the chemicals neatly labeled on a shelf, the photographs drying on a rack safe out of harm's way, everything precisely where it should be.

"That first day, your grandfather said you had the chance to go to art school. Don't you think you'll miss not going?"

"*Pourquoi*—why? Running the antique shop is what I've always known I would do. Grandpère would be heartbroken if the shop died after he could no longer run it. *Non,*" Paul Henri said, "that decision was made a long time ago."

Reminded of how happy I felt just that morning as I sat sketching the silhouette of a bird, and beside it, the geraniums in the window box, the range of color contained in a single petal opening up to me as I drew, I knew I could never be satisfied doing something else.

"What about Luc?" I could taste the risk of this question, but I couldn't resist, not after the incident with the hat.

"What about him?"

"You said he was an artist."

"No, I used the word 'kitsch.' I said he made so-called art out of scraps of junk. The work may have its fans, but it's not the sort of thing that will stand the test of time. In one hundred years," he said with a little too much satisfaction, "Luc's chrome horses and birds will not be in a museum."

124

"You're that sure?" I said. "Why?"

"Taste," he said in his haughtiest voice, made haughtier because the pronunciation of the French word for taste, *goût*, required a certain torque of the lips. "Luc Duplessis's work is faddish."

"You can be a real snob, you know that?" I said.

"I'm sorry. That was unfair of me. I'm in a bit of a mood today."

"You? Why?"

"My father," he said, "The man is—to put it, as you say, mildly, a foolish *rêveur.*"

"I don't know that word, I'm afraid."

"A dreamer, one with his head in the clouds."

I stayed quiet, sure he had no idea that Marie France had told me about his father.

"Papa calls himself an inventor, but it's Maman who worries about the electric bill and the groceries and works Saturday and Sunday while Papa tries to come up with some gimmick to make his fortune. My poor mother used to have to pretend to believe in him. We all did.

"So," he said. "You asked about the heavenly scent of chocolate. Perhaps it is heavenly to you. But it reminds me of how hard my mother has to work. Today she was up before five a.m. There are some repairs to the house, and then my sister's dancing tuition." Paul Henri spoke matter-of-factly, but I could feel the undercurrent of unhappiness.

"Your sister is a dancer?"

"Monique is the next Pavlova," Paul Henri said, the elitist in him returning. "She dances like a swan and in another year she will begin her apprenticeship at the Ballet Nationale.

"Now, tell me about you. Hankla is not a typical name for an American, is it?"

"Hungarian," I said, seeing no point in telling Paul Henri that the only real 'American' names belonged to the Cherokee, Sioux, and other tribes. "My mother's parents came to Chicago in the sixties. They were farmers in Hungary, but they didn't do so well after the war."

"Unusual for you to have your mother's name, isn't it?"

I stared back at Paul Henri, and then the words just sprang to my lips. "Not when I know next to nothing about my father."

For the first time, Paul Henri looked uncomfortable. "I had no idea. It was not my intention to—"

"It's okay. Honestly, I've been thinking about him a lot lately," I said, relieved, almost, to bring him out into the open. I remembered the Ferris wheel, and what Mom always said about confronting your fears if you're going to overcome them. Paul Henri wasn't exactly the person I imagined confiding in, but maybe the fact that he wasn't emotional or even very sympathetic would make it easier. He wasn't going to dole out a lot of fake feeling.

"Lately? As in, since you've been in Paris?" Paul Henri looked puzzled.

"That's right. My mom met my father here one summer while she was in graduate school. He's French, an artist." I hurried the words out. "The relationship didn't last. At least that's how she put it."

"That must have been terribly difficult for your mother, and for you."

"Yes," I said, relieved to be finally talking about this. "It was really hard when I was younger. Now, it's mostly strange. Here I am in Paris. As far as I know, I'm half French, and I don't know anything about that part of my history."

"But you know enough to realize something's missing," he said.

"Yes, I do," I said.

Maybe that's what working with antiques did for a person, I realized, as we retraced our way through the market, on the way to the exit. It gave them a perspective larger than a single life. "Let's stop a minute," Paul Henri said when we passed the rack of hats.

"I thought you said the cloche wouldn't fit Marie France," I said.

"That's true," he said, selecting the hat. "But it looks very good on you."

Fifteen

WE DIDN'T REACH the cemetery until nearly five thirty, since the last hour involved a serious hunt through some silverware, and the careful examination of a tea service at what Paul Henri called "an incredible price," though the four figure number seemed astronomical to me.

A light rain was falling, and all around us the air smelled like leaves, grass, and something much older—a fragrance I would have compared to a sadness infused by sunlight. 'Nostalgia' meant the same thing in both English and French. But it was only now, surrounded by ancient trees and crumbling monuments, the rain falling, that I felt I understood this longing for something beautiful that was now lost.

I thought of Oma, who we buried next to my grandfather in an old cemetery on the South Side of Chicago. Her only request had been for us to plant hollyhocks and something white and lacy there, using seeds from the flowers in her garden that she'd brought with her from Hungary. How far from her own country she traveled during her lifetime. How much she must have missed Hungary's countryside during all those years she lived in Chicago where the streets were concrete, the view of the sky often blocked by the apartment buildings and factories in the distance. Not that she complained. But there was something in her expression sometimes, and in her voice—

"As I said, Modigliani and Jeanne Hébuterne are buried in the Jewish section," Paul Henri said, while we hiked up a cobbled walkway littered with fallen leaves.

Paul Henri didn't have to explain to me why the Jewish section was tucked into a more remote and hard-to-get-to part of the cemetery. Even if Madame Becerra hadn't talked about the reputation of Modigliani and his paintings being negatively affected between the First and Second World Wars, I knew the Jews had suffered a great deal in France, as they did almost everywhere in Europe, during the twentieth century.

"There's an old Jewish neighborhood in the Marais," Paul Henri said, checking a map along one of the markers. "Even though the synagogue there is beautiful, the artistry of the prayers carved into stone exceptional, it's been empty since the 1940s."

"What about after the war ended?" I asked. "Didn't the people who used to live there come back, the survivors I mean?"

Paul Henri shook his head. "There were few survivors."

"What happened to those who did make it?" I asked, careful not to slip on stones made slick by wet leaves.

He didn't answer. I was reminded of the piece by Anselm Kiefer in the gallery, Rafi's description of it as 'an offering' to those who died during the Holocaust. Rafi spoke of that Hebrew command to remember—*zakhor*. It was a responsibility, a burden to be among those who lived, to carry the necessity of remembering all that had happened.

Once we reached the Jewish section, we had to make another long uphill climb before we found the row containing Modigliani's grave. The landscape twisted and turned. If Paul Henri hadn't been with me, I'm not sure I would have found it.

"Here," he said, pointing to a plot obscured by the fallen leaves of a nearby oak tree.

I looked down at the gravestones.

Modigliani's art had always been so simple, and his life, especially at the end, so poor; but nothing prepared me for the plain stone marker bearing his name and dates, the writing already obscured by time and weather. Beside him Jeanne's gravestone was equally spare.

I picked a delicate, yellow wildflower and laid it on her headstone, understanding that Jeanne and Modigliani's daughter, Giovanna, must have come here, too, in search of some clue, some connection to the parents who'd died before she could get to know them. *A street full of shadows*, Chana called Giovanna's search.

What had art meant for her? It must have been a part of her journey towards her mother and father; but after or beyond that? Had it provided Giovanna with hope and comfort? Had it helped her find a place for herself in the world? And what of my place? A voice deep within me asked.

"Why don't I leave you for a few minutes?" Paul Henri said quietly, though there was no one else around. "A friend's grandmother is buried close by. I always water the flowers planted there."

I nodded, too overwhelmed to think of Paul Henri, or anyone close to my age, taking care of the flowers on someone else's grandmother's grave. He wore sneakers and knew the subways and flea markets inside out, and he was probably the most judgmental person I'd ever met, on either side of the Atlantic; but there was something gentle and incredibly old-fashioned about Paul Henri, or at least old world, from the wicker basket in which he'd packed lunch to his knowledge of old china, and especially, his commitment to his grandfather.

I touched the brim of my hat, reminded of the unexpected kindness of Paul Henri buying it for me.

That was one of the remarkable aspects of my time in France and perhaps one of the most difficult to explain. Here, I continually seemed to find myself stepping into several new worlds, one overlapping the next. I traced the letters of Jeanne's headstone, and as my fingers felt the cold, smooth stone I felt the questions about my own past, stirring, pressing to be brought up into the light.

I love you enough for both of us, my mom said once.

It had been weeks since I found that paragraph about Gustave Fermiere, weeks since I copied it. By now, I'd read it so many times I knew it by heart.

AT HOME THAT night, I sat before the computer, reminded of how easy it had been for Paul Henri to find that information about Chana Sadkine's daughter.

I typed his name and the place where he used to live—maybe still did live—into the search engine again. It came up with a dozen results for Gustave Fermiere.

I tried again, this time adding 'art restoration' to the description:

Gustave Fermiere, Art Restoration, 13 Rue Placide, Provence.

Who would have imagined it would have been so easy? That he'd been there all along?

Part Two

Sixteen

Dear Father, I began, only to cross it out immediately. 'Father' sounded too intimate. He'd never met me. He's still your father, that voice inside me said. *Dear Father,* I began once more. *I'm in Paris for the summer, working for a friend of my mother's. I'm taking care of her daughter...*

I read this first sentence over and over again, second-guessing the smallest things. Should I put more emotion into the writing—or less?

Just get to the point, the voice said again. *I want to know if you and I might meet. I see that you are involved in art restoration. Do you still paint? I have seen the painting you made of the red room with the view of Paris. I don't know the story behind it, though my mother keeps it above her desk. I don't expect anything out of this meeting,* I wrote, only to cross these words out right away.

Of course I expected something. Otherwise, why would I try to get in touch? But what could I say were my reasons? I want to know why you never wanted me. I want to know if you have any other children—if I have any half-brothers or sisters—for all these years, all my life, it's just been me and Mom, especially now that my grandmother has died. Coming to France, where so many people have such deep roots, centuries of history all around me, I've started questioning the meaning of family and home over and over again. Growing up, all I had was Mom and Oma. Now she is gone, and with her, the history she carried.

I couldn't put this down in writing. I sounded confused (which I was). He would probably tear the letter up and try to forget he'd ever heard from me.

I've been through a lot of changes these last few months, I wrote instead. *The art school I always wanted to attend didn't accept me. That's the reason Mom sent me to Paris—to widen my perspective. This has happened, but in more unexpected ways than I could ever have dreamed possible…*

In the next room, Genevieve stirred in her sleep. Sometimes she murmured the word 'Daddy.' She was going to see him in a few weeks, and she was growing more and more excited as the day drew near.

I crumpled up the paper and threw it in the trash.

Dear Father, I began again. *My name is Julie Hankla. I'm seventeen years old, and I'm in Paris for the summer working as an au pair. I would like to meet you, though I know very little about you, except that you are now living in Provence. That's only a few hours away by train. Please, will you meet me?*

Really, what else was there to say?

Seventeen

ALL THROUGH THE next three days, it rained. Not a drizzle but a soaking rain that required umbrellas, galoshes and slickers. It was the kind of rain that encouraged you to curl up with long novels, movies, and warming cups of tea. I'd look out the window at the street below and sketch the dozens of colors and patterns, even count the number of dogs wearing slick yellow ponchos. (A few actually wore booties. The Parisians took their wardrobes and their dogs very seriously; the booties being the icing on the cake.) Normally, I would have loved this break from the summer sun; but now I was totally focused on the letter I'd sent. The tick tock of the clock reminded me of the time that would pass before the letter reached Gustave Fermiere, if he was even here in France. After all, he could be away for the summer. Or maybe he'd moved, and failed to update his address.

Then, on the fourth day, the sun came out.

Relieved to hang up Claire's extra slicker (safety red and a good three inches too short in the arms), and even more relieved to plunge into the bright, fresh air, I put on my floatiest sundress and the pale blue cloche, packed a lunch, and Genevieve and I set off for the Luxembourg Gardens, Annie hurrying alongside us.

"I'm going to buy some cotton candy," Genevieve said when we arrived, nodding towards a balloon-crowded stall run by a toothless man who could have been a walking advertisement against sweets.

I knew I should remind her of her sandwich and nectarines, but she'd been so patient throughout the last few days, playing with her doll house, sketching fashion designs, flipping through every *Teen Vogue* and *Paris Chic* in her possession at least twice, and watching movies that I liked almost more than she did, including *My Neighbor Totoro*, which we sat through four times, and *Lady and the Tramp*. Besides, I was tired, my sleep fitful since I posted the letter. How long was a reasonable amount of time to wait for Gustave Fermiere's reply? Ten days? Two weeks?

"I'll meet you over there," I told Genevieve, pointing to a pair of chairs, nowhere near any shade. After the rain, I didn't want to hide.

I lay back and closed my eyes, letting the sun hit my face, the sounds of the garden—a mix of children's laughter, intimate conversation, and muted street noise—washing over me.

"Hey there!" A voice called.

At first I paid no attention, assuming the person was talking to someone else.

But when he called out again—"Hey!"—louder this time, I looked up. The dreadlock-threaded hair, the topaz eyes. *Luc.* Dressed in a plain white t-shirt and faded jeans, he seemed younger and less overwhelming than I remembered, while remaining every inch as gorgeous, and I could feel myself blushing up to my eyebrows.

"The girl from my grandmother's restaurant, right?" he said, sitting down on Genevieve's seat. "Marie France's friend?"

"Yes, I'm Julie," I said, the questions ricocheting through my mind. Did he know I came to the park? Was there a chance he'd been hanging out in the hopes of seeing me? A tingling sensation rushed down my spine.

"*Enchanté*, Julie," he said. "The other day, you left before I had a chance to introduce myself."

Given how long I sat there eating my soup while he chatted with diners at the bar, I didn't believe this for a minute. But I couldn't deny it: his words set the butterflies fluttering within my chest.

He motioned to the drawing pad on top of my rucksack. "Marie France said you're very good. May I have a look?"

"Okay," I said, pretending casualness I didn't feel as I handed him my drawing pad.

They actually talked about me!

He turned the pages, lingering in such a way that suggested he was seriously interested, and I began hoping that Annie would get distracted sniffing the shrubbery and Genevieve would take her time coming back.

The muscles in his shoulders and arms were as well-defined as Clay's, and up close his skin looked boyishly soft: kissable. His lips were full, and they turned down with concentration—what I wouldn't have given to trace the outline of his mouth. And there was a tiny scar, shaped like a crescent moon, along the base of his chin; the kind of scar one would get from falling against a concrete step. Had it happened when he was a child? Had his mother been alive then?

"I like this one," he said, then held up a sketch I'd done of a cat curled up in one of the geranium-filled window boxes that were nearly everywhere in Paris.

"*Vraiment*—really?" I would have expected him to choose one of my portraits; lately I'd taken to drawing people wherever I went. There was a particularly good one of an old fisherman beside the Seine who I'd come across while walking there at dusk. And on the last page I'd drawn a ballet dancer having a cup of tea at a café, her hair still tied up in a neat bun, her satin toe shoes slung over her shoulder. "What do you like about my cat?"

"The sinuous line from head to tail, the languor that could instantly transform into something else: it's clear you pay attention."

"Thank you," I said. Luc himself was catlike. In a weird way, he reminded me of the snow leopard that Genevieve and I saw at the Paris Zoo, though that poor creature had paced his glass room continuously. Nothing about Luc gave the impression that he was caged.

"Hey," Genevieve said, returning, her mouth and her fingers sticky with the purple spun sugar swirl.

"Your sister?" he asked, even though Genevieve and I looked absolutely nothing alike.

"I'm taking care of her for the summer."

"Ah, so you are an au pair."

"More or less," I replied.

"Who are you?" Genevieve looked from Luc to me, trying to puzzle out our relationship. "A friend of Clay's?"

"Clay?" he said. "As in sculpture?"

"No," I grinned, imagining what Clay would look like sculpted by Rodin. "He's a friend here."

"Ah," he said. "A good friend?"

"We hang out," I said, aware I wasn't exactly being truthful. The last time we said goodbye—the way we looked at each other just after I gave him my drawing—hinted at something much more.

"But who are you?" Genevieve asked again.

"Manners, Genevieve," I said and frowned.

"Not at all. I like her *détermination*." He held out a hand. "I'm Luc Duplessis," he said.

"How do you know Julie?" Genevieve asked, ignoring the gesture as she pulled off a chunk of the cotton candy.

"Julie," his eyes lingered on my face, "came into my grandmother's restaurant a few weeks ago."

"Oh yeah," Genevieve said, stretching out on her chair. "She told us."

"Oh she did? Tell me, what did she say about me?" He leaned back, a little expectantly.

Genevieve poked the pebbled path with her shoe but held his eye. "Nothing."

Lùc burst out laughing. "Nothing?"

Genevieve shrugged, plucked another finger full of cotton candy. "All she said was she liked the soup, and she told us about the painting in Modigliani's studio."

"The one on the back of the door," I qualified, realizing Genevieve's attitude here was a real asset.

Luc's topaz eyes came alive. "Jeanne's painting," he said.

"You really believe it's hers?" I said, reminded again of the letters. If all went well, Monsieur Rimbaud would have an answer about them in five more days.

"I know it's hers."

"How?" I said, wishing I could tell him about letters, and just imagining the impact. "How do you know?"

"Who else, besides Modigliani, could have brought such tenderness to those long, fluid brush strokes, the qualities that Modigliani is known for? A woman who looks so much like Jeanne?"

I thought back to the biography, pictured Jeanne in the studio, sewing or cooking or caring for their daughter while Modigliani worked. She'd been an art student when she met him, but afterwards the biographer said she gave everything up.

Unless she didn't—unless, as Marie France suggested— Jeanne had helped to finish his paintings. Unless, as the letters indicated, and as Luc so clearly believed, she kept up with her art all along, stopping only during those terrible last few months before Modigliani's death.

"Has Julie told you about the painting by Modigliani at the gallery where my mother works?" Genevieve had nearly devoured her cotton candy by now, her lips and her fingers a purplish-blue that matched the color of her smock dress, this one flecked with iridescent flowers.

"A Modigliani?" Luc sat up straighter. "No, I don't know anything about it."

Surprised, no, amazed he hadn't heard of it, I sat back in my chair and let Genevieve be the one to tell him about the portrait, which she did, with surprising detail.

"You've piqued my curiosity," Luc said, placing his hands on his knees and leaning closer.

Paul Henri would have tried to make me suspicious of Luc's interest.

But on this balmy afternoon, with the pigeons hunting crumbs at our feet, and the sun filtering chartreuse light through the leaves of the horse chestnut trees, Paul Henri wasn't here. And even though I was wearing that exquisite pale blue cloche he'd bought for me at the flea market (which Genevieve said was 'to die for'), I basked in Luc's attention, the worry about finding Gustave Fermiere nudged to the side, for a little while anyway.

"The gallery's not more than a twenty minute walk from here," I heard myself say, the scarf around my neck fluttering in the breeze, giving me a cosmopolitan, confident look that went well with my windblown summer dress.

"Well then," he said, looking from Genevieve to me. "Let's go."

Outside the garden gates, Luc showed us where his motor scooter was parked. "I could give one of you a lift."

For a split second, I fantasized sitting on the back of Luc's scooter, my arms wrapped around his waist, my palms aligned with his breathing, as we burned through the city streets.

"Julie," Genevieve said, touching the chrome handlebars. "Could I go with Luc?"

"No," I said, unable to imagine what Claire would say if she learned I let her daughter ride around Paris on the back of a near stranger's scooter. As for me going, no matter how much I was dying to find out what it would feel like, to hold onto Luc, whose torso was almost as sculptural as Michelangelo's David, it was outrageous. Genevieve may have known the metro system a hundred times better than I did, but she was still a child.

TWENTY MINUTES LATER, Genevieve and I hurried into L'Espace Stein to find Claire and Luc standing before that faux-Impressionist painting, the pretty one of a city street in the rain. Luc, who was easily six two, towered over Claire. It was only a slight exaggeration to say that two of her feet could have fit into one of his shoes. From the way she was looking at him, I could tell he was making an impression on her, though what kind of impression seemed difficult to say.

"It seems your friend here knows the artist," Claire said to me, pointing to the tulips.

"You do?" I turned to Luc, liking the way 'friend' sounded since Claire used the French 'ami,' which was close to the Spanish 'amor.'

"Madame Delmar is a friend of my grandmother," Luc said. "She comes into the restaurant every Tuesday, studies her sketchpad, and orders the same meal: bouillabaisse with bread and a portion of potatoes."

The gallery door opened, and Rafi stepped in, his Albert Einstein-wild hair in more disarray than usual, his wire-rimmed glasses perched unevenly on his nose. In his arms, he carried a paper bag. His week's supply of Orangina.

"*Je vous reconnais*—I recognize you," Rafi said, studying Luc's features, once Claire introduced them.

Luc shrugged. "I have that kind of face—"

Hardly, I thought, for I'd never seen anyone who looked like Luc.

"No, I'm sure I know you from somewhere. Ah yes," Rafi said, righting his glasses. "Now I remember. You were in a show recently, no? An exhibition at the Cartier Institute?"

"*Twenty-Five Artists Under Twenty-Five*," Luc said.

Was this for real? Paul Henri said Luc made so-called art out of junk metal, and Monsieur Rimbaud made it sound like Luc was a real struggling artist, trying to do what he loved without many resources.

But this! Even after only a few weeks in Paris, I knew the Cartier Institute showcased the work of the most prominent up-and-coming artists.

"Cartier showed one piece," Luc said, hands in his pockets.

"A dog, wasn't it?" Rafi said, enthusiastic. "And it was made out of metal, yes of course. The body was made out of a re-fashioned fender and the ears and paws—"

"Old fry pans and spatulas," Luc said, his slow smile proof of his pleasure at Rafi's attention.

"Most imaginative and very good," Rafi said, his eyes not once straying from Luc's face. "Tell me, where do you find your materials?"

"I've been scouring the junkyards around Paris since I was seven," Luc said. "Much of what I make depends upon what I find. I thrive on improvisation, or at least what *objets trouvés*—found objects—suggest."

How differently he presented his habits, I realized, reminded of the scorn in Paul Henri's voice, the elitism—or maybe just jealousy and a deep grudge—for really I knew nothing about what their relationship was like.

"Well, you're obviously very good. And the idea of recycling materials is very au courant."

"I never thought of it that way," Luc said, scooting his hands into his jeans pockets. "I just never had much money. Scavenging made sense. Besides," he grinned, revealing a chipped front tooth, "I enjoy it."

"Yes, of course," Rafi said. "Tell me, are you exhibiting anywhere?"

"A friend of my old teacher's has a place in the Marais," Luc said. "A hole-in-the-wall really, not far from the famous falafel place. I'm comfortable there."

"I know it." Rafi said. "A good location, though it's not the Left Bank. If it doesn't work out, come and talk to me."

"That's quite generous of you," Luc said.

Generous? I thought. Are you kidding? It was beyond amazing. Luc couldn't have been more than twenty. To have a prominent art dealer offer to take on his work at that age, well, it was extraordinary, huge, and simultaneously a business venture that Rafi thought worth his while.

I turned towards Luc, who had stepped over to the Modigliani. He stood there for a long time, arms crossed over his chest, legs slightly apart. The quality of attention captivated me, as if he'd forgotten the rest of us were even here. I couldn't help imagining what it would be like to touch or draw that body: the sinuous arms, tight belly, a fine line of dark hair beginning at his navel.

"According to Julie, you, or at least your grandmother, know a lot about Modigliani," Claire said, her gaze drifting over to me a little too often—thank god she couldn't read my thoughts—as she talked to Luc.

He turned away from the painting. "I wouldn't say that."

"Modest?" Rafi said, taking off his glasses, as if this would enable him to see Luc more closely.

"*Non.*" Luc laughed, revealing that chipped tooth. "Nobody knows much about Modigliani. Almost a century later, and he's still a mystery."

"And so is Jeanne," I could not resist adding.

"*Vrai*—true," Luc said, meeting my eye.

"Julie is very passionate about Modigliani and especially about Jeanne," Claire said.

"Passionate, yes, I can see that," Luc said.

I turned away, self-conscious and yes, flattered.

"Your grandmother must be doing very well if she's managed to hang onto that property all this time," Rafi said, once we gathered in the back, and he opened a box of the corner bakery's Madeleines while Claire poured Oolong tea into small blue cups. "In Modigliani's day, the Rue de la Grande Chaumière may have been inexpensive, but it's hardly that today."

"Doesn't that filmmaker, the one who made *Amelie*, live there?" Claire asked, cuddling up against Genevieve whose eyes had that muzzy look, as if she was ready for a nap.

"A few blocks over," Luc said, reaching for a Madeleine. "But you're right. The old street is becoming expensive. My grandmother is very old world. She knows how to be *regardant*— I don't know the English word," he said, and looked at me.

"Thrifty," Rafi translated.

"Why haven't you or your grandmother done anything to make the public more aware of Modigliani's studio?" Claire asked.

"The place would need a lot of renovation, and that would require an architect and contractors. Paris is very strict about building codes. Besides," Luc said, the teacup looking tiny in his big hand, "my grandmother has a lot of respect for the past. She's not interested in having crowds of people poking around."

"What about you?" I said, tasting the risk of this question, the threat of Paul Henri's criticisms balled up like a fist.

"The property belongs to my grandmother," Luc said, his eyes intense, focused. "She makes the decisions."

I nodded, gratified at the way his answer, the immediacy of it, pushed the harsh things Paul Henri had said into the background.

"Are you often at the Luxembourg Gardens?" I asked, once we stood outside the gallery, the skirt of my dress swirling around my calves, as the wind blew, and Luc unlocked his bike.

"Every once in a while. A friend lives off the Rue des Fleurs," he said, the topaz in his eyes, in the late afternoon light, softening to amber. "And you?"

"Genevieve and I go a few afternoons a week. She loves it there," I said, my eyes tracing that small, crescent-shaped scar along his chin. Would I hear the story about it one day? Would I touch it? And why did Clay's face swim into my memory so that I felt more than a little guilty—the French 'coupable' sprang to mind? After all nothing had happened between us. And yet—

"And you love the Luxembourg, too, no?" he said, stepping closer. "How right you looked sitting there, how I would have liked to draw you, the light on your face, the shadows from the trees—"

I stared down at my feet. Was my interest in him that obvious? "Who wouldn't love the garden? The flowers, the fountains, such atmosphere—" I could hear myself rambling.

"Next time I'm up there, I'll look for you."

"Promise?" The word was out before I could reclaim it.

"I am not good with promises, but you are not the sort of girl I will forget." He smiled at me, just as he'd done that day at the restaurant, a smile that seemed amused and distant and definitely unreliable. Still, it was the kind of smile to turn my knees to melting candles, to warm my belly like hot chocolate on a December day. Then he leaned over and kissed me on the cheek.

His lips were warm and smooth, and his skin smelled of sunshine, cinnamon, and a trace of garlic.

People kissed hello and goodbye all the time in Paris, I told myself, as he climbed onto his bike, revved the engine, then pulled into traffic, the noise startling a drowsy cat in a doorway.

Yes, people kissed hello and goodbye all the time here.

Even so, deep inside, my world was spinning.

Eighteen

WAS IT JUST coincidence when Marie France telephoned that same night? I asked after Genevieve handed me the phone. "What's up?" I said, trying to sound casual.

"Those sketches you did at Shakespeare & Company were fabulous. I called to see if you'd like to be the resident artist at a very special party at Madame Marthurin's restaurant."

My hand strayed to my cheek. Luc's kiss. "What's the occasion?"

"His birthday is coming up in the middle of July—"

"Birthday?" Had I missed something? "Does Luc know about the party?"

Marie France laughed. "No, no, not Luc's birthday, it's Modigliani's birthday. Madame Marthurin says Luc was born during a snowstorm, one of the only real storms in Paris's history."

"I don't understand," I said. "Modigliani's birthday? But he's no longer alive."

"*Mon Dieu*," Marie France said. "I see that I have not set this up well. Here's the situation: every year on Modigliani's birthday, Madame Marthurin serves an Italian-influenced meal in his honor. Instead of two seatings for dinner, she serves a lavish buffet, and she opens up the courtyard for dining. There are paper lanterns, some intriguing guests. A few gypsy musicians come and play. I told Madame about your artwork, and we both agreed it would be *merveilleux* to have an artist present—"

Caught up in imagining what that courtyard would look like filled with the lightning bug glow of lanterns and guests, and somewhere in that courtyard, Luc and his disarming smile, I heard myself say 'yes.'

A door into the unknown had opened, and I was stepping through.

"*Fantastique*," Marie France said. "Madame Marthurin will be so happy!"

Afterwards I sat there staring out at the Eiffel Tower, picturing myself standing along its balcony by starlight, Luc at my side. He would tell me about the scar on his chin, and I would tell him about Oma.

"And Luc is Madame Marthurin's grandson, right?" Claire asked, once I told her about Marie France's invitation.

"Yes," I said. "Why? What's wrong?"

"I'm a little concerned, that's all," Claire said, reaching up to massage a sore shoulder.

"You don't like Luc," I said.

"I wouldn't say that," Claire said, the edge in her voice like sandpaper against rough wood. "Besides, he's older."

"Maybe two years," I said. "That's hardly older. Really, Claire, he's the same age as Paul Henri."

"Oh Julie, Paul Henri is so responsible. Luc seems like someone who could get you into trouble."

Had she seen the two of us outside? I made myself poker-faced and said, "What are you saying?"

"Just that you're dazzled by him. That's a dangerous position to be in. Take my word for it: I've been there. One doesn't made good decisions under such circumstances."

"Come on, I just want to draw some portraits at a party. I thought you'd be happy for me. You told me that I had talent," I said, playing a trump card. "This is a chance to practice my art."

"Of course I'm happy for the opportunity. It sounds like a terrific one, but as your mother's oldest friend—"

"What is it?" I said, sure there was something she wasn't telling me. "This isn't just about Luc, is it?"

Claire shook her head, rubbed her shoulder—she spent way too much time slumped over the computer screen.

"Just tell me."

"Here," she said, walking over to the computer. "I found Gustave Fermiere's name and his address among the recent searches. I wasn't trying to pry, but I have a blocker on my browser because of Genevieve, a sort of screening process when someone goes to an unknown site."

"Oh," I said, a butterfly-fluttering beginning deep in my belly. "How long have you known?"

"Since yesterday. I've been trying to figure out how to approach you about this."

"Just say what you need to."

"Right. Okay then," she said. "I think you need to talk to your mom."

It amazed me, that she was bringing this up into the light, she knew. And to my surprise, it wasn't panic I felt—but relief.

As Claire punched in the international codes and then the number, I pictured my mom sitting down at her desk beside the window, staring out at the garden, the little painting of the red studio just in front of her—why had she kept it all these years? What did it mean?

Meanwhile, instead of being a wreck as I'd been that day on the Ferris wheel, I just sat there, absolutely calm.

Claire said 'hello,' then handed me the receiver.

"Hey Mom," I said.

"Julie, it's so good to hear from you." Mom sounded a little breathless, and I wondered if she and Claire had already talked about this. "How are you?"

How to begin? I wondered, then blurted out the news of my internet search, and as the silence thickened on the other end, I repeated the paragraph from the biography, word for word, described that picture of the gargoyle.

She didn't speak right away, and I pictured that focused, faraway look she got when she was really concentrating.

"A part of me expected this to happen," Mom said at last.

"You did?"

"Yes. You're in Paris, after all."

"Mom," I said. "What if he had the breakdown because he regretted what happened?"

"What do you mean?" she said, a catch in her voice.

"Leaving us, or letting you leave with me: what if that's the reason he had the breakdown? The dates—"

"—No, darling, I don't think so."

"Why not?"

"Oh Julie," she said, her voice breaking a little, "I don't know where to begin."

"Just try," I said. "Please, Mom."

"You're right. I owe this to you. Okay, so here goes: There's a great deal I haven't told you about your father. First, you were too young; and then as the years passed, well, it just got easier for me to try to forget."

"What do you mean? What haven't you told me about him?" I said, tasting the fear in my voice.

"Your father, Gustave, was not a consistent person. He had these wild highs when he'd be so full of confidence, so incredibly alive. At those times, it was magic to be with him. He'd meet me at a café with a bouquet of wildflowers. He'd buy us a bottle of champagne and tell me that a gallery was going to give him a one man show. Another day, he'd tell me he was going to be part of an exhibition in New York or Rome."

You never mentioned any of this, I almost said, except I couldn't find my voice.

"I was so happy, for a little while, so full of expectation, but then a week would go by, and none of it ever materialized, except that his high would give way to a low that was so much worse. He'd sleep late, forget his commitments, forget to wash. His laundry would pile up, and I'd find dishes in the sink at his apartment. I may have been naïve, young, and in love, but I knew enough to realize that something was terribly wrong, that he was—"

My breath caught in my throat. "What?"

"Ill, sweetheart, mentally ill: what you read just now, about his history, well, the breakdown fits the pattern."

"What pattern?" I said, everything around me beginning to spin.

"I think your father was suffering from manic depression," Mom said, "those highs and then those deadly lows. Once I came back to the States, I started looking for clues, and I started reading about this disease."

How could this be true? How could this have been my mother's life? How could she have kept all this inside?

"That's the reason we didn't stay together," she said finally. "When I found out I was pregnant, we'd been together for two months, and I knew that I couldn't keep deceiving myself by believing that one of the galleries was finally going to showcase his work. It wasn't just about me anymore—I had you to think about."

I sat there in silence, a terrible question taking shape inside me. "What are you saying? You did tell him about me? He knew you were pregnant, right?"

No answer.

"You're not telling me that he never knew, that you lied, all these years—"

"It's not that black and white, Julie."

"But all my life I believed he didn't want me. All my life I thought he'd chosen to forget me on my birthday and each and every Christmas." Fury swept into my voice. "And the truth is he never even knew about me."

"He wasn't well. I didn't know how he would react, and the truth is I was terrified—"

"—Of what?"

"Of losing you, and," she hesitated, "of losing myself."

"But you lied," I said, my voice sharp as a butcher knife. "You lied to me—and before that, you lied to him."

"Please, baby, I'm trying to explain—"

I sat there staring, the receiver pressed against my ear, the pigeons on the windowsill pecking at the glass. All I believed about my life was a lie. My mother, the person I trusted more than anyone else in the world, had lied to me. What if my father had wanted me after all? What if—?

"After you were born, I wrote to Gustave. I told him then."

Still, I didn't speak, not because I didn't want to, but because for that space of time I seemed to have forgotten how to make words. I was back on that Ferris wheel, only this my little cabin hung on by a tether and was in danger of crashing to the ground. "Tell me this," I said at last. "Did he write back?"

"I didn't include a return address," she said.

"Why?" I nearly shouted.

"I wanted to protect you. I had to protect us."

"Does Claire know the truth?" I asked.

"Yes," Mom said.

"What about Oma?" I said, picturing my grandmother's gentle, brown eyes, the way they shone when she smiled. "Did Oma know?"

"No, Claire's the only one."

Static crackled on the line and inside me. Mom had preferred to let her own mother think she'd been abandoned. What would Oma have said if she'd known the truth?

"I'm sorry," she said. "I did what I thought was right at the time."

"But you lied," I said, never having seen this side of Mom before: scared, unsure. She and my grandmother had been so close. If she'd lied to Oma, then—

"All I'm saying is that I love you," she said, her voice husky, "and that I can't tell you what to do about your father, not now. You're old enough to decide for yourself."

"You're right I am."

"I just want you to be careful. I don't want you to get hurt."

"It's a little late for that, don't you think?"

On the other end, I could hear my mother crying. "I'm sorry."

"Me too. I wish I'd known the truth a long time ago."

"Julie—"

"Please, Mom, you don't need to say anything else. I need some time to think about all of this."

After I hung up, I sat beside the window, the lights of the Eiffel Tower ranging from gold to blue to red, the surge of colors as complicated as my own emotions. Always, I'd believed there were no secrets between Mom and me. How totally wrong I'd been, at least about this one hugely important thing.

After a while, I heard footsteps.

"Julie?" Claire said, laying a hand on my shoulder.

"She lied to me. My whole life, I believed my father didn't want me, but the truth is Mom didn't want him in our lives."

"That's not fair," Claire said, sitting down beside me. "You've always been the center of your mother's world. What she did, she did because she believed it was right. That's all any of us can do at the time."

There was weariness in Claire's voice that reminded me of the day she told me why she'd stopped making art. Was it inevitable then? Did you grow up and have to compromise or let go of what you believed? Or, like my mother, did you feel you had to lie? And once you did, what happened to your life? And to the lives of the people who loved you? I shivered, though it had to be eighty degrees outside. If I followed this train of thought, I'm the one who's going to go crazy, I realized, then went to fetch a sweater.

Nineteen

OVER THE NEXT few days, Claire pussyfooted around me, so polite I almost wanted the bossy, I-know-best-Claire back. If it wasn't for Genevieve, who kept after me to work on the doll house and go to the Luxembourg, I would have felt like a House Guest. The afternoon that Claire took Genevieve to the movies, I begged off, emailed Clay, feeling that surge of guilt given the time with Luc; but really, I told myself, wasn't Clay just the friend I needed right now: *I've got another gig as an artist at a swanky party*, I typed into the computer. *Must find a dress. Meet me at Bon Marché at one? Please!*

"Nice of you to ask me and all, but I have to say I'm pretty surprised," Clay said some two hours later, once we were navigating the brightly-lit aisles, a lively jazz score playing in the background, the fragrance of too many perfumes wafting through the air.

"Surprised, how come?" I asked, aware of the exquisitely dressed Parisian women browsing with a confidence that would have made Genevieve stand up and clap.

"Isn't it obvious? If you were looking for a bike, I could understand, but dresses? I'm not exactly the kind of guy one takes clothes shopping," he said, stepping out of the way of a woman in flamingo-colored mules and matching lipstick .

"Sure you are," I said, thinking he might still be self-conscious about what Genevieve said about him and pedicures and his shaved legs. "Besides, I don't need a *Vogue* stylist here (although Genevieve would have argued otherwise). What I need is a second pair of eyes."

"Okay, then, how about this?" Clay's first pick was chocolate-colored and school-girlish with what looked like calico, or possibly an old quilt, acting as a ruffle.

"Um, I'd look like a rerun of *Little House on the Prairie*, don't you think?"

"You know that show, too?"

"My mother loved it."

"Seriously?"

"Uh huh. She kept the whole dog-eared series from the time she was nine. One Halloween she actually decked me out in a bonnet and pinafore and these old riding boots from one of her students. Everybody kept asking if I was Holly Hobbie—that rag doll."

"Poor you," he said. "Almost beats my year as a light bulb."

My hand closed around his bicep. "You are not seriously telling me that you were a light bulb."

"I am, Mickey's old ice skating costume: white satin with silver sequins and a silver Styrofoam cap that reached one foot high and was wound round with black sequins."

"Oh my god, that is beyond mortifying. How old were you?"

"Six and a half."

"Well, eight would have been horrors, but six—"

"Speak for yourself," Clay said. "My best friends were a cowboy and Superman, totally cool, right? And I was a light bulb."

"It does sound pretty awful."

"Point made. Hey," Clay said, stopping so fast I nearly bumped into him, "check this out." He produced a fluorescent dress whose primary colors were pink, orange, and purple.

"Only if I'm auditioning for Austin Powers."

"Think rainbows after a storm," he said, draping the fabric against himself and sort of shimmying his hips.

"That's not quite the image that comes to mind," I said, grinning.

Clay grinned back. "Like I said, I'm not the kind of guy one takes shopping. Besides, isn't this Genevieve's territory? Where is our future *Vogue* editor today anyway?"

"Claire wanted some mother-daughter time."

"Mom and Mickey do that sort of thing," Clay said. "Usually, it means Mom drags my sister to Paris's equivalent of PetSmart."

"Poor her."

"Yeah, my sister's friends get manicures and clothes, and she comes home with squeak toys and dog chews for the Chihuahuas. I have to hand it to her, though, she never complains."

"I really have to meet your mother," I said, "and Mickey."

"You may live to regret those words," he said, then picked up the psychedelic dress once more. "Actually, this is just the sort of deal my mom would wear."

With anyone else, I would have been offended. Imagine choosing a dress for a friend that he could picture on his mother. But with Clay, it was impossible to be annoyed. He was just so—

"What?" he said, as if he could read my thoughts.

"Nothing," I said, retrieving a sort of slinky but refined black cocktail number. "What do you think of this?"

"It's a little—"

"Audrey Hepburn in *Breakfast at Tiffany's?*" I said, the simple elegance reminding me of one of Mom's all-time favorite movies.

"Can I just say it doesn't remind me of you," he said.

"You're saying I'm not the little black dress type?"

"No, it's not that. You'd look great in that. It's just that Lacy used to wear black ninety-nine percent of the time. I have bad associations."

"Oh, sorry." I returned the dress to the rack. This Lacy person: did he still think about her, or had cycling exorcised her presence?

We browsed in silence until Clay showed me his next pick. "Well?" he said.

"Anything that green and sequined and shimmery belongs on a mermaid," I said. "That Australian girl in *Aquamarine* could get away with it."

"I keep my distance from mermaid movies."

"Your mom again?"

"No, Mickey, she was totally obsessed with Ariel for years."

"But you didn't have to dress up as a mermaid, did you?"

"Good one; and no, I didn't."

After an hour of searching, I disappeared into the dressing room with an armful of dresses, including something subtle and purple that Clay happened to find. But nothing seemed right, except a dream of a dress in cream silk that cost way more than I could afford.

"So where next?" He slipped his arm through mine. "You have other boutiques lined up?"

"Lunch," I said, "I'm starving."

"I was hoping you'd say that. The perfume in this place is giving me a headache."

"But you must breathe a lot of car exhaust while biking."

"I'll take car exhaust over too much perfume."

"I'll make a note of that."

"So, what do you feel like?" he asked, as we rode the escalator downstairs to Le Bon Marché's food court, a sort of overwhelming restaurant slash gourmet grocery store.

"Would you believe I've had enough French food for a while?" I said, staring down at maybe one hundred baguettes.

"I hear you. I've been here long enough that even the buttery-est croissants and baguettes can get old. So, how about pizza? I wouldn't mind loading up on some carbs."

"I thought you'd never ask."

Outside we crossed over to the Boulevard Raspail, one of the major thoroughfares along the Left Bank. Mid-afternoon, and the traffic was fierce and noisy. By the time we found a pizzeria, both of us were hoarse.

"I'm going to order a mega-sized Coke with ice," I said, still unable to figure out why Parisians didn't put ice in their soft drinks.

Inside the waitresses may have been French, but the atmosphere was kitschy American. Only a few blocks from the Luxembourg Gardens and the Musée d'Orsay, we found ourselves surrounded by mirrored advertisements for Coca Cola and Miller Light (an outrage in a country known for its wine), overblown posters of performers like Madonna, Michael Jackson, and Prince, and countless athletes. I recognized Michael Jordan from his days with the Bulls—Oma had been a huge basketball fan. There was even a photo of John McEnroe, the middle-aged former tennis star known most for his temper tantrums on the court.

"Get the feeling this place is a couple of years behind the times?" I asked.

"Decades," Clay replied. "That's the weird thing about the French. They pick up on American pop culture, but often it's more retro than current." He leaned across the table. "I'm saying I've actually met people here who think Cyndi Lauper is current."

I laughed, reminded of the ultra-hip woman who owned the shop that sold Madeleines. Her all-time favorite rock song was

"Highway to Hell." No matter how I tried, I couldn't see her—a woman who wore espadrilles and floral dresses—singing, much less dancing to heavy metal.

It was comfortable sitting here with Clay, soaking up the familiar smells of melted cheese and oregano, as I twirled my straw through a slightly-flat but really big Coke in a red plastic cup. (Extra ice got me two cubes.) But I couldn't deny that no matter how hard I tried to reign them in, my thoughts kept straying to Luc. I would see him at the party. He would have loved that little black dress. So, I thought, sipping my bottomless Coke, should I go back when Clay wasn't with me and buy it?

"Double cheese," Clay told the waitress, then added on pineapple, extra onions and green olives, sundried tomatoes, and peppers.

"That's a lot of stuff," I said, once the waitress set it down. The smells, a mixture of spicy and sweet, proved a little overwhelming. "Maybe we should have spread out the toppings over a couple of pizzas."

"Go on and try it," Clay said, biting into his own slice.

I took a reluctant bite and felt like my taste buds were navigating an obstacle course.

"Good, isn't it?" Clay asked.

"It is, actually." I would never have expected pineapples to go with olives, but they did.

Clay told me about the day he ate a whole pizza—"just like this"—just before his first race.

"And?" I said. "Did you win?"

"I placed third," he said. "Heartburn. I should have left off the onions."

I hadn't planned on saying anything to Clay about my father, for one of the things I liked about hanging out with him was how uncomplicated it felt, how natural. I didn't want to mess that up with family issues. I mean, the most I knew about his obviously weird mother was that she was passionate about Chihuahuas, owned stock in Target, and was fond of bizarre girls' names.

But the crust was way better than I expected, chewy without being too dough-y; the pizzeria felt cozy; and the soundtrack slipped in "Leaving on a Jet Plane," a silly sentimental song I'd loved since I'd learned it in chorus in the fourth grade; and then there was the fact that Clay was, well, Clay. "I mailed the letter about a week ago, and I still haven't heard anything," I finally confessed, as I picked the olives off my fourth slice of pizza.

"He'll write back," Clay said, so naturally it was as if he heard this kind of thing every day.

"How can you be so sure?" I asked, the candlelight magnifying the gold flecks in his eyes. "I mean, you don't even know anything about him."

"Trust me: it may take some time, but he'll write back."

I looked hard at Clay, amazed by his certainty.

"Listen, Julie, call it intuition, but he'd be a fool not to want to meet you."

"Thank you."

Afterwards, we were both so full from the pizza that we sat in one of Paris's many postage-sized parks. Instantly, about fifty pigeons swooped down at our feet.

"The international bird," Clay said, as they eyed us in that expectant, curious way of theirs. "You know they're actually sea birds. They nest along the cliffs. City living isn't that different, I guess, except they look a lot less rugged out here. Sorry, guys," he said, leaning towards them, "we don't even have breadsticks."

"Maybe they only understand French," I said, when they continued to hang around, a few even daring to peck at Clay's cycling shoes.

"*Allez!*" he cried, but they continued to hang around until an old lady tottered into the park and actually called them over.

"Get the feeling she's a regular?" Clay asked, for she'd begun distributing baguette crumbs, completely unfazed when two pigeons perched on her knees and another settled on her shoulder.

"Absolutely."

It had been cloudy earlier, but as we lifted our faces to the sky, the sun came out, and pretty soon we were both warm.

"Right now, I'd love a swim," I said, reminded of the university at home's leisure pool, the silky feel of the too-blue water.

"You serious?" Clay said.

"Of course I am, but it's impossible unless you want to consider the Seine."

"We have other options," Clay said. "I know an indoor pool at the Sorbonne. Picture floor-length windows looking out on the city, skylights cut into the roof, mineral baths. I think they even do henna tattoos, not that I've tried them."

Instantly, I knew Clay headed there after particularly hard workouts. And the henna tattoos? Maybe he was just a little bit metro-sexual. "But I don't have a suit."

"Have a little imagination here," he said. "We're in the middle of Paris. Don't tell me we can't pick up a pair of suits between here and the Sorbonne."

Minutes later, we were fast-walking down the pricy Boulevard Saint Germain, eyes peeled for anything resembling affordable swimwear. The suits we found, not here but on a grungier side street much further down, were beyond awful. Mine was a skimpy one piece in seaweed green. Clay's was baggy and tobacco-colored.

"Maybe we should have looked a little bit longer?" I said.

"You want to swim, right? Besides, it's not going to make a difference once we're in the water," Clay said. By now we stood in the line to pay at the Sorbonne pool, above my head a list of at least twenty rules which I studied carefully.

"The important rules are these," he said, pointing out item two. "'All women and men must wear bathing caps.'"

"But—" I said.

Clay motioned to a vending machine where you could buy anything from a bathing cap to shampoo.

"And the second rule?"

"Don't forget your cabin number," he said, as we neared the front of the line, and I glimpsed two stories of cabins, at least fifty on each floor, in a sort of atrium that surrounded the pool.

"Sorry?" I said, as a growly man with a huge mustache scowled at me.

"Each person gets assigned a changing room, and it's there you stash your clothes and other stuff. The first time I was here, I got confused, and the attendant had to open up a whole row of cabins until he found my stuff. Believe me, he was pissed, and I was really, really cold by the time we finally found the right one."

"How awful," I said, picturing myself shivering beside some furious cabin attendant.

My second thoughts skyrocketed once I saw my reflection in the cabin mirror. The bathing suit was even worse in the green-ish cabin light, and the bathing cap was too tight. Genevieve, I knew, would never be caught dead in such a get up.

I found Clay poolside. "Don't even say it," he said, the nicotine shade of his suit almost as bad as the baggy fit.

"Not a word," I said, though the bathing cap looked better on him than me.

There were four sections to this pool. In the furthest two, people were swimming laps. There must have been twelve people in each. But the middle lane was empty.

"Private," Clay said. "You pay extra. Follow me," he said, pointing to the fourth lane where everybody else floated on their backs or just relaxed in the water. Most of the people were older women over sixty-five, and many of them obviously knew each other, for they chatted in French as if they were at the park or in a *boulangerie* instead of in a swimming pool. I felt a little out of place.

"Come on," Clay said.

"Okay." I couldn't deny it, as soon as I stepped into the chlorinated heaven of the Sorbonne's pool I knew this was the right thing to do. Immersed in water, I felt as if I were shedding the layer of myself that was weighing me down.

"Heaven, isn't it?" Clay said, as we floated on our backs, looking up at the blue sky through the cut-out skylights.

"Beyond heaven," I said, fanning my hands around my hips to stay on the surface of the water. At that moment, I think I could have lingered there forever, or at least until my skin turned all prune-y.

"Where'd you learn that?" Clay asked, as I scissor kicked while keeping my hips afloat.

"Water ballet," I said, then ducked my head underwater, so the whole world went quiet. The next thing I knew, I was swimming the length of the pool. When I opened my eyes, Clay was swimming right beside me.

He swam so close that our legs touched beneath the water. Despite those breathless moments outside the gallery with Luc, I leaned into him, and the next thing I knew we were treading water and laughing. Our knees bumped, and our lips met with that staccato electricity I hadn't felt in ages, the kind of zing that sings *this is the real thing.*

Or is it? a needling voice within me asked. I couldn't deny that I had wanted—that I still wanted—to feel Luc's arms around me. And yes, if I was honest, I'd have to admit I'd looked at

166

every dress for the party and wondered what he would think. Even so, I was here now with Clay, and I closed my eyes and let the water and our kiss surround me.

Twenty

ON THE EVENING of the party, I met Marie France at the entrance to Madame Marthurin's restaurant where she stood printing the menu on a chalkboard, an old-fashioned touch I'd only seen in Paris. "What a dress," she said, reaching out to touch the float-y fabric.

"You like it?" I gave a little twirl, watched the aquamarine shimmer in the evening light.

"*J'aime cela*—I love it." Just then, her admiring glance felt as reassuring as the sketch pad under my arm, the careful assortment of crayons and pencils tucked into my tackle box.

"Wherever did you find such a dress?"

"Genevieve has a friend here whose mother is a designer," I said, then told her about the showroom above the expensive boutique where sample dresses in fabrics I had not known the name for—until Genevieve clarified—could be bought at a serious discount.

Marie France smiled. "That Genevieve: she's eleven going on twenty-nine."

"Actually," I said, "she's ten."

"*Mon Dieu.*" Marie France tipped her head back and laughed. "Well, she'll have a boutique of her own one day, and I'll have money enough to be one of her patrons. Don't tell me that this little Coco Chanel did your hair, too?"

I touched the chignon secured with a bit of silver ribbon at my neck. "Claire," I said. "Genevieve's mother."

"*Très chic.* How I wish my hair would lie smooth like that."

"You?" Who was she kidding? Marie France's hair was the hair of the woman in *The French Lieutenant's Woman*. It was every woman's dream. And every man's.

"Well, as you Americans say, the grass is always greener in another pasture."

"On the other side," I added.

"What?"

"The grass is always greener on the other side."

"Oh yes, of course, though I like pasture better."

We stepped inside, and I caught sight of my reflection in the glass. With the candles glowing gold in their sconces, and the mottled stone walls, the aquamarine silk seemed ocean-cool, summer-light.

"*Bon soir*, Julie, what a lovely dress," Madame Marthurin said, waving to me as she bustled past; in her arms, a tray bearing more than a dozen baskets of bread that still smelled of yeast and the oven.

"She's been working since before sun up," Marie France explained, wiping sweat from her own brow. "Every year, the party is spectacular, but tonight's celebration—there'll be three courses plus a chocolate torte and crème brulee. She's outdone herself."

It was true.

In the courtyard dozens of paper lanterns—yellow, purple, red, and blue—had been strung up on a clothesline. The effect was that of an opalescent necklace. "Who did this?" I said.

"Luc."

The word brought back his kiss, and my thoughts drifted toward the possibility of other kisses. "For someone who's supposed to be so much trouble, he certainly seems to do a lot."

"That's Luc for you," Marie France said, bending over to re-light a tea light. "He disappears for days, leaving his poor grandmother to accomplish the tasks he's left undone."

"But he's not like that all the time," I said.

"No, it would be unfair to suggest that, especially when it comes to his grandmother. He adores her, and well he should, for she'd do anything for him."

How I wanted to ask her more about their relationship, but I didn't know how. "What about his mother?"

"Listen, Julie," she said. "I like Luc, but I would never trust him with anything I valued too much—or with anyone."

Georges, the old waiter, drew near, and Marie France called out to him. "Would you fetch the easel? Luc said he would do it, but he hasn't."

"*Oui, mademoiselle.*" Georges was still shaking his head as he strode towards the steep coil of stairs that led to Modigliani's studio.

"But it's not up there, is it?" I said, pointing to the top floor.

"Oh no." She frowned. "I must have forgotten to tell you. It's in Luc's studio on the floor below. He's probably there now. He said he wanted to get something right on one of his sculptures."

He's here.

I helped Marie France with some last minute preparations, and while we laid napkins on the tables and straightened the silverware, the empty courtyard, with its bauble of lights and its rose-bedecked tables, was deliciously transformed by the arrival of guests.

Soon the courtyard no longer magnified every echo, so that I almost forgot restless spirits lingered here.

Instead, a chorus of voices shared the air with a guitarist and a woman on a violin. The atmosphere itself seemed to absorb the festive scene.

The air, though, smelled strongly of garlic.

"'Like kissing the lips of a beautiful woman,' Modigliani told Madame Marthurin's grandmother," Marie France said, her voice bright with the night's merriment. "You do like garlic, don't you?"

"Sure," I said, as an extremely elegant old woman stepped into the courtyard. She wore her still-lustrous hair in a silvery chignon, and she was dressed from head to toe in a cape that Genevieve would have called lapis lazuli. "Madame Dupont," I said.

"Chic, isn't she? And she's fantastically wealthy thanks to a marriage to some old count. They say he bought her a chateau in Chantilly and a ski lodge in the Alps." Marie France's eyes flickered with interest. "How do you know her?"

"I don't, at least not really. She was at L'Espace Stein the day the Modigliani was presented to the public."

"Ah, but of course," Marie France said. "She owns several Modiglianis. She's terribly opinionated and can be difficult. If the soup is too hot or too cold, she sends it back. If the bread is a touch stale, she will not hear of eating it." Marie France tossed her head, smiled. "And god forbid one should forget butter. But if she takes a liking to you, well then, it's like a golden ticket—"

"She's influential then?" I asked, watching Madame Dupont speaking to an equally old man wearing a crisp white suit.

"*Sûrement*. To her credit, she gets on very well with Madame Marthurin." As if she sensed my inability to couple the two, Marie France added, "They were in school together. Madame Dupont started out as a tailor's daughter. She lived in a small apartment above a shop not too far from here."

After Georges brought me an old-fashioned easel, I set up my drawing pad and crayons while Marie France and Georges walked around the courtyard offering canapés to the first guests, who chatted and listened to the music, the stars switching on like lights in the Paris sky.

It wasn't long before I had my first sitter, a small woman who seemed even smaller beneath a cascade of curly brown hair. "I'm Nicolette," she said. "Marie France tells me you're very good."

"*Merci*," I said, as Nicolette sat down and proceeded to tell me that she was an aspiring actress.

"In theater here?"

"*Non*." She pouted. "I make, how do you say, commercials for deodorant, hairspray."

"Ah," I said, capturing her pout before it faded, and she went on to tell me of her dream to play Juliet or at least one of the spirits in *A Midsummer Night's Dream*.

The canapés were followed by a chilled watercress soup which Luc carried out in an enormous terrine. Like Marie France, he wore a white shirt and black trousers, his long hair hidden tonight beneath a black woolen cap, the kind fishermen wear. I waited for him to notice me, but he was too absorbed in serving the guests, and often paused to make conversation with someone.

After the soup, there were garlicky prawns served with plenty of crusty bread. "*Bon appétit*," Marie France said, bringing me a hearty portion and a full goblet of delicious red wine.

MAYBE AN HOUR later, I sat sketching Beatrice Folkins, a reed thin dancer in the Paris Ballet with a coil of red-gold hair and calf muscles that were beyond sculptural.

"I hoped you would come," Luc said, finally appearing at my side as he topped off my wine, letting his free hand brush my shoulder.

"Stop distracting the artist," Beatrice said, swatting at his arm. "I don't want her to hand me a mass of smudged lines."

"You know each other?" I said, tripping over my French.

"We met at an opening," Luc said casually.

"At the Cartier Foundation," Beatrice said, as if she hung out there all the time. "Luc was one of ten artists showing." She crossed one leg over the other, and completely changed her pose, mid-sketch.

"Luc!" Madame Marthurin's voice.

When I looked up, she was motioning to the bread baskets. They were empty again.

"I'm perpetually being sent to fetch bread," he said slyly. "Not what you'd expect from an artist, eh Beatrice?"

"But you're so good at fetching, darling," she giggled, her gaze trailing after him as he walked towards the kitchen, so that I pictured her in Luc's bed with him fetching her tea or chocolate. Once again she re-arranged her pose, craning her long neck to get a last look at Luc.

"I'm afraid I'll need to start over again," I said, tossing aside the drawing.

She sighed. "I feel like I'm at an audition."

"Sorry," I said, trying to reflect the serene cool of my aquamarine dress. "It would help if you would just keep still."

She narrowed her blue-black eyes, reached into her purse to draw forth a cigarette. "You're not interested in Luc, are you?"

I shook my head, amazed she would take me seriously until I remembered the effect of the aquamarine dress, the deep 'v' of its neckline making me look older than seventeen. "Classic," Margaret's mother had said, after asking me to slowly turn around. "Debutante meets Grace Kelly." Catching sight of myself in the dressing room mirror, I hadn't actually agreed with her, but I had been happily startled—is that girl really me? I asked, the same question reoccurring when I'd dressed earlier that evening.

"What about you?" I said, determined to play the role she saw me in.

"For a few weeks I was mad for him." She sucked on her cigarette and continued to study me. "I found out fast that he isn't exactly the faithful type."

I took a deep swallow of wine. "No?"

"When he met me after my last performance, he seemed to know at least three other dancers, a bit too intimately. And at restaurants—well, all I can say is a few too many waitresses always know his name. Too bad," she sighed, re-crossing her legs yet again, "there is something about him I cannot resist. Despite his teasing, he can speak right to the heart of what matters to a person, you know?"

I found myself reminded of what he'd said to me outside the gallery, the way he seemed to understand not just my love for the Luxembourg Gardens, but something far deeper.

But I wasn't about to tell her that.

"Are you almost finished?" Marie France said, laying a hand on my arm. "There are several others who'd like to have a sketch, and Madame Dupont is among them."

I looked in the old woman's direction. She'd taken off her lapis lazuli cape to reveal a gown of the same color, and seemed entranced by the music of the guitarist, who was playing a lively, gypsy melody.

It took me a few minutes to recognize the person beside Madame Dupont. That copper hair shiny as a new penny, those dramatic gestures: Madame Becerra, the full-of-herself art historian from L'Espace Stein. I should have known she'd be here.

THE MUSICIANS CONTINUED to play as twilight turned to azure darkness, the glow from the lanterns creating an even more enchanted feel as color and sound blended with the aromas of the meal and the conversation and laughter of the guests.

Just as I was putting the finishing touches on a joint portrait of a husband and wife—"newlyweds at fifty-four," they told me—Madame Dupont strolled over, her cape once again drawn around her shoulders.

"I insist you draw me next," she said, though another man—a rather fat one with a scowling, jowly English, not French, bulldog face, a crucial difference—was ahead of her.

"But Madame—" he protested.

"Where is your *chevalerie*, sir?" she said, drawing forth that same golden cigarette case. "I'm an old woman. I made up my face hours ago. I cannot predict how long the effect will last."

Having seen her talking to Luc, as flirtatiously as Beatrice, I didn't believe for a minute Madame Dupont would appear in public unless the effect would last.

But the man gave up his place.

"Now then," Madame Dupont said, carefully arranging her cape so that it fanned out around the chair on which she was seated. "I want a flattering drawing, mademoiselle, nothing abstract and nothing too realistic. Is that understood?"

"*Oui*," I said, a little disappointed she didn't remember me from the gallery. Maybe it was my dress? Its transformative effect? Maybe I looked like someone else entirely?

I was reminded of the way I'd felt trying on all those dresses. The many possible identities each one suggested, from the bohemian caftan—a little too Jeanne or, at this point in history, just a little too much like shouting 'I'm an artist'—to the silver slip dress—a little too sexy especially if Claire was going to let me out of the house—to the aquamarine silk which was demure, sophisticated, just right. If only all things could be as easy as slipping into a different outfit and a different skin.

With special care, I shaded in the area behind Madame Dupont, an effect that brought her small figure into the foreground more. I wanted to please her without compromising what I saw before me, and as I sketched, I realized how much I reveled in the challenge.

Meanwhile Luc began to dance with Beatrice in the circular space at the center of the courtyard, moving his hips as lithely as she did, and perhaps with more natural grace, the way a cat moves, or a fox. Soon, another very thin girl joined them. She wore her white-gold hair in a high ponytail; another dancer I assumed, reminded of Beatrice's story. They drew closer together, then swirled apart, the necklace of lanterns encircling them. The dancers moved with the trained lightness of their profession, but it was Luc who held me captive.

I set down my glass of wine—it was making me dizzy—and tried to concentrate on the drawing, but my gaze kept straying to him. In the very corner of Madame Dupont's portrait, I actually began sketching the way he moved. One minute he was here, the next—he wasn't.

"He interests you," Madame Dupont said, piercing my concentration.

I looked up, met her sharp eye.

"One piece of advice, *cherie*. A young woman must never expect too much from someone like Luc. Otherwise," she tilted her head and looked at me closely, "he will leave her heart in tatters."

"I hardly know him, Madame," I said.

"Perhaps not yet," she said, lighting another cigarette, "but all that will change, I think, and *bientôt*—soon."

We did not speak again until I finished her portrait, and it took all my concentration to focus on her instead of dwelling on what she'd just said.

"*Très bon*," she said, when I handed it to her. "You're the girl from the gallery, are you not?"

"Yes," I said. So she had recognized me!

"I thought so," she said, keeping her shrewd gaze on my face. "You impressed me from the first. At your age, to understand that art cannot be separated from life, *cherie*, well, I commend you. There is something very wrong with the world of art if we forget the brave souls who created the masterpieces.

"Here," she said, then reached into her evening bag, "my card." It smelled of perfume and cigarettes. "Come and see me sometime. I may have some work for you. My house is on the Rue Récamier."

"Any connection to Juliette Récamier?"

"Clever girl." She smiled, and something in her gaze opened, as if she was admitting me into the light. "You've seen David's portrait of her in the Louvre then?"

"Several times," I said, recalling Juliette's shy but seductive expression as she reclines, barefoot, on a chaise lounge the same creamy white as her slip of a gown.

"An unfinished masterpiece with quite a story attached to it."

"Unfinished? What do you mean?"

"David seemed to take a bit too strong a liking to my ancestress, if you understand my meaning," she said, lighting a cigarette. "Juliette had no choice but to end her sittings with him. Her *réputation* was at stake."

"Wow," I said, "I had no idea."

"Not the stuff of history books," Madame Dupont said, and stood. "Now then, I will give the next person their turn. Remember what I said, eh?"

"I will," I said, breathing in the perfume of the card, sure I detected a hint of intoxicating but poisonous oleander among the prettier scents of rose, narcissus, and freesia.

Twenty-One

IT WAS NEARLY ten thirty, and one by one a steady stream of guests continued to sit for a portrait. I drew the bulldog-faced man and a shy woman with lily white skin and onyx hair. I drew a cartoonist named Jacques Zborowski, who was not, as I hoped, a distant relation of Modigliani's art dealer; and after that, a woman with powdery skin and a cap of platinum hair who told me that she was the second most famous woman in Paris, though something about her cotton candy lipstick and the way she slurred her words told me that she was either delusional or more likely drunk. I even drew the other dancer, unsure if I was relieved or concerned when she did not mention Luc.

They were all competent drawings; but none possessed the energy of Madame Dupont's. In drawing her, I'd tried and succeeded in capturing the glint to her smile and a quality that resembled the yellow-gold light of the candles in the sconces.

I kept hoping—and fearing—that Luc himself would ask me to draw him. Would I be able to capture the steep height of his nose, the sharp cheekbones in his long face, the feline topaz of his eyes, the hint of moon in his scar, without breaking into an embarrassed, dreamy smile? And what of Luc's shoulders, the strong line of collarbone visible above the thin fabric of his shirt? Whenever someone approached me from behind, I felt a rush a little like the feeling I had the first time I went canoeing and came precariously close to the rock falls, entranced by the surging water, and simultaneously terrified. Luc caught my eye a few times, smiled, or toasted me with his glass.

But he never came.

By the time Madame Marthurin brought out the much-awaited trio of desserts, he seemed to have disappeared, and I caught myself looking around for that dancer, relieved when I spotted her coiled up in a candlelit corner, an expensively dressed man, his hair slick with pomade, at her side.

Dinner was spectacular, but it was with dessert Madame Marthurin truly outdid herself. There was crème brulee and some sort of elaborate chocolate torte, each of its three layers filled with almond paste, said to have come from Modigliani's home town: Livorno. As the guests tucked into their sweets, Georges and Marie France circled the courtyard, their silver trays filled with glasses of champagne.

A few toasts were made in Modigliani's honor, the first by Madame Marthurin. Dressed all in silver—a simply elegant apron over an equally simple and quietly elegant dress—Madame Marthurin looked lovely and graceful and of another time. Modigliani's and Jeanne's. Standing there, her silvery dress took on the iridescent quality of a moth's wings or a rare butterfly's.

"As almost all of you know," Madame Marthurin said, "Modigliani and *la pauvre* Jeanne Hébuterne and their small daughter lived just upstairs. The little studio was the place where they began and ended their lives together. It is inevitably a place touched by *la tristesse*. And yet," she said thoughtfully, "Modigliani did some of his best work there, and then there was Jeanne, his muse. Thirty-one portraits he made of her."

"Thirty-two," Madame Becerra qualified.

"Ah yes, thirty-two. Jeanne may not be remembered in the art books, but her presence lingers in his paintings." I waited for Madame Marthurin to mention the painting on the back of the studio door, but she dwelt instead on the quiet mystery the place exuded after all these years. "As if Modigliani's and Jeanne's spirits lingered here, restless, yes of course, inevitably; yet aware of how much I cherish the guardianship of their memory."

Madame Dupont stood next, surprising me when she introduced herself, not as a great collector, but as one of Madame Marthurin's oldest friends. "Tonight, as she has done for more years than I can remember, my dear friend Marta has filled the space with bright lights and music and good food. The simplicity in this courtyard is very much in keeping with the clean lines—with the purity—of Modigliani's work. He would only have been honored by such a tribute, as would his beloved Jeanne."

Madame Dupont raised her glass to toast the artist's birthday, and everyone else, including me, followed.

It was shortly after that the bulldog-faced man passed out at the table.

"That's the trouble with these buffets," Marie France said, sitting down beside me and wiping the sweat from her brow. "The guests pay a standard fee, and then they eat and drink what they like. Always, there are a few who over-indulge. Last year I had to help sober up half a dozen guests with black coffee, but one man was so drunk, Luc had to carry him out and put him in a taxi."

AROUND MIDNIGHT THE last guests gathered up their jackets and purses, many of them nodding to me as they left. I leaned against the wall, the effects of the wine and the two very full glasses of champagne catching up with me at last. I looked over at Beatrice perched beside the fountain, her coil of red-gold hair washed through with moonlight, her bare feet trailing through the water. Would she try to catch Luc's attention before she slipped away? Would she wait for him?

In a few minutes I would ask Marie France to call a taxi, but just now all I wanted was to sit and let the night's events soak in. Though I'd given the portraits to each of the sitters, the impression of the drawings lingered on the blank pages of my pad, just as the impression of tonight seemed inscribed within me, a hidden but necessary calligraphy.

It wasn't long before my eyes drifted towards the studio. There was a light on. Marie France said Luc had a studio in that tier. Was that the one? Was it possible he was there now? I moved closer to the stairwell, curious, my senses keen as a cat's. And then the door to the studio opened, and someone stepped out—a woman with coppery hair. Madame Becerra. She was followed by someone swathed in a cape as dark as the night. But of course—it was Madame Dupont.

Once they made their way down the stairs, I stepped into the shadows, but I did not rejoin the last remaining guests.

I felt a hand on my shoulder. "Julie— " Warm breath pungent with garlic.

I turned. "Luc, I—"

He shook his head, gently placed his fingertip on my lips. "No need to explain. It's enough to find you— how beautiful you are tonight—outside my studio."

I touched my hand to my dress, silky soft and cool, and now the color of moonlight. "What were they doing up there?" I asked, thrilling to the fact that he'd called me 'beautiful.'

"Madame Dupont is my—" He hesitated. "The old-fashioned term is patron, but I find it difficult to call her that when I've known her since I was in the cradle."

I thought of her sitting for her portrait, cigarette in hand, scarlet words on her lips. She was not the sort of person I pictured with a baby. "She invited me to come and see her," I heard myself say.

"And you must go," Luc said, brushing a stray lock from my face. "She can be haughty as a queen, but she's quite a character, and she's made several artists' careers—"

"She told me the craziest story about Juliette Récamier."

He laughed. "I can only imagine. Go and see her, and you will hear many more crazy stories and some truly fantastic ones."

We stood there looking at each other until I said, "Could I see your work?"

He touched my shoulder. "I would like nothing better than to show it to you."

I followed Luc up four flights of stairs. As we climbed, the remaining voices in the courtyard—Marie France's and Madame Marthurin's among them—seemed further and further away. I felt light-headed, a little dizzy, an experience not unlike the Ferris wheel, except it was not terror I felt.

No, nothing like that.

Luc opened the door, and I followed him inside.

What are you doing? a voice within me asked, Paul Henri's warning echoing around us.

But much louder, or at least more enticing, was the iridescent wish I'd packed with me when I came to Paris. Didn't I want to find love? and who better than a Parisian who was also a fellow artist? And Luc wasn't just any artist—

For just a moment that kiss with Clay tingled on my lips, but I pushed the memory away, waited for Luc to turn on the light.

Instead he stepped over to the window to draw back the curtains, and moonlight poured into the studio, revealing wood floors polished to a warm sheen, the reflective surface filled with dozens of sculptures. Paul Henri had spoken the truth when he said Luc made things out of scrap metal and other junk, though 'made' did not do justice to the enchantment he brought to the bits and pieces others had thrown away.

"I think of my work as a kind of metamorphosis," he said.

I stood, spellbound, before a pair of swans, for that was the only way to describe the effect of his art. The swans' long-throated bodies had been shaped out of what looked like car fenders, their magnificent sheet metal wings covered with hundreds of silver spoons that had been beaten or molded to resemble feathers.

"*Leda and the Swan*," he said, reaching for a slim glass decanter containing deep green liquor. He poured us each a small glass, and retold the myth in which the Greek god Zeus made love to Leda after taking the form of a swan. So intimate was his voice, I imagined the swan god's white feathers brushing my neck, my shoulders, my breasts. "The daughter Leda bore was Helen of Troy," he said.

"I know the story," I said, and sipped the liquor. It was both sweet and bitter. "What is this?" I said.

"Green chartreuse," he said. "A taste of paradise thanks to the alchemy of pine needles."

"Delicious," I said, as he poured a little more into my glass. "Does it come from Chartres?"

"*La cathédrale?*" Luc smiled. "*Non*, lovely Julie, it's made by monks in the Swiss alps." He watched me for a while, and I wondered what he was waiting for, what he was thinking.

"Your work is incredible," I said, longing to stroke the wings of the two swans, so smooth and cool did the silvery metal seem on this warm night made even warmer by the heat of the room.

Not far from the swans stood a life-sized sculpture of a woman at a loom. "Penelope waiting for Odysseus," he said.

I knew this story, too, though given what I'd heard about Luc, it surprised me that he would have taken so much care in recreating a woman so faithful she waited a lifetime for her voyaging husband to return, discouraging her suitors by telling them that she would only marry once her weaving was complete. Little did they know she unraveled her work each and every night. "Odysseus was unfaithful to Penelope," I heard myself say. "He did not deserve her love."

"That does not change the fact that he was fortunate enough to find her waiting for him when he returned," Luc said.

The words reminded me of the history of the studio upstairs. How many hundreds of nights had Jeanne waited for Modigliani to come home? No, he was never gone for very long—a few weeks, sometimes only a few hours. Yet she knew he could not be faithful. And always, she hid her reproach. Or perhaps, I realized now, she understood him well enough to know he could not be any other way.

I'd read far enough in the biography to know that during that last year, especially during the autumn when

Modigliani was increasingly ill, and Jeanne, halfway along in a pregnancy that would never result in a birth, she not only waited for him, she went to look for him at the cafés and in the parks around Montparnasse. Once, the biography said, she even searched for him in the cemetery of Père Lachaise.

"The truest sort of friend," the artist Ossip Zadkine called Jeanne during this time, setting her apart from those who wanted something from the dying Modigliani. "Good and beautiful," he called her, "with a beautiful soul."

Once, I thought, she danced beneath the plane trees in Montparnasse, marguerites woven into her long hair, her own future as bright as the colors in her sketchbook. Less than five years later, in the ninth month of her second pregnancy, she jumped from the window of her childhood bedroom, leaving behind her small daughter...

And what of my own mother waiting for Gustave Fermiere to make good on one of his own promises? Was his illness anything like Modigliani's? The words *manic depression* came back; and yes, I'd looked it up, and it did seem frightening, especially if left untreated. Those last days, what kind of fear had my mother experienced?

Thank god. The realization hit me with the force of a fall onto the concrete—the force with which Jeanne fell—that my mother's fate had not been Jeanne's. My mother, I realized then, had saved herself, and in so doing, she had saved me.

"You seem far away." Luc's voice reached me in that desolate landscape where I pictured Jeanne searching for Modigliani, her auburn hair echoing the color of the autumn leaves, though at that time of year when nightfall came early, she would have appeared as a dark figure in an even darker landscape calling to the man she loved.

An almost dreamlike fuzziness was creeping over me, so that I would have liked to lie down, rest my head on my hand, Luc beside me. "Do you ever find it uncomfortable to work beneath the studio?" I asked.

"Ah, so you are thinking of Modigliani and Jeanne," he said, the moonlight giving his own skin an otherworldly glow. "What you must understand is that, for me, they have always been here. I came to live with my grandmother when I was just a small boy. I heard bits and pieces of their story. You'll find it bizarre, perhaps, but their story—sad as it is—well, it wove itself into the fabric of my life. It never lost its sadness, but it became familiar, a part of me."

I gazed back at him, remembered what Monsieur Rimbaud and Paul Henri had told me of Luc's childhood: his mother's early death, his father's abandonment. He would not find Modigliani's story—and Jeanne's—as impossibly sad as someone else would.

Fatherlessness was something we shared. Would I have the courage to speak those words to Luc one day? Would such closeness root itself between us?

His sculptures shimmered before me. They must have always seemed impressive, but I felt sure they made the strongest impression at night, lit as they were by the moon, that agent of transformation.

"I've taken much of my inspiration from Ovid," he said, as I continued to admire his work, "but I'm not interested in transformation for its own sake."

"What then?" I stood before a sculpture of a tree, its branches and the sinuous shape of its trunk still bearing echoes of a woman's form: Daphne, the woman who asked to be changed into a laurel tree so as to escape Apollo, her very limbs retaining the beautiful litheness with which the god fell in love even after her transformation.

"The world itself is always in flux," he said. "Take Paris: a hundred years ago, this neighborhood was filled with struggling artists. Today—"

He didn't need to finish. I'd seen the Mercedes and the Passats parked along streets lined with fancy shops like Sonia Rykiel and Henri Bendel, restaurant dinners costing as much or more than two weeks of my wages.

"Time moves so fast so that the leaves of the horse chestnut trees inevitably yellow and fall, and the gardens wither; but the swiftness of time means winter, too, will end. When it's sleeting, and the trees are skeletons against a January sky, and my own head is cold and dull with winter, I relish knowing this will soon change. It is then I picture the yellow and purple crocuses," he said, and smiled, the edges of his mouth curling up just slightly, his words the closest to poetry I could imagine. "I try to listen for the song of the *petite merle*—the little blackbird."

Caught up as I was in this picture, the moonlight swathed Luc and me and the sculptures in its silvery glow, and time slipped away. I may even have forgotten where I was.

Until I felt his hands on my shoulders, his breath on my face. That hint of garlic.

His palms felt warm against the thin silk, and the next thing I knew, his mouth reached for my own. I lifted his cap. Against my neck and shoulders, the dreadlocks had the not unpleasant feel of seaweed. When I was small, Oma had taken me to the ocean. How I'd relished the cool feel of it between my toes, the warmth of the sun overhead. At this moment, it was as if I stood beside the ocean again, the salt smell on my skin, in my hair, the rush of surf echoing in my ear. I stopped thinking about anything else then. All I wanted was for that kiss to continue. Metamorphosis, I thought, feeling the blood pumping within and through me. What was the word in French?

With Luc, who could say who or what I might become. The kiss deepened. My shoulders felt the strong warmth of his hands. He drew me to him, and it was as if I was swimming through very deep water, weightless for the moment, though I knew I would soon need air.

Twenty-Two

WHAT COULD I have expected when I dialed up the internet the next morning: an email from Luc telling me that he couldn't live without me? a telepathic warning from my mother? some sign that my father intended to get in touch?

Instead there was a message from Clay. The subject read: 'How did it go?'

Hey Julie,

I'm dying to hear about the party. Yes, I'm clueless when it comes to fashion, but I'm sure you looked amazing in that dress. I even googled aquamarine to find the color, and I must admit it's a better choice than mermaid green (despite the fun at the Sorbonne pool. Speaking of which, I've been thinking about you a lot.) The Louvre has re-opened its Decorative Arts Museum, and I thought you and Genevieve might want to meet me there. How's three o'clock? I'll be biking thirty-five kilometers earlier, and after that I'll need a nap. But by three o'clock I'll be golden. Don't say no!

Guilt wracked through me as I pictured myself standing in Luc's studio, the two of us kissing, his enchanted sculptures looking on. I could never say a word about what had happened there to Clay; and if I was really honest, I would hold off meeting him until I knew where things stood with Luc.

But when I thought of the hours Clay and I had spent just a few days ago, talking over pizza and later drifting through the water at the Sorbonne pool where we stared up at the rectangles of blue sky pouring through the skylights, I felt an intense yearning to re-experience that calm sense of security he alone brought me. "I'll be there," I wrote back.

"HEY," CLAY SAID when we found him waiting by an Empire chaise lounge, as promised, at three o'clock sharp. Today he was wearing shorts, and his legs were even more freckled by the sun, his eyes raccooned by sunglasses.

"How was the bike ride?" I asked.

"Grueling," he said happily. "I decided to enter the race to Mont St. Michelle."

"Saint Who?" Genevieve asked.

"Not 'who,' 'what,'" Clay said.

"A cathedral, isn't it?" I said.

"Not just a cathedral, but the most amazing cathedral anywhere on earth. It was built in the tenth century and sits on high ground on an island off the coast of Normandy. At low tide you can walk out there, but at high tide it's totally cut off."

"Sounds dangerous if you don't know what you're doing," I said, aware that these words came a little too close for comfort.

"I do," Clay said, in that casual way of his, a confidence that propelled me back to that pizza lunch, his certainty that Gustave Fermiere would want to meet me. "The race starts about fifty kilometers away in St. Malo. If I bike twenty kilometers an hour, I'll reach Mont St. Michelle at low tide."

I remained unconvinced by Clay's tour guide description but grateful—under the circumstances—for the ways in which cycling completely absorbed, no, obsessed him. With a race on his mind, he would be unlikely to press me for details about the party, and so I would not (I hoped) find myself in need of lying.

Genevieve tugged at my hand. "Come on. You can talk about biking inside. I want to see Marie Antoinette's jewels."

"Right," Clay said, his cleats clickety-clacking against the tile floors.

We meandered through a museum that was beyond lavish, and Clay asked me about the party—bike obsessed or not, he knew this was my big deal—and I managed to speak truthfully about the food, the toasts, the incredible atmosphere, the fun I'd had making portraits, especially as I described many of the weird characters; and Madame Dupont's offer. The only thing I left out was Luc.

"Sounds like a great night," Clay said.

"Come on," Genevieve called out, for we'd fallen behind.

"Yes," I said, his wide smile bringing back my guilt times ten.

To reach the jewelry galleries, we passed rooms filled with enough furniture to fill Versailles, from gilt armchairs and brocade sofas to silk tapestries and mahogany armoires. Beyond the furniture, more than two thousand years of jewelry were housed in a mazelike network of rooms, all of them dark, and all of them filled with spot-lit, plexi-glass boxes, each one containing some fabulous necklace, pair of earrings, ankle bangle, or other adornment. There were Sumerian wedding bracelets of beaten saffron gold, onyx and jade pendants from Pharoah's Egypt, even sixteenth century lockets containing miniature portraits from England.

The highlight, though, was the French jewelry, the eighteenth and nineteenth centuries in particular. We planned to focus on the room housing Marie Antoinette's jewels, which were beyond spectacular. A pendant contained a sapphire the size of a small plum, and there was a necklace threaded through with rubies and black pearls. "Not so hard to understand why the people of Paris turned on her, is it?" I said to Clay, the two of us standing before the plexi-glass box, Genevieve between us.

"Actually Marie Antoinette's 'Let them eat cake,' was taken completely out of context," Clay said.

"Sorry?" I was reminded of how many hundreds of times I'd heard the tired phrase that had cost the queen her life, most recently in some advertisement for a new bakery chain.

"'Let them eat cake'—Marie Antoinette may not have understood the common people, but she wasn't trying to be vicious."

"You're saying she was just stupid then?"

"Harsh, Julie. She was brought up to be a queen, and her teachers were pretty behind the times. She learned embroidery, dancing, singing, that sort of thing. If only she'd learned some history."

"So she was basically a spoiled girl in the wrong place at the wrong time."

"That's the gist of it," Clay said, "though I thought you'd have a little more heart."

"Hey, we're talking about Marie Antoinette here," I said.

Clay just shook his head. "My father's a historian. He's trained me to look at a situation from different angles—"

"Alright already," Genevieve said. "I get it. You're both saying that Marie Antoinette would have been better off if she'd stayed in some castle in Austria. Now let's look at her jewels."

"You know," Clay said, "her head disappeared after her death—"

"What's wrong with you today? You are both being so weird," Genevieve said. "I don't want to talk about cut off heads going missing."

"Correction," Clay said. "The head was probably smuggled out and preserved in something like formaldehyde—"

"Please," Genevieve said, wrinkling her nose. "This is a museum full of jewels. You're spoiling the whole experience for me. I want to go and see the Lalique."

"But you wanted to see Marie Antoinette's jewels," I said.

"Yeah, sure, but not like this," Genevieve said. "I'm off to the Lalique."

"Not on your own?" Clay said.

"Why not?" Genevieve said. "You two can talk about Marie Antoinette's head all you want, and I can look at the jewelry without feeling like I'm in a horror movie."

"Gen," I said.

"No, you two clearly have something going on, and it's distracting me. I'll just be down the hall. I'll see you in the gift shop at five."

She turned to go.

"Hold on." Clay reached for my arm.

"I'll be fine," Genevieve called over her shoulder. "I have a map, and I'll see you at five."

And with that, she strode off, leaving me alone with Clay.

"You're really going to let her explore the museum alone?" Clay said.

"You heard her. She's carrying a map, and she knows exactly what jewelry she wants to see."

"Okay, but I don't think it's the greatest idea," Clay said.

"She'll be fine," I said, more concerned just then with what Genevieve had said about the two of us having 'something going on.'

When Clay reached for my hand, I hesitated, but despite the little voice inside me screaming 'traitor!' I wound up interlacing my fingers with his.

We strolled through rooms heaped with treasures including the most gorgeous necklace of gold filigree strung with teardrop diamonds. The placard said it had originally belonged to Juliette Récamier. As I counted the number of teardrops, fifty-five, I replayed Madame Dupont's invitation to come and see her sometime. Replayed, too, Luc's certainty that I must go—"She's made many an artist's career."

"Exquisite piece," Clay said. "Do you know who Juliette Récamier was?"

"You mean you honestly don't know?"

"No idea." He smiled that orthodontic-bright smile, for he said he'd worn braces for three years, beating my record of twenty-six months.

"She was the Julia Roberts, no the Jacqueline Kennedy of post-revolutionary Paris."

"I'm sorry, Julie, but could you be a little more specific?"

"Excepting Marie Antoinette, Juliette Récamier might just be the most famous French woman from the eighteenth century."

"I already told you that Marie Antoinette was Austrian. That was part of the problem—"

Aware that we were straying back into those dangerous, severed-head waters again, I said, "You are missing the point."

He smiled, and his hazel eyes crinkled up at the edges. "And that is?"

196

"Juliette Récamier was considered the most beautiful woman in Paris after the Revolution." Clay's expression suggested a bad joke was coming. "Jacques Louis David painted her on a chaise lounge," I said, leaving out the details Madame Dupont had shared. "That painting's in the Louvre. She married her mother's lover during the Reign of Terror so as to ensure that she held onto his fortune."

Clay stared. "Sounds like a soap opera."

"It was a strategy. Her mother and her lover, Monsieur Récamier, wanted to make sure they lived in style if he went to the guillotine."

"Why couldn't the mother marry him? God," Clay shuddered, "the guy must have been old."

"She was married already, that's why."

"Like I said, a soap opera."

"Uh huh, and you're the one who defended Marie Antoinette."

"I didn't defend her. I just said that she wasn't the bitch that history's made her out to be."

"Right," I said, figuring out at last what Genevieve had meant. There was something going on between us; in formal terms it was called sexual tension.

It wasn't long before we were standing very close together before the most elaborate jewelry cabinet either one of us had ever seen. It stood nearly as tall as Genevieve and was made of what the placard described as rare yew and purple-heart wood, and inlaid with mother of pearl and gilt bronze.

"Seems Napoleon gave the cabinet to Empress Josephine in 1809, not long before he divorced her," Clay said, doing the math.

"Do you think it was a sort of settlement gift then?" I wondered, aware that one could live the rest of one's life—very well—by selling off one piece of jewelry at a time, if the cabinet was any proof of how many jewels this Josephine possessed.

"No," Clay said. "If you read further down, you'll see that after the divorce the cabinet went to Napoleon's second wife."

"Rough deal," I said, though the truth was I knew virtually nothing about the personalities or politics of this trio, except for the fact that the luxury in which they obviously lived stood in the face of all that the Revolution had stood for. Face to face with this beyond-extravagant cabinet, Marie Antoinette's 'Let them eat cake' really didn't sound so bad, though I wasn't about to get Clay started on her again.

"Rough deal or not, this cabinet is incredibly cool," Clay said, motioning to the many locks and other mechanisms concealed within. "Look closely: it houses all sorts of secret compartments and drawers. Just imagine what might have been hidden within."

"You're right," I said, not quite ready to veer any closer to the subject of secrets.

"Hey, check this out," Clay said, drawing my attention to a scene at the cabinet's center depicting the birth of some sort of goddess—Josephine, maybe? 'To whom Cupids and Goddesses hasten to bear their offerings,' the caption read.

"Do you suppose Napoleon had any alterations made to this goddess picture once he took the cabinet away from Wife Number One and re-gifted it to Wife Number Two?" I asked.

"That is a really good question," he said, the guard near the door motioning for us to step away from the display, "the kind of question worth tracking down the curator for and pressing to have answered."

I could not tell if he was serious or joking; all I knew was that he was standing super close to me, and his hands were at my hips. The next thing I knew I was closing my eyes, and despite Luc and all that I wasn't telling Clay, when he kissed me, I kissed him back; and yes, traitorous or not, I reveled in that kiss. It was better than the one at the pool, or maybe I just put more of myself into it on account of what had happened with Luc, or so I told myself later.

I NO LONGER remember how much time passed before Clay pointed to his high-tech watch.

"Oh my god," I said, already in motion. "Five o'clock already!"

We ducked in and out of the rooms, their mazelike network seeming to increase in number, until we reached the gift shop at ten past.

But when we got there, the place was overrun with middle-aged Englishwomen, all of whom wore fanciful millinery confections (a.k.a. hats) that Genevieve would have died for.

"I don't see her," Clay said.

"Neither do I, and if she was here, I think she'd be trailing behind someone like her." I pointed to a woman whose feather and foliage-laden hat resembled a rain forest complete with tangerine bird.

"Maybe she said to wait for her at the exit," Clay said.

"No," I stammered, "she said the gift shop, I'm sure, but let's check the exit just in case."

As we rushed out, I felt myself beginning to hyperventilate and sub-consciously wondered if this wasn't my punishment for deceiving Clay.

Seriously, Julie, a voice within me said, *that sounds a little too self-involved. Focus on finding Genevieve, not on your deservedly guilt-wracked heart.*

"Pardon, Monsieur," Clay said to the security guard, then described Genevieve in rapid French.

"Non," the guard said.

"Okay," he said, trying not to react to the panic in my face. "I say we stand outside for a few minutes and see if she comes back. She might have gone across the street for a soda or something."

"Right," I said, though I doubted this, given the smoothies on the museum restaurant menu.

Unlike the main branch of the Louvre, which sat in a football stadium-sized courtyard filled with fountains and street vendors, tourists and pigeons, the Decorative Arts Museum squatted right up against the phenomenally busy Rue de Rivoli. It was now rush hour in Paris, and the noise was deafening. The smell of petroleum and pollution intensified in the heat, and I started feeling sick and very itchy.

"What could have happened to her?" Clay said, as five ten became five fifteen and then five twenty-five.

"She's never done anything like this before," I said, what was left of my cool giving way to full blown panic. What if someone kidnapped her in the museum? I'd heard stories about that sort of thing happening. A friendly stranger comes up to a child, offers her a drugged candy.

A choked sob escaped my throat, and once I started I couldn't stop, the stress of losing Genevieve—and the fear of what may have happened to her—compounded by the emotion that had been building for weeks now.

"Hang on there, Jules," Clay said, digging around in his pockets for something that could work as a handkerchief.

"A sock?" I said between sobs. "You are handing me a sock?"

"It's all I've got. Besides," he said, "at least it's clean."

I blew my nose, tuned out the people who were staring, unable to imagine what we were going to do next—call the police? Claire?

Just when I thought the earth was going to crack open and swallow me whole, the door to the Decorative Arts Museum opened, and the security guard stepped out, accompanied by a girl in a tie-dye dress and matching sandals: Genevieve.

I raced towards her, flung my arms around her neck, and hugged her close. "Where were you? Why didn't you come and find us? I thought we'd have to call the police."

"Sorry. I fell asleep on a chair—it was very comfortable, an antique, I think—in the women's lounge. I started feeling dizzy while looking at the Lalique."

"You don't have a fever," I said, touching my hand to her forehead.

"Motion sickness," Clay said.

"What are you talking about?" I asked Clay, keeping my eye on Genevieve.

"Those dark rooms and all those bright little boxes," Clay said, after thanking the guard, who looked equally relieved to have restored Genevieve to us. "The eye has trouble focusing."

"Maybe. I'm just glad you're here," I said, hugging her even closer.

I turned to Clay, my eyes holding his own. "Thanks," I said, "for everything. If you hadn't been here—"

"Genevieve wouldn't have taken off."

"He's right, you know," Genevieve said.

He looked straight at me. "Honestly, I was glad to help."

"Thanks."

"Soon," Clay said, leaning in to kiss me before we parted.

"Soonest," I replied, then whispered, "thank you for helping me stay calm."

"No problem," he said, though we both knew I had been anything but.

"So are you and Clay together now?" Genevieve asked once Clay was out of earshot.

I studied Genevieve who sounded twenty right now and not ten.

"I'm just saying, he's a much better pick than that Luc guy."

Perspiration prickled my brow. "What do you mean?"

"Come on, Julie, isn't it obvious?" Genevieve said, before turning towards the metro station.

Twenty-Three

BACK AT THE apartment, my worries about Genevieve telling Claire that she'd gotten, if not lost, then dangerously separated, not to mention motion sick, were immediately trumped by the note we found on the coffee table.

> *Julie and Genevieve,*
> *Monsieur Rimbaud just telephoned. He said something about a group of letters that Paul Henri found in an art book he picked up in a flea market. He said you, Julie, already know about this!??? Gracious, you are good at keeping secrets—too good perhaps! Monsieur Rimbaud has spoken to Rafi who, as you can imagine, is ecstatic. I thought I'd find you at home—I waited, but it's now six thirty, and I've gone back to the gallery. Please telephone me there as soon as you return. I expect you'll want to come right over. We can order takeout.*
> *Claire/Mommy*

"I admit, I had some grave doubts, but the letters are authentic," Monsieur Rimbaud was saying, once we stepped into the gallery. Rafi and Claire were there, and so were Paul Henri and Madame Becerra.

"So everything in those letters about Jeanne is authentic?" I said.

"We have no reason to believe otherwise," Rafi said.

"In a strange way, we owe it all to you, Julie," Monsieur Rimbaud said, stroking the edges of his well-tended mustache. "As I was just telling everyone, Paul Henri would never have picked up the book if it weren't for you."

I tried to catch Paul Henri's eye to find out what he thought about all of this, but I had the strong suspicion he was trying hard not to notice me. Why? Had he heard about me and Luc?

"Once the media gets hold of the news there will be a resurgence of interest in Modigliani," Rafi said. "More people will want to see the painting in the gallery."

"The reputation and the longevity of all of Modigliani's work will benefit," Madame Becerra added, a trio of bangles on her wrist tinkling while her own voice remained cool, her expression composed.

"What about the portrait on the back of the studio door?" I asked, returning in my mind's eye, to the studio, where the woman in the vibrant pink tunic waited. Almost a century, she'd been hidden away like that. "Jeanne's portrait—"

"But of course we will display it alongside the 'Madonna and Child.'" Rafi nodded towards the shadows where the portrait itself seemed to watch and listen. "Imagine: a great reception, an unveiling of Modigliani's late masterpiece alongside the work of his beloved muse."

205

"I must admit," Madame Becerra said, positively glowing, "it is a major coup. I congratulate you."

"Just be sure to keep Madame Marthurin's grandson Luc out of it," Paul Henri said, a deep furrow marring his high brow.

Rafi turned towards him. "Why? Will he cause problems?"

"He might just demand a share in the profits," Paul Henri continued.

"Nonsense," Monsieur Rimbaud said. "Luc and Paul Henri are like two alley cats fighting over territory that others would have the sense to abandon. Unfortunately, my grandson is the more tenacious."

Paul Henri's now wintry blue eyes met mine. He did not smile.

"About the book—" Rafi said now.

"It's mine, isn't it?" I said.

"My dear," Monsieur Rimbaud said, stroking his moustache. "I'm afraid the book is no longer some flea market treasure. It's a valuable artifact. We will have to share it with other art historians and perhaps, ultimately, with the public."

"I will choose another book on Modigliani for you myself," Rafi offered, laying a hand on my arm.

I bit my lip, afraid I would start crying. It may have seemed childish, but I didn't want another book. I wanted that one.

Part Three

Twenty-Four

"I WONDERED WHEN you were going to look me up, *cherie*," Madame Dupont said the following afternoon, ensconced in what Genevieve would have called a 'dressing gown,' this one of the luxurious silk I associated with drapes or queens, and the color of frosted grapes, once her butler—what else could you call the aquiline-nosed man in a pseudo-tux?—showed me into a salon lined with mirrors, its colors confectionary pink and gold, its ceiling and walls fitted with Plaster of Paris moldings that resembled clouds or ice cream; and on every table, a crystal vase of pink and yellow anemones.

"Yes, well," I said, entranced, "I've had a whole lot going on."

"So I've gathered," she said, and smiled so that her teeth showed, all of them white and straight, incredible since she seemed to smoke nearly as much as she breathed. She reached for a lacquered box on the table beside her. "Care for one?" she asked, holding out what looked like a hundred gold-tipped cigarettes.

I shook my head, amazed that all that smoking didn't affect the flowers, for there were bouquets everywhere, the majority of them overly-fragrant tiger lilies or heavy-headed roses.

She raised an elaborately plucked eyebrow, her expression echoed in the surrounding mirrors. "The cigarettes are Egyptian, so smooth you would think you were Cleopatra."

"I don't think Cleopatra smoked," I said. "I sure don't."

"Wise decision on your part, *cherie*. Cleopatra, I believe, was game for anything. I took it up before all those warnings. Blame it on Bette Davis, Jean Harlow—all that 1930s glamour." She laughed. "You're too young, I suppose to realize how divine smoking looks in black and white."

Her butler brought tea in a Limoges pot—white decorated with violets, a print I recognized from the antique shop—and a plate of English biscuits. We both drank the tea, which was smoky and bitter Lapsong Souchong, but I was the only one who ate the biscuits. They were dry and tasted as if they'd been in the pantry for too long. We talked about painting and Modigliani and the studio door and even the letters. But she didn't mention Luc, though I was dying for the slightest news. I mean, why hadn't he called?

"Extraordinary," she said, pouring tea. "Dear Marta wept when she phoned last night. She has been waiting all her life for a chance to prove the studio door was painted by Jeanne, you see."

I thought back to that first day at Madame Marthurin's restaurant, the way she looked at me when I asked her about Jeanne, a look both haunted and hopeful. Sitting opposite Madame Dupont, my eyes traced the papery beauty of the nearby anemones, their petals like the crinkled skirt of a can-can dancer, their black hearts like a woman's eyelashes. "Madame Marthurin's daughter," I began.

"Yes, what about her?"

"She was an artist, too, wasn't she? And something terrible happened to her, didn't it?"

"You are intelligent, *cherie*," she said, continuing to smoke, "and correct. Madame Marthurin's daughter struggled for years, auditioning for every play, making ends meet with those ridiculous commercials. Once she played a minor part in *The Winter's Tale*, a very prestigious production; but despite all her efforts, and her talent, she never saw success as an actress."

"What was her name?"

"Marguerite."

The French word for daisy, the flower the young Jeanne was fond of weaving through her own hair. "What happened to her?" I asked.

"You are bold to ask," Madame Dupont said, but there was approval in her voice, not criticism. "How can I explain? She was high strung, as is Luc. He has his art, but his mother—" She looked away—did a tear glint there?

"Please," I said, watching the smoke rise and disappear.

"His mother was hospitalized for a while. There was medication, shock therapy, so many doctors, but she never really recovered."

211

"Is her daughter, losing her, I mean, is she the reason Madame Marthurin cares so much about Jeanne?"

"It's not so simple, but you are right in thinking that her death deepened Marta's commitment to the past, particularly to women artists. I haven't the same dire reasons, but it's in my blood, too, and it's become a bond between us." She drew on her cigarette.

"What are your reasons?" I said.

"My parents specialized in the repair of heirlooms: wedding dresses, a baby's christening gown, the sort of things a family holds onto. Suits and christening gowns may not be paintings," Madame Dupont said, the ash from her cigarette spotting the purple velvet, "but they are masterpieces that ennoble ordinary people's lives."

From anyone else, I would have mistrusted such words. Ennobled? Be serious. But this was not just anyone else. This was Madame Dupont, a woman wearing a dressing gown as cool and shimmery as frosted grapes, her sterling silver hair glinting in the light, her perfume hearkening back to a time when women wore gardenias in their hair, twined pearls round their necks and dressed for dinner. A time, too, when very few women dared to dream of becoming professional artists.

I had to listen.

"You recognized the name of Récamier," Madame Dupont continued. "Too many young Parisians don't know her, but an American? It's quite a *marque de distinction*. Now," she walked towards the mirrors, her figure refracted there, a calculated effect I had no doubt, and one she must have practiced often. "I want to show you something."

"This is her house, isn't it?" I said, feeling as I had when I stepped into the Great Hall at the Louvre.

"*Oui.*" Her smile, just then, matched the Cheshire cat's. "My boudoir once belonged to her. It is the art in my boudoir I wish to show you."

Be casual, I reminded myself, absolutely and totally cool. "Of course."

She stood, opened the heavy, gilded doors, and I followed her down a long hallway that had been painted a smoky blue. It was lined with portraits, among them several Modiglianis, a sad-looking harlequin by Picasso; and what looked like one of Matisse's interiors, the doors flung open to the sea.

"Here," Madame Dupont said, once we reached the end of the hallway. She opened a door, and instead of smoky shades of gray and dim light, I beheld a wedding cake of a chandelier, hundreds of crystal icicles stemming from a base of gold. The cream-colored walls, too, were trimmed with gold.

"Incredible." The walls of this room and the ceiling had been painted with a series of related images that unfolded into a story.

"What you see before you is the story of Eros and Psyche told in a dozen pictures. All of post-revolutionary Paris, but especially the legendary Juliette, was spellbound by the story being retold here." Madame Dupont dropped her cigarette in a silver bowl, where it smoked. "Are you familiar with the story?"

"A little." I had a basic knowledge of the myth, having studied it during sophomore year as part of a unit in English on fairy tales. What I mostly remembered was that the story of Beauty and the Beast found its beginning in the tale of Eros and Psyche. A beautiful young woman named Psyche marries an amazing man who is also an amazing lover named Eros, a.k.a. Cupid, Aphrodite's son. The only trouble is he will not let her see his face. If she does, he tells her that they will lose each other. Psyche, like any other human being, cannot resist his warning, especially not once her jealous sisters convince her that he must be a monster, this being their only explanation for his not letting her see his face.

"The tale of Eros and Psyche is a love story, but it is also a quest, rather like Odysseus's journey back to Penelope."

The words brought back Luc's sculptures, my own belief that Odysseus did not deserve Penelope, the faithful wife who waited years for him to return. "Why was Juliette Récamier captivated by Eros and Psyche?"

"Because the story is as much about the search for oneself—for one's true identity—as it is about the search for love.

"What I like about the story is the fact that the search, the quest, belongs to the woman." Madame Dupont went on to tell me that after Psyche beholds her husband and discovers a face more beautiful than her wildest imaginings, she loses him, just as he predicted.

I sought out the painting depicting Psyche as she flees, her face buried in her hands, her body bent as an old woman's. "Aphrodite sends Psyche down to the Underworld, doesn't she?" I said, my own memory of the story returning.

"Yes, eager to be rid of her, Aphrodite tells Psyche to return with the box of beauty belonging to Persephone, the queen of the Underworld."

"So, does she go? And does she try to steal Persephone's beauty?" I asked, searching the panels for this part of the story.

"Psyche may be young, but she's not naïve," Madame Dupont said, recovering her cigarette from the bowl. "She knows a mortal cannot return from the Underworld. But she's so miserable without Eros she doesn't care. Young as she is, she's ready to lay down her life."

I shivered, pierced by the similarity to Jeanne's love for Modigliani.

"It's only once Psyche's down there that a voice whispers to her not to open the box containing Persephone's beauty," Madame Dupont continued. "That voice belongs to—"

"Eros," I said, figuring out the sequence of these panels as she spoke, and jumping ahead to the last one which depicted the lovers, their bodies entwined.

"Yes." Madame Dupont's silvery eyes regarded me closely. "Thanks to Eros, Psyche survives the Underworld, but the lovers cannot be together until Eros begs the gods to restore Pscyhe to him."

Suddenly, I remembered: "Psyche is the word for 'soul,' isn't it?"

"*Oui*. It is the soul's journey the myth captures. That journey is the source of its power."

We stood in silence for a while until Madame Dupont said, "Stunning as these panels are, if you look more closely, you'll notice they're in need of restoration." She pointed to a depiction of Eros, his wings chipped.

"Yes," I said, my eyes tracing the cracks in Eros's face, and in Psyche's, the way they distorted his beauty, just as time did ordinary human beings.

"To restore artwork like this would cost a fortune," she sighed, her gestures mimicking those of Aphrodite in one of the final panels. "And a fortune, *cherie*," she lowered her voice, as if someone, the butler perhaps, might be eavesdropping, "despite what I allow others to believe, a fortune I do not have."

I swallowed hard, amazed at the success of Madame Dupont's deception, for everyone I'd met believed she was phenomenally rich.

"One positive of living in Paris is that Paris has always been filled with artists of extraordinary talent and little income. Poor darlings." She drew on her cigarette, tapped its ash against the edge of an empty vase. "I've found just such a person to do the major restoration, but she needs an apprentice, someone who shows promise and would be willing to work."

My heart was beating wildly with the possibility she seemed to be holding out to me, and its parallel to my own father's life. Restoration was his field.

"*Exactement*. As you can see, it's a vast undertaking," she said. "If you were to work with my artisan, Emma Lyttleton is her name, you would have to learn the techniques of the age in which the panels were created. There's a course at the Louvre, and it would involve studying many works from the late eighteenth century. I would pay for the study, certainly, a serious financial commitment," she said, grinding out her cigarette, "but other than paying for your studies, I would not be able to pay you."

"I understand," I said.

"*Bon*. I would of course give you a room here and meals—and the gift of experience." She blinked, and her fabulous lashes fluttered like butterflies.

We stood there, the story of Eros and Psyche enclosing us, and I was suddenly afraid she would ask me to make a decision right there. I needed time to think.

"A week's time for your decision, eh *cherie?*" she said, and laid a cool hand on my arm.

"A week," I agreed.

OUT ON THE street, the sun resembled a tangerine. It made the pavement glisten and haloed the horse chestnut trees. A warm breeze lilted through me, tangling my hair. I crossed over onto the Rue de la Cherche Midi, promising myself that I would always hold onto this moment. My god, I thought, dodging a cinnamon-haired woman on rollerblades and her galloping, cinnamon-furred standard poodle, this must

217

be one of the gifts of my time in Paris, an invitation to remain here and restore art.

I walked on, marveling at the chance to understand, not just with my mind but with the muscles in my fingertips, an eighteenth century painter's brushstrokes, composition, secrets. My father understood this kind of work. What had drawn him to it? When would I find out? Would I find out? I closed my eyes, lifted my face to the sun, and smiled. The opportunity had arrived at last. If I wanted to, I could stay in Paris.

Ten minutes later, I stood outside an old-fashioned ice cream parlor with two scoops of strawberry piled into a steep cone when someone called my name.

I turned. *Luc.*

Was this just coincidence? Or did he know about my visit with Madame Dupont?

"Hey," I said, trying to sound casual, a nearly impossible task.

"You're looking *très chic*," he said, taking hold of my sticky hand and turning me around. "Did you take my advice? Have you been to see Madame Dupont?"

"Oh yes, her house is incredible. My god, to think it once belonged to Juliette Récamier. All that art, and her stories—"

"Yes, yes, I know. To spend a few months with her is reason enough to stay in Paris."

"You know about the invitation then?"

"*Oui*," he said, taking a handkerchief from his jeans pocket and wiping my chin, the corners of my mouth, "I have selfish reasons for hoping you'll stay."

My face broke into a giddy grin, and I felt about ten years old, ice cream dripping down my fingers.

"Are you on your way home then?" he asked.

"Um—" It was nearly five o'clock, and Claire, I knew, expected me for supper, and what about Clay? How could I deny that I'd let him believe that I cared for him? And the truth was: I did care for him.

But Luc was smiling at me, and in his tattered jeans and navy blue t-shirt he looked boyish and beautiful, the sun having sprinkled his cheeks and the bridge of his nose with freckles. Of course I thought of Eros.

"Say you have an hour. Please," his voice turned gentle, and he reached for my hand, "don't disappoint me."

I could tell Claire that Madame Dupont had kept me longer, couldn't I? She'd never have to know. "Let me just make a quick phone call," I said.

Five minutes later, having left a message on Claire's voice mail, I was riding around Paris on the back of Luc's scooter, the hot July wind tousling my hair, as I breathed in the smell of gasoline and something earthier, Luc's sweat mingling with my own. "Where are we going?" I asked, once we came to a red light.

"Bellevue," Luc said, as a Mercedes nosed its way in front of us. "The murals there are something every young artist must see."

A sudden vision of the two of us—up-and-coming artists taking Paris by storm—flashed through me. The afternoon at the Louvre with Clay pulsed in my memory, but I pushed it far back. Luc was the one. He had to be.

"THEY CALL THIS street La Kommune now," Luc said, once he parked his bike, and helped me down. "The fortunate artists, those who are really trying to make something powerful, live down here. It's much less expensive than the Marais."

"And you?" I said, shaking out my hair and feeling exquisitely Parisian.

His topaz eyes held my own. "Of course I'd love to have a place here, and maybe one day I shall, but for now I'd never do that to my grandmother."

"She depends on you a lot, I think."

"*Cherie*, we depend upon each other," he said, letting his fingertip caress my cheek.

I was dying to hear about his history—how long he'd lived with Madame Marthurin, and especially what had happened to his mother. But there was no way to ask.

"You've seen the murals outside the Musée Picasso, yes?" he asked, as we walked, hand in hand, down the cobbled streets, the heels of my sandals gently slapping the stone.

"Honestly I've only been to the Marais once," I confessed, not quite ready to tell Luc that with the exception of the moody blue period, I wasn't a huge fan of Picasso, who I didn't think had the talent of Modigliani, though he did have the business savvy.

"Well then," Luc said, tucking a loose strand of hair behind my ear, "I must take you there, and soon. *Bien sûr*, what you'll see here is just as good. The artists here are in touch with the pulse of the city. Now then," he said, steering me around a corner. "Have a look."

220

Still holding Luc's hand, I found myself face to face with a monumental mural: part El Greco Madonna and part Kandinsky abstraction dominating a building that ran the length of a city block, the colors so bold it was as if the paint was still wet. "Incredible."

"Isn't it?" Luc said, his own gaze riveted by the Madonna-esque woman painted in a range of purples; behind her, a giant boot filled with children—a la the nursery rhyme?—and a gleaming but slightly menacing high-tech desk. "The artist is Sua-yin Chen. We met at the Cartier Institute. He's trying to express the self-division in contemporary women—torn between family and career."

I nodded, stabbed by all I knew about Claire's choices, and my mother's.

"Part of the reason I wanted to show you this one is the legacy of Modigliani. You see it, don't you? *La mélancolie? L'élégance?*"

I took in the long lines of the woman's throat, the elongated fingers, the wistfulness of her gaze. "It would be impossible not to."

"Maybe I'll invite him to the gallery," Luc said. "He'd love the Modigliani on display, and I think you'd like him. There will be a party, no?"

"Yes." If I had wings, I would have lifted into flight. He would introduce me to other artists. A door was opening. We would have a future.

"Come on," he said, and tugged me forward. "There's more."

The building on the next block, too, had a mural. It was a landscape of trees in winter. The day was overcast and gray; the only sign of color, a red cardinal perched on a lonely branch.

"It's so sad," I said.

"Yes, Charlotte Giselle, the artist, is a master of emotion."

"Tell me more about her," I said, sensing they had a history.

"Impossible. She no longer paints."

"What does she do then?"

"A friend says she's more of a performance artist now. Once she even dressed up as a gargoyle and climbed Notre Dame, but she didn't get very far. The police forced her down—the media went wild."

The breath left my lungs. Did this artist know anything about my father? Had she been copying him?

"You okay?" Luc said, pressing his hand to my cheek. "You've turned so pale."

"Just a little dizzy," I said, unable to mention Gustave Fermiere to him, at least not yet.

He reached into his backpack, and pulled forth a bottle of water which he uncapped, then raised to my lips.

Drinking it down, I shivered a little, realizing only now how thirsty I was.

Luc ran a fingertip along my mouth, his eyes not once straying from my own. When he took hold of my hand and pulled me close, cupping my face between both of his hands to kiss me, I once again felt as if I was plummeting many leagues under the sea. Was this a feeling I could get used to?

"I'd love to sketch you," he said, brushing a tangled lock of hair from my face. "How about going back to my studio?"

The idea both thrilled and frightened me, and I began to play out a script in my mind, one that had come into my thoughts several times since the night of the party. I would sit down among those magical sculptures, and even if he drew me, it would not be long before he came over, knelt at my feet, then nudged my dress down around my bare shoulders, unclasped my bra, bent to kiss my breasts.

"Well?" he said, stroking my chin, the topaz-gold of his eyes brighter than the late afternoon sun. "Say you'll come, Julie. You want to. God knows I want you to. You've been on my mind so many times—"

There was no denying that I wanted to go with him, at least part of me did, the part of me that wanted to experience everything, and who better to teach me than Luc? Why then hadn't he called?

"Say you'll come, lovely Julie," Luc said again, his tone as irresistible as a caress. "Please."

There were two Me's at that moment: there was the Me in the aquamarine dress who'd kissed Luc and drank green chartreuse and the Me who slept in the bed beside Genevieve, the one Claire trusted.

And I felt caught between them.

"Well?" he said.

I pictured Genevieve's open gaze, her smile.

"I'm afraid I can't today. I'm Genevieve's au pair, you know," I said, though I was the one who felt about ten years old just then. "Claire and Genevieve, well, they're both expecting me."

HALF AN HOUR later, Luc dropped me off a good three blocks from the apartment. I'm sure he understood the reasons behind this, but I was relieved when he didn't mention them. "I'll see you soon," he said, and kissed me so deeply I felt as if we were becoming one of his sculptures, engaged in some strange and wonderful transformation.

Madame Dupont and Marie France could be wrong about him, couldn't they? I thought, walking away, the sound of his scooter diminishing. Wasn't the gentleness in his voice, the way he held me, proof of this?

It wasn't until I climbed the stairs to the apartment that I began to ask myself how I was going to pull this off in front of Claire. On her voice mail, I'd said I'd be two hours at most. It had been nearly three.

Just tell her you stayed longer at Madame Dupont's, the voice within me said.

I turned the key in the lock and walked in to find both Claire and Genevieve waiting for me. My first thought: They know I lied. They saw me with Luc.

"Hi," I said. "What's up?"

Claire stood. "It came," she said, her own voice breathless.

"What? I don't—"

"Your father wrote." Genevieve thrust the envelope into my hands.

Dear Julie,

I have thought about you often—at least I have thought about the daughter I knew I had—since your mother wrote to me nearly seventeen years ago. If I am truthful, I will confess that at first I thought of that daughter with a mixture of fear and mistrust.

My health was not good. I was far too preoccupied with my art. In other words, I was not ready for fatherhood, but this information is not suitable for a letter. It must unfold slowly, over time…

During the last fifteen years my attitude has shifted, or perhaps the more accurate statement would be—in the last fifteen years, I began to think about my daughter with a growing desire to come to know her—to come to know you. Hence my wonder, my joy, at your letter.

A lot has changed for me since I knew your mother. I am no longer a person who moves quickly in anything, which is why I am so well-suited to the restoration of old paintings. The craft belongs to a slower world, a world we must recreate through the pieces we have, the relics of another time.

Yes, I am willing, even eager, to meet you. But I am also afraid. My own path has been a strange one—why I think it best that I come to Paris for this first visit.

It is a city with which you are already familiar, and Provence is a day's train ride away. Thank you for enclosing a telephone number. I am in the midst of finishing a project, but I will call, within the week, or at least very soon, to make the arrangements.

Sincerely,
Gustave Fermiere

Beyond the window, a boy on a bicycle hurried past, ringing his bell before ducking around a truck. The letter was formal, even a little distant, and certainly not what I expected.

But what did I expect?

More emotion? Definitely some news about the circumstances of his life. Was he married? Did he have other children? *My path has been a strange one…* What did that mean? Did it mean he missed me? Regretted what had happened? Wished he could have held onto my mom?

At least he's willing to come to Paris, I reminded myself. *Eager*, the letter said.

"You okay, Julie?" Claire asked, laying a warm hand on my shoulder.

I nodded, all I felt with Luc fading fast in the face of this news. While I stood kissing him on the street, Claire and Genevieve had been sitting here with my letter. All this time, my father's words had been waiting for me.

Twenty-Five

"OF ALL DAYS to drop this in my lap, Mark couldn't possibly have picked a worse one," Claire said, scowling into her coffee cup.

It was the day before the big reception at L'Espace Stein, the one to celebrate the unveiling of the studio door portrait by Jeanne Hébuterne alongside Modigliani's "Madonna and Child."

"Genevieve's father must have given some reason?" I said, though I had to admit almost any reason would have been pretty lame. Who, in his right mind, disinvites his own daughter for a week-long holiday just months before he gets married again, to a pregnant woman who is not her mom?

"He's busy with wedding preparations, he says, and then there's the honeymoon. Those are his reasons." Claire sipped her coffee, continued to scowl, frown lines etching themselves into the corners of her mouth. "He and Margot are going to some wildlife refuge in Costa Rica. Mark is not the outdoorsy type, and he's definitely not an animal person. I find it hard to imagine him hiking through rain forest and looking at rare species of birds and monkeys."

This was the closest to bitter I'd heard Claire get, and it brought back what she'd said just after I came to Paris, the fact that she'd given up her own art after she became pregnant. Because there couldn't be two starving or at least two struggling artists, not if they wanted to raise a child in a place with air-conditioning, not if they wanted money in the checking account, a reliable car.

Madame Dupont, Luc, the turmoil I felt about Clay, the anticipation about meeting my father, and now this; again, I was back on that Ferris wheel. I called up that feeling of me in my white dress standing in the sunlight, the days ahead full of possibility just after I left the house of Madame Dupont, only to run into Luc.

Three days had gone by, and still no word. Well, he'd said he wasn't reliable, as had everyone else—including Genevieve. So, why was I so slow to catch on?

"Mommy," Genevieve said, padding into the room in her hot pink slippers, Annie trailing behind her.

"Hi there, sleepyhead," Claire said, the lightness in her voice coming out forced. "Good to see you're up. I bought brioche—your favorite—and there are a few macaroons for later."

It wasn't just the t-shirt from Clay emblazoned with Mont St. Michelle, size extra large, that made Genevieve look small. It was the quiver in her voice, and the way she stood there with her shoulders slumped, watching us. Even Annie seemed to sense

PARIS, MODIGLIANI & ME

something was wrong for her stub of a tail, usually a flag of attention, drooped.

"It's true then, what Daddy said over the phone: does he really have no time for me?" Genevieve asked, scooting into a chair.

"Daddy has so much to do before the wedding, pumpkin, you know that."

"But he promised," Genevieve said. "He promised it would just be us two for the week. We were going back to the beach house. How could he do this to me, Mommy? How?"

"I'm sorry. I wish I could change it." Claire reached out and covered Genevieve's hand with her own.

"Do you really have to go to the gallery today?" Genevieve asked Claire.

"I do, I'm afraid."

"I don't want to stay here anymore," Genevieve said.

"Well, Gen, for now Paris is our home. And I promise you: once the reception is over, you and I will drive out to Fontainebleau. A night at that fancy hotel we read about. Room service."

Genevieve's cheeks regained a hint of pink. "The one with the marble bathtubs in the rooms?"

"Yes."

"We can go and see the famous horses while we're there?" A sliver of sun entered Genevieve's voice.

"Yes." Claire smiled, but her face looked tired.

Given Claire's budget, this must have been a big deal dream of Genevieve's, and for an hour or so she rallied, going over to her closet in search of a very

'equestrian outfit,' and something to wear to dinner—
'everyone dresses up.'

But then Claire left for the gallery, and pretty soon
Genevieve climbed back into bed and leafed listlessly
through an old *Paris Vogue*.

"Come on, Gen," I said, sitting down beside her.
"It's too pretty to stay inside. We should go out and do
something."

Genevieve's green eyes held my own. "I don't want
to."

"Sure you do. What good is it going to do to be
miserable?"

"I don't know, she said. And then more sharply:
"Aren't you angry?"

I felt suddenly light-headed. I stared at her,
wondering if I'd missed something. "Why would I be
angry at you?"

"Not at me," she said. "at your father. Aren't you
angry at him?"

"Oh," I said, "I see. I was angry or at least hugely
hurt when I was younger, and I thought about him
plenty, convinced he didn't want anything to do with
my life."

"That's pretty much what my dad's telling me," she
said.

"No, he's not. He's getting married again," I said.
"People can get pretty weird when they get married. It's
like this loss of perspective sets in, but it's just
temporary."

Genevieve didn't look convinced.

"Did I ever tell you about my friend Hannah's mother?"

She shook her head.

I'd seen enough bad movies to come up with a plot that had Genevieve actually laughing. "Hannah's mother went completely nuts. She'd been married before, but it was like she was a first-time bride: fancy dress with a train the length of a mini-van; a bouquet of roses so big she could barely hold it up, even maids of honor. Sixteen of them. The woman was forty-five years old, and she acted like she was twenty-one and had never been kissed—"

"What were their dresses like?" Genevieve asked.

"Pink, cotton candy pink with the most outrageous ruffles," I said, exaggerating wildly now. "Hannah nearly died of embarrassment."

Genevieve nodded, giggled just a little. "They do sound hideous."

"They were, and they were impossible to dance in. So, my point is too many people just sort of lose it when they get married, but it doesn't last. Your dad will figure it out," I said, hoping this was true; hoping, too, that my own father—would I ever call Gustave Fermiere that?—had as well.

"Now come on, the sun's out, and we have the whole day ahead of us, what do you say?"

"Okay," Genevieve said, then climbed out of bed.

That day, we did all of Genevieve's favorite things. At the Costume Museum we looked through a hundred years of clothes by designers like Givenchy, Dior, and Prada. We bought triple scoops of ice cream on the Isle de la Cité and wandered around the flea market in the Marais, spending about an hour rummaging through boxes of unimaginably cool buttons. We went to the Luxembourg Gardens, and she rode the carousel. No, she didn't catch the bronze ring, but when she climbed down from the white unicorn her cheeks were flushed, and she radiated happiness.

"IF YOU GO and work for Madame Dupont, we could still spend time together, right?" she said, taking hold of my hand, as we walked away from the carousel.

"Absolutely. We'll keep coming to the Luxembourg until you catch the bronze ring."

Genevieve smiled. "I'd like that, but it might take a long time."

"That's fine with me," I said, reminded of Madame Dupont's invitation.

"Hey, look over there," Genevieve said, as we passed the rose garden. She was pointing to the amazing display of roses, all of them with exotic names. "Isn't that Luc?"

It was Luc, his dreadlocks no longer tied back. In the slight wind, the tangled coils swirled around him. Reminded of that day in Bellevue—the fierceness of his kiss, the pure exhilaration of riding behind him on his bike—I almost called out.

Until I recognized the dancer from the night of the party; not Beatrice, but her friend. Today she wore her white-gold hair loose, and it streamed around her shoulders and down her back like running water seen through blinding light. Her gauzy floral dress swirled out around her as Luc lifted her into the air.

When they kissed, that underwater swirl of emotion returned, but this time I felt I might drown. There wasn't enough air, and I struggled up towards the surface, the seaweed tangling around my feet and ankles, holding me back—

My first thought: Thank god I didn't go back to his studio.

My second: If I had, would he be here with someone else?

Seriously, Julie, have a little more self-respect, the voice inside me said.

At least I'd been smart enough to wear sunglasses. I would have died if Genevieve had seen the tears stinging the corners of my eyes.

"Julie?" Genevieve said, reaching for my hand. "Are you okay?"

"No," I said, keeping my voice as still as possible. "No, I'm not. And please don't do anything to get his attention."

"I won't," Genevieve said, and this time her voice dropped several octaves. "I'm really sorry."

"Thanks," I said, fearing I might actually start crying. "I'd like to leave now."

"Sure." Genevieve's voice stayed quiet. "Okay."

Twenty-Six

"ARE YOU GOING to wear the aquamarine dress tonight?" Genevieve asked, once I stepped into our room where she'd laid maybe half a dozen outfits out on her bed, each one arranged with matching shoes and socks, or tights, as the case may be.

"Not sure."

"I can't believe you haven't thought about it," Genevieve said, holding a salmon-pink sundress up to herself.

"Um, I've had a lot on my mind."

"I know, I know, same goes for me, but clothes should help."

I grinned. "You sure you're ten?"

"That's what my birth certificate says."

"Right. That will look good on you," I said, admiring the way the sundress brought forth the pink in her cheeks.

"It's going to be this one," she said, scrutinizing the dress, "or the Suisse point or maybe—" She reached for a pale blue wisp of a dress with a Peter Pan collar that reminded me of Alice in Wonderland.

"Go with the blue," I said. "Definitely."

Genevieve frowned and then held the Wonderland dress up. "Don't you think it's too little-girlish?"

"Seriously, Genevieve?"

She giggled.

For me, the aquamarine dress I'd worn to Madame Marthurin's party instantly trumped my one other option: the vintage muslin with the slightly ragged hem. This time Genevieve, not Claire, helped do my hair: skinny braids at the front clipped in back with fresh tea roses and baby's breath.

Genevieve didn't wear the pink or the Suisse point or even the Alice in Wonderland, deciding instead on tie dye pants she'd found at a flea market in the Marais and a gauzy white blouse.

TWO HOURS AFTER Claire left dressed in a teal pantsuit that Genevieve insisted she wear over the more formal cranberry cocktail dress, Genevieve and I stepped into the evening air. The sky was a soft gray, and an unusual quiet had settled over the city. Instead of the distant whir of taxis and traffic, I could actually hear the end-of-summer birds, the whoosh of warm air in the trees. "I don't want to take the metro," I said.

"Me neither," Genevieve said, "but I don't want to ruin my shoes."

"No problem," I said.

After running upstairs for walking shoes and a backpack to store Genevieve's silver slippers and my own, we set off. I looked a little bit ridiculous in sneakers and aquamarine chiffon, but the sight of a woman in a baggy burly sweater trumped me hands down.

Besides, it was nice walking along the Seine, our umbrellas sheltering us from the misty drizzle. The barges and a few brightly-lit tourist boats passing by, their names—Gypsy Rose, Delphine, Wanderlust, Last Hurrah—as enticing as the primary colors of their deck furniture on which many a dog, from an overweight mastiff to a pair of freckled spaniels, slept.

Just before we made the long climb back to the street, Genevieve waved to an old fisherman who was now gathering up his things. The light and his old-fashioned nets and buckets were so perfect I would have loved to sit down and sketch him.

A whoosh rushed through the sky above. "Look," I said to Genevieve, and pointed towards Notre Dame's steeples in the distance.

With our heads tipped back, we stood and watched maybe a hundred snowy white birds—some sort of crane or wild goose—fly into the gray-blue beyond. "It's like they're swimming through the sky," Genevieve said.

"I can't imagine what it would feel like, that kind of freedom." Staring up at the birds, my thoughts strayed back to my father. What role would he play in my future life? Why hadn't he gotten in touch by now?

Claire had told me to be patient. My mother, who I'd called after receiving the letter, said not to expect too much.

"AT LAST," CLAY said, coming towards us. "I've been waiting for you to get here. It's not like I fit into this crowd, if you know what I mean."

"Don't be silly," I said, faking the casual thing, for I'd been really jittery about Clay being at the gallery tonight, not because of his cleat thing, but because Luc was on the guest list, too. Question was: could I pull it off? Or would Clay figure out that something had gone on between Luc and me? And Luc? How would he behave?

"Nice threads," Genevieve told Clay.

"Very nice," I agreed. Tonight, for the first time, he wore no trace of cycling gear. Instead, his attire included perfectly pressed khakis, a white linen shirt, and honey-brown kidskin oxfords.

"For a party as swanky as this one, I let the cleats sit the night out," Clay said.

"Good decision," I said, catching sight of Paul Henri and Monsieur Rimbaud beside the buffet, and nearby Marie France, talking to the friend with the curly hair I'd sketched at the party. But I didn't see Madame Marthurin—or Luc.

"So this is the dress you wore to that swanky party?" Clay said to me, taking my hands in his own. "It's a knockout."

"Thanks," I said, propelled back to those moments in Luc's studio—*snap out of it*, I told myself, then turned towards the paintings, wishing we could go over; but there were already so many people crowded around the two portraits, their goblets of wine and their jewelry sparking in the light. Besides, I didn't want to see them side by side for the first time, while people knocked into me, or breathed down my neck.

Claire said two collectors had already approached Rafi about purchasing the Modigliani. I knew this was inevitable. Still, Modigliani's painting brought hollowness to my belly, the thought of separating it from the studio door portrait, now that they had been brought together. It was like separating Jeanne and Modigliani all over again.

AN HOUR LATER, the crowd had thinned enough for us to look at the two portraits. Seen side by side, I felt as if I were looking at two parts to a story that needed a third part to be complete.

"A triptych," Clay said, surprising me a little with his knowledge of this art term.

"Yes. The first portrait, of mother and child, is unbelievably idealized, the Madonna-like tilt of Jeanne's head, the serene smile."

I closed my eyes, fighting back tears, as I thought back to my own mother's decision to leave Paris without telling Gustave Fermiere about her pregnancy. Oma would never have cast her daughter off as Jeanne's parents had; but if Mom had stayed with him, she would have dropped out of school to live with a man, one who was unstable, mentally ill. Under those circumstances, what would have become of me? And what of her?

"And the second portrait, the woman in pink— Jeanne's painting?" Clay asked, his question puncturing my thoughts. "Julie?" he said again. "Are you listening?"

Perspiration prickled my brow. How long had I been quiet? "Sorry, could you repeat the question?"

When he did, I answered, "I can't help but see that painting as a wish, on Jeanne's part, that she could stay happy with Modigliani. Her pink tunic and her smile—less ideal than just plain happy—seems to suggest that."

"And the third part?" Clay asked, his own voice hushed, as if he really understood what these paintings meant to me which of course he could not. "What would the third part say, if it existed, I mean?"

I thought about all those nights Modigliani disappeared during the last months of their lives, leaving Jeanne and their child in the draughty studio where firewood had become a luxury. I couldn't imagine the despair he must have felt, and the anger; but he must have known, too, how deeply his actions were damaging Jeanne, who was pregnant again. The biography said Jeanne would go out looking for him. Sometimes, the weather was very bad: snow and freezing rain. How terrible those walks must have been for her, descents into the underworld, one after the next, as deeper and deeper she fell.

And where was their daughter during these outings after dark? Did Jeanne leave her with their friend Lunia? Or did Jeanne take the child with her, calling out Modigliani's name as the little girl shivered against her thin breast?

I shuddered. My art mattered, but not that much.

And what about Gustave Fermiere? How had my mother felt during those last days as she struggled to decide what to do? She'd told me about the professor who'd tried to ban her from university when her pregnancy began to show. Mom may not have been living in Jeanne's day, but the idea of an unmarried woman having a baby on her own was still shocking. How much shame she must have endured, and what bravery she must have mustered.

"Are you okay, Julie?" It was Genevieve's voice, her hand on my arm.

"Here," Clay said, producing a napkin. I looked into his eyes, found the russet and gold flecking the hazel.

"No sock this time?" I said, managing a smile.

"I'm a gentleman tonight: no socks, no cleats," he said, and touched the napkin to my eyes.

I smiled at him, grateful, and my thoughts returned to the flock of white birds flying overhead, their wings iridescent in the evening light over Notre Dame. Only now did I understand, really understand why birds, too, were a symbol for the soul.

Twenty-Seven

"GENEVIEVE, JULIE," PAUL Henri said, approaching us from across the gallery. He carried a package in his arms.

Genevieve grinned. "For me?"

"For Julie," Paul Henri said, and handed the package to me.

I un-wrapped the brown paper slowly, taking note of Paul Henri's meticulous folds. Inside I found a book about Modigliani, and it was huge and brand new.

"I wanted to get you a replacement for the other," he said. "This one may not have the sentiment, but it's comprehensive."

"Thank you," I said, struck again by the many sides of Paul Henri.

"Here's your drink," Clay said, returning. "Champagne and pomegranate juice."

My mind flashed back to Madame Marthurin's boudoir. Did Clay the historian know that the pomegranate was the fruit of the underworld? "Isn't that a weird combination?"

"Not really, just a healthy one. You're looking pale, and pomegranates are high in anti-oxidants."

"Right." I took a few big swallows, waiting for the champagne to relax me.

"Anti-*what?*" Paul Henri said.

"Anti-oxidants," Clay said.

"Vitamins," I added. "Clay is a serious cyclist. Very serious."

Clay grinned, and then he introduced himself. I knew, at once, he appreciated my saying he was *sérieux* to Paul Henri, and not obsessive.

The two of them talked for a while, about Paris's history, but also cycling, a sport Paul Henri liked as well, and pens. Paul Henri obviously appreciated Clay's knowledge of the various brands, from Mont Blanc and Luno to Waterman and Parker. They got along well, their loose-hipped way of standing and easy voices proof of that.

Ordinarily I would have been thrilled, for I'd never have put these together; but I remained anxious, on edge. When one of the waiters came around with another tray of champagne, I reached for a second glass. Pretty soon the gallery lights seemed too bright, and I felt dizzy. Or maybe it was the room—it seemed to be spinning.

"Once again the girl in the heartbreaking dress," said a voice behind me.

Luc. A queasy sensation filled my belly. Of all moments to turn up, he had to pick this one.

"Hi," I said, our last kiss returning full force, despite my willing it not to.

"You are?" Clay said, his voice an electrical wire.

"Luc Duplessis, and you?" Luc was not unfriendly, but he didn't seem exactly interested either.

"Clay Ranger," he said, keeping himself between me and Luc.

"Ah, the ravishing little sister," Luc said, smiling at Genevieve who just glared back at him, loyal to the core.

Paul Henri laughed. "When will you outgrow this act? Ravishing: who calls a child ravishing?"

"Ah, you're here," Luc said and frowned. "Given the possible business contacts, I should have known."

"I'm not a child," Genevieve said, a fierceness coming into her voice I hadn't heard before.

Clay stepped away from me and tucked an arm around Genevieve's shoulder. "It was a stupid thing to say," he told her.

But Luc and Paul Henri were no longer paying attention to Genevieve, Clay, or even to me.

"When will you grow out of playing a fifty-year-old at nineteen?" Luc said. "And that scarf. How pretentious can you get? Who do you think you are: Cary Grant, or some contemporary incarnation of Oscar Wilde?"

"Look who's talking. Since when have you become a Bob Marley fan, or has some love-struck *jeune fille* taken you to Jamaica? There's always a love-struck *jeune fille*, and to what lengths the poor creatures go only to discover, too late, their mistake—"

Was he thinking of me?

"Julie, please, this is getting weird," Genevieve said, tugging at my hand. "I want to go."

"Yeah," Clay added. "I need some air."

I was about to do just that, but then Luc turned away from Paul Henri and seized hold of my hand. Literally. I felt myself pulled away from her, even though her eyes pleaded with me, and she called out, "Julie—"

"In a minute," I said to Genevieve, feeling the heat of his grasp. "Okay?"

"But—" Genevieve said, her face a pale moon.

"Julie, you need to come with us now." Clay's voice was razor-sharp.

Given all that had happened, all that I knew about Luc, and the hurt I would inevitably bring to Clay, how could I have been stupid enough to let him lead me away from the others, grabbing another glass of champagne on the way? I felt like the leading lady in a Hitchcock movie, one who is often a decoy or a target as much as a star, and not just because of my dress.

The party may have been happening inside, but Luc kept hold of my hand long after we pressed through the crowd, the intimate feel of his pulse alongside my own weakening Clay's expression and especially Genevieve's plea—"Come with me"—to an echo.

It was after nine o'clock by now, and the sky was the color of lilacs. Standing on the street with Luc beside me, the breeze stroked my shoulders and bare arms; and despite everything I knew about him, everything I'd seen, I thought back to the Closerie des Lilas where I waited for Marie France all those weeks ago. What would it have been like to have been alive when the café was still the hot meeting place for artists and writers? With the city lights winking in the distance, and a river scent drifting in on the breeze, I could almost picture myself there. That day in Bellevue, riding around on Luc's scooter, the two of us walking hand in hand, kissing before the murals, and talking about art, I felt like I'd stepped into a modern-day equivalent.

Luc reached out and stroked my cheek. *You fool!* that voice inside me said. *You know better!*

Even so, I leaned into him.

Until I remembered…

Give your heart to someone like that, and it'll soon be in tatters.

I stepped back, swatted his hand away.

"Ah, so you are not so happy to see me," Luc said.

I just stood there, dizzy from the champagne and my fears.

"Madame Dupont told me that you still haven't given her an answer," Luc said, keeping his voice soft, as if to ensure I'd listen.

"That's right," I said.

"I don't understand. It's an incredible opportunity. You know it is, and you seemed so excited the other day. So," he said, looking genuinely baffled, "what's changed?"

"I was at the Luxembourg Gardens the other day."

"Ah." I wanted him to say the other girl meant nothing to him, wanted to hear that he was just biding time until we got together.

But he said no such thing, and how could I actually expect him to? *Get real, Julie, what are you doing here with him?*

"Say you'll stay in Paris," he said at last. "Madame Dupont will work magic on you. We could spend so much time together." He stepped closer, tried to draw me close, but I didn't move.

What do I mean to you? I wanted to ask. *Am I just another* jeune fille *as Paul Henri suggested? Are you playing with me?* The questions ricocheted through my mind but before I could ask a single one, high-heeled footsteps clattered along the pavement, and then Claire yanked my arm hard.

"Julie. What in the hell has gotten into you?! You're supposed to be looking after Genevieve," she said. "Instead, you're out here carrying on with—"

"Luc," he said calmly. "Luc Duplessis."

"No need to remind me," she said fiercely. "I know who you are." She swiveled around to take in the scene: Luc, me, the champagne glass glinting beneath the streetlight. "Do you know where I found Genevieve just now?"

I shook my head, simultaneously flashing back to the way Genevieve had pleaded with me not to go.

"She was sitting in the storage room sobbing," Claire said. "That door locks automatically. Thank god Clay was looking for her; or should I say, *looking out for her.* Otherwise, who knows what might have happened?"

I bit my lip, tasted blood. "Is she okay?"

"Yes. She was cold, and she was terrified, but the timer hadn't gone off yet; so she wasn't in the dark. You know that room is set for forty-five degrees. With all the people here tonight, no one would have heard her—"

"I'm sorry," I said. "Really, I am."

"*Sorry* is just not good enough," Claire said, with such fury I thought she would fire me on the spot. "Sorry is what you say when you spill a glass of milk or show up five minutes late. Sorry is not the appropriate response to abandoning your responsibility for my daughter just because some French bad boy wants to lure you away."

You messed up big time, but this is not just about you, a voice inside me said. It's about Claire taking Genevieve to Paris and keeping her here, even though Genevieve is dying to go home, though that place no longer exists. It's about Claire's ex-husband getting re-married next month. And most of all, it's about Claire having to make up for the fact that her ex-husband isn't bringing Genevieve to L.A. a week early to spend time with just her, despite his promise.

Luc nodded to me, mouthed the French word for 'later' and walked away.

"Look," Claire said, a little less severely, "I know you're under stress—all this suspense about your father. I've been relying on you too much, especially lately with what's happened with Mark. It's unrealistic, unfair, but I'm worried about you too. This guy, this Luc, he—"

"No," I said, "you're right. I blew it."

She sighed, rubbed her brow, worn out. "Yes, you have; and I can't afford another night like this. I'm near a breaking point right now."

I touched her arm, felt her goose bumps. "Please, Claire," I said. "Nothing like this will ever happen again."

"I'd like to believe you," she said, "but this really scared me. *You* scared me. I mean, we're talking about Genevieve. I trusted you, Julie."

"Claire, I'm sorry—"

"Right. Now," she said, tears threatening, "find Genevieve and take her home."

Back inside, not one person stared or whispered. Why would they?

This was Paris, where Genevieve and I actually saw a woman strip down to her bra and panties and jump into a fountain on a hot day; where Monsieur LaBoeuf, the downstairs neighbor, serenaded or pleaded with his wife on those nights she locked him out after a quarrel; where certain dogs were as well-dressed and as well-coiffed as their owners.

Madame Dupont waved to me, very discreetly, and then a woman's voice, followed by several other voices, Rafi's among them, and Madame Becerra's, rose above the conversation of the guests.

The woman was tall and elegant and a few years older than me. Twenty-two, maybe twenty-five. She had dark red hair—rouge-colored—that fell past her waist in a perfect curtain. Her eyes were large and almond-shaped and ringed with shadow, and she was wearing an expensive-looking Kimono-style dress with bell sleeves. Maybe it was the light or the alcohol or the chaos churning inside me, but she reminded me of Jeanne. Given all that had already happened, I felt myself sway on my feet and reached for the wall, nearly putting my hand through that faux-Impressionist painting, the pretty one of the woman walking in the rain.

The stranger's gestures were urgent, distressed, and Rafi was trying to get her out of the gallery. Given what Claire had said, I should have gone to look for Genevieve immediately; but I stayed rooted to the spot, compelled to find out why she was here.

"*Cherie,*" Madame Dupont said, choosing this moment to join me. "You are looking at Chana's great-granddaughter."

My whole body seemed to catch fire, as I thought back to the letters pressed in the book. "The Chana?"

Madame Dupont lit one of her interminable cigarettes. "*Oui.* I recognize her from a retrospective of her grandmother's work. *Mon Dieu,* it must have been eight years ago. She was still a girl then."

"Julie." Claire hurried over, exhaustion tugging at her voice. "It looks like I'm going to have to stay here for a while. Go find Genevieve now and take her home."

"Of course, right now," I said, and looked pleadingly at Madame Dupont.

"You must go, I understand. Remember my offer, Julie. I meant every word, but I am not one used to waiting long. You have just a few more days."

"Yes, of course," I said, then hurried after Claire. "I'm going to take Genevieve home, but please, I have to know, what's happening?"

"Not now, Julie, please." She touched a hand to her brow, closed her eyes. "Look, if I ever needed to count on you, it's now. I don't want to say it again: take Genevieve home. This is going to be a really long night."

I found Genevieve and Clay stretched out on the purple-blue sofa in the back. Genevieve's head rested on his shoulder, and she was sleeping. The soft look on her face and her small smile suggested that the events of tonight hadn't left their mark. I wasn't sure if I felt guilty or relieved.

"Hey," I said. At first he didn't answer, and his hazel eyes seemed darker, almost brooding. "Clay," I said again, more softly now.

"Well if it isn't Miss Heart Breaking Dress."

How much had Clay seen?

"I'm sorry," I said lamely.

"You are the most self-absorbed person I've ever met," he said. "You know that? Forget about stringing me along like some puppy on a lead. You were supposed to be watching her."

Beside him the sleeping Genevieve stirred.

"But she was with you," I said, hearing how stupid I sounded as soon as the words were out.

"With me? I'm not the one who's supposed to be watching her. I'm not the one Genevieve asked to stay, though begged is more like it. How responsible are you? Some French pseudo-artist decides to show you the time of day, and you're out of here. Interesting," he said, his cheeks now as red as his hair, "the fact that you never mentioned him, this Luck Guy, that day at the Sorbonne when it's clear you two know each other. Really well, too, from what I can see."

"Clay, I—"

"Don't bother with the explanations," he said. "I was stupid enough to think you were different. But believe me, I won't make that mistake again. From now on, I'm sticking to bicycles."

"And dogs?" I said, wishing he would crack the hint of a smile.

He remained stony-faced. "Get real, Julie."

"Please," I said, reaching for his hand. "You don't understand."

"Actually, I understand too well," he said, yanking his hand away. "See you around, Miss Heartbreaking Dress." He nudged himself free from Genevieve so carefully she didn't wake, then turned and walked away, his loafers, unlike his cycling shoes, making no noise at all.

Twenty-Eight

I FOUND MYSELF running down a long white corridor in a place that vaguely resembled the gallery but wasn't: down, down, down, my breath ragged. I was wearing my chiffon dress, except the skirt was torn and ratty; it was freezing, and Genevieve had vanished. "Where are you?" I cried again and again.

"Here!" she called. "I'm right here."

Around a corner, through a door, I kept running, only to be confronted by the cold dark. Again and again. My feet throbbed. What had happened to my shoes? I was reminded of Cinderella, except there was no prince.

"Genevieve?" I cried. "Genevieve?"

At last I reached the end of the corridor, certain now that she must be here, for I could hear her. I tried to open the door, but it stuck.

"Here," Genevieve called. "I'm right here. Help me, Julie, please."

I pulled, but the wood was swollen, which didn't make any sense given the freezing temperatures. Harder I pulled, bracing my feet against the weight.

At last it gave way.

Emptiness engulfed me, the echoing whiteness bringing back the sorrow and fear I'd felt in Modigliani's studio.

Behind me pottery smashed against the floor.

When I turned—nothing.

Then Clay entered.

I rushed towards him. "Please, you have to help me."

"Sorry, Miss Heart Breaking Dress."

"Please."

"It's too late, Julie," he said, backing away.

"You can't go," I cried, keenly aware that Genevieve was still out there somewhere—"Please, I need your help—"

But Clay was already gone, and my voice alone echoed in the chill air.

I WASN'T SURE if I was more relieved or exhausted when I finally jolted awake, bathed in sweat, the sun too bright on my swollen eyelids; had I been crying? My cheeks were dry. In the bed beside my own, Genevieve slept on, her small face resting against her hand, as if last night hadn't happened, or if it had, it had at least been forgotten, for the time being anyway. Annie, who was still tucked into her basket, opened her amber eyes, but she didn't make a move, not even a wag of her tail. "I know," I whispered. "I disappointed the lot of you."

I climbed out of bed, slipped on some socks and padded into the bathroom to brush my teeth. Face to face with my reflection, all I felt was ashamed. How could I have treated Clay like that? Or Genevieve? And what about Claire—would she trust me again? Over and over again, I told myself the dream was not real. Why then did its presence hang about me like a shroud?

Because I'd messed up big-time, and may have broken Clay's heart in the process. And what if Genevieve had gotten locked in the storeroom and no one found her? And then, yes it was true, now that it seemed to be too late, my own heart ached for Clay. He was the one I should have been focused on all along. He was right. I was self-absorbed. A complete fool.

I found Claire sitting at the table outside the kitchen, and when she didn't say anything to me, kept reading the newspaper, I feared the worst. "Claire?"

She looked up from the Culture Section of *Le Monde*, her eyes ringed with dark circles.

"I can't believe this has already made the news," she said, as if continuing a conversation she'd started without me.

"What?" I asked, at a loss again, and afraid somehow that I was still stuck in the dream.

Until I poured myself coffee, savored its bitter, gritty heat.

"What happened last night at the gallery: that journalist who turned up didn't waste any time in getting the word out," she said, tapping the paper. "The story's all here in black and white."

I knew what and whom she was thinking of—the woman with the curtain of rouge-colored hair who'd trailed after Rafi; the woman Madame Dupont had said was Chana Sadkine's great-granddaughter.

"What happened?" I asked. "What does it say?"

"It goes over last night's events exactly," Claire said. "Germaine Toulouse, the woman who caused all that commotion, has some pretty indisputable proof that the Modigliani in the gallery was actually painted by his daughter, Giovanna."

I sat down beside her, tried to make sense of the French, but the text just blurred before me. "But how could that happen? I thought this painting came from a collector."

"It did," Claire said. "But that's not what matters anymore. Germaine claims that Modigliani's daughter painted it, and she has some documents, including the fragment of a letter written in Giovanna's hand, that reveals Giovanna to be the artist. We have no reason to doubt their authenticity," Claire said. "Germaine Toulouse has nothing to gain."

Instantly I recalled that first day in the gallery— Rafi's comment about the unusual feel of the child in the painting. *As if she'd been added later,* I'd replied. And then there was Chana Sadkine's letter, what she said about Giovanna Modigliani's search for her parents. She, too, had grown up to become an artist. So wouldn't it make sense for her to copy her father's work?

"What if Giovanna Modigliani was trying to make a place for herself in art that was never there in life?" I heard myself say.

Claire stared at me, and I had the impression her face was opening. "Go on."

"How else, other than by making art, could Giovanna find a way back to her mother and father?"

"And so she drew herself as a child in her mother's arms." Claire shivered, took a sip of coffee. "Good god, it does make sense, but it's so overwhelming too. What I wouldn't give to just go back to bed and sleep for like a month. Remind me, how did all this begin? How'd you find your way to the studio? I can't seem to be able to put any chronologies together right now."

"Marie France," I said. "I ran into her that night at Shakespeare & Co, the night I came home so late."

"Oh, right." She smiled, but nervously, or just with weariness. "Look, I've been feeling a lot of pressure. I'm sorry I freaked out last night. I know how much you care about Genevieve."

"But I let you down," I said, still shaken by the dream. "You were right about Luc, and I was beyond naïve."

"Yes, you were," Claire said, but kindly. "The thing to remember is hindsight's always twenty-twenty. Just try to learn from experience."

"Yeah," I said, that ache for Clay growing stronger. Always, he'd made me feel so good about myself.

"Julie," Claire said, and touched my hand. "It's okay, really."

"No, it isn't. I hurt Clay really badly."

She nodded, cradled her coffee cup, and I knew she was not going to make the situation with Clay any easier. Why—how could she?

"Listen," she said. "You may have blown it last night, but that doesn't erase the last few weeks." She reached out and squeezed my hand, her green eyes clear, focused. "I've been thinking about the fall—about the coming year."

"Madame Dupont's offer, you mean?"

"Maybe," she said. "I know it's a good, possibly a great opportunity, but I want you to know something."

"Yes," I said, leaning close.

"Regardless of what you decide about Madame Dupont, you can stay on here next year, if you like. You have that possibility. There's always a bed here for you. Not just me but Genevieve would insist on it. In fact," she giggled, "Genevieve has insisted on it, though she may also insist on redoing the walls, the bedding."

"Honest?" I said. "You mean, you'd let me stay here, with you two, after last night?"

Claire's eyes turned up at the edges, and she smiled. "You mean after all that you've done. Like I said, Genevieve's a lot happier since you got here—and so am I. You've been a great help, Julie, and I'm grateful."

"Thank you," I said. "I'd love that, staying here, I mean."

"Good. Now," she said, glancing at her watch, "I'm afraid I have to get to the gallery. Call me if you need anything. And let Genevieve sleep in. She's had more than her share of excitement."

After Claire left, I sat there for a while, amazed at what she'd said.

It's true, you know, the voice inside me said.

Genevieve *was* happier.

Clay was a different story. How was I ever going to fix that? The furious hurt in his eyes last night came swimming back. And then there was that awful, awful dream—

If I went on like this, I was going to drive myself crazy, I knew, so I sat down on the sofa and opened the book of prints that Paul Henri had given me, the thick weight of the paper reassuring against my fingertips. Page by page, I followed Modigliani's journey as an artist; a journey that began in Livorno with his mother's promise that he, a sick child, could study art; a journey that took him to Rome and then Florence and on to Paris where, some ten years after his arrival, he fell in love with Jeanne. The pictures of her were the same here as in every other biography: Jeanne in the caftan dress; Jeanne sitting at his side in a café, a wide-brimmed hat shielding her eyes; Jeanne walking beside him along the ocean-bound quay at Nice, her body swollen with their coming daughter.

It wasn't until the end that I found a picture of Giovanna Modigliani as a grown woman. She was raven-haired like her father, but her eyes and her small smile—these were Jeanne's. In the photograph, she stood before an abstract painting. "Giovanna Modigliani at an exhibition of her own paintings," the caption said.

I made myself a cup of tea, spread jam on another croissant, my thoughts straying back to Clay. *He has to forgive me*, I told myself, reminded again of the day we went dress shopping, what he'd said to me at the pizzeria.

How confident he'd been that my father would want to be a part of my life. How could I have taken all of that for granted? He made me laugh. To think I believed it was a French artist I was looking for. All along, Clay had been there, from that first morning at the bakery when he caught on about that stylist in front of Genevieve's awful classmate. Clay was worth his weight in saffron, as Mom would have said. Should I tell him that? Question was, even after I explained that saffron was a costly, highly-prized spice derived from the stamens of mountain crocuses, would he believe me? Would he even listen long enough for me to get the words out?

I went over to the computer and dialed up the internet, hoping against hope that there would be a message there from Bikerman.

Nothing.

My stomach was a tangle of knots. *Calm down*, I told myself. *You have to calm down.* I took a deep breath, stood, and opened the windows. It was such a clear day, and everything—from the chimneypots along the rooftops to the Eiffel Tower in the far distance—stood out in bold relief. It was the kind of day, still warm, that held the promise of autumn in the angle of the light, the whiskey tint to the air. Ordinarily, I would have picked up my sketch pad and drawn what I saw.

Today I just sat and watched a pair of chimney swifts dipping through the air, missing my mom, wishing the Atlantic Ocean didn't stand between us.

I leaned back in the chair and closed my eyes. Remarkably, the only sounds were the hum of a delivery truck below, the furious bark of some small dog, the voice of a mother singing to her child.

When the telephone rang, in the same way that my dog at home knew what time I was coming home, I knew who it was on the other end of the phone.

Twenty-Nine

IT SEEMED MORE than coincidence that when Gustave Fermiere phoned, his voice far softer than I would have imagined, he asked me to meet him at a small church just six tangled blocks from L'Espace Stein.

After I dropped her off there, Genevieve took one more admiring look at the outfit she'd so carefully helped me pick out: a pair of blue jeans that we'd refashioned into a skirt and a peach camisole. "You look great," she pronounced. "I'll be waiting up for you, no matter what time you come home."

"I'm counting on that," I said, and hugged her tight. *Claire said I could stay another year!*

I said goodbye to both of them, then pressed on into the dense network of streets that make up Saint Germain de Près, the tarnished but still majestic spires of the cathedral rising up above the rooftops lending the neighborhood the feel of an earlier century.

The Rue de la Cherche Midi was the major thru street linking little streets like the Rue de Confiance where L'Espace Stein was located, and I followed it now. The first time I walked along the Cherche Midi, as Parisians called it, I misinterpreted the meaning, reading it as 'The Street on Which I Seek Myself.' The real translation was 'The Street of the Middle Way.'

"I like your meaning better," Clay had said when I told him.

"Me, too." It was much more suggestive, full of possibility, and contained the feel of a real journey. If there was anyone I wanted to talk to right now, it was Clay.

Don't think about this now. I quickened my pace, my footsteps carrying me toward my father, a man I knew only from a photograph older than I was.

I found Gustave Fermiere waiting outside the church. He told me that he'd be wearing a khaki jacket over a t-shirt, not black or white but powder blue, and he was sitting midway up a flight of stone steps. He seemed slighter than I'd imagined him. His hair was no longer ebony-dark as it had been in the photograph Mom had held onto, but salt-and-pepper gray. But his eyes were the same charcoal dark. Like my own. Looking at him, I found traces of myself, and I shivered with fear, possibility, hope.

"Julie." He spoke my name as if he'd known it all along, and came towards me.

I stood at the bottom of the steps and stared up at him, amazed at how ordinary it all seemed: the pigeons fluttering around us or pecking for seeds on the concrete, the sound of traffic in the distance, the gasoline scent in the air, the faded jacket he was wearing, the threadbare knees of his jeans.

It could have been any other day.

He kissed me on both cheeks, gently.

"Come." He took my hand so naturally I understood how my mother could have loved him.

"Where are we going?" I asked, having assumed we'd find some café and sit and talk.

"I want to show you something inside, something that has been here longer than either one of us, a fact I take great comfort in."

I let him lead me up the endless flight of stone steps, the heat from my palm merging with his own. It was a relief not to have to speak right away; a relief for him, too, I felt sure. How much better for the two of us to get used to each other first without words getting mixed up in it.

The inside of the church was shadowy and quiet, the air scented with incense. Tucked into corners, luminary candles burned in small red glasses. I didn't go to church much anymore, but as a child I'd always gone with Oma, lighting candles for my grandfather and for Oma's sister, Sabine. Always the feel of a church had comforted me, the sunlight slanting through the stained glass and casting patterns along the stone floors, the sound of doves in the rafters, the cool quiet of the air. For just a moment, I wondered if Oma was witnessing this. I knew she would have felt at home here.

The possibility of this, of her presence beside or around me, filled me with warmth.

"I want to show you the painting at the very front," he said, still holding my hand, guiding me towards the altar.

There, just to the left, hung a painting of Mary.

Usually Mary appears only as the innocent, pious Mother of God, more saint than woman, qualities that made her less than real. Divine, yes, but not close enough to really approach.

This painting, however, was different.

Sure the symbols were all there: the blue robes, the white veil, the tilt of the head that Modigliani took for his own portraits; a quality that gave an ordinary woman a Madonna-like quality, one of sadness and grace. But there was fierceness in this Mary, too, in her piercing gaze and in the sharp angles of her face. And I loved these qualities, for it made clear what so many paintings about her forgot: she was a human being, too, a woman who had loved and suffered and struggled to survive. Like Jeanne and her daughter. If only Jeanne had possessed such strength. Like Oma and my own mother had.

"Whose work?" I asked, turning to him.

"An artist named Anne LeBrun. The painting was done in the midst of the French Revolution. Anne LeBrun was a royalist, you see. She painted it after Marie Antoinette's death."

"What happened to her?"

"She managed to escape to England and left the painting in an old man's safekeeping. But it was more than ten years before the church dared to show her work."

We stood before the portrait, and I found myself wondering if there was some secret meaning to his words. Something he couldn't tell me in any other way.

"Sixteen years ago, when your mother sent me the letter, when she told me that she'd had a child, I came here and stood in this very spot and looked to her, as if she might offer me some advice."

"And did she?" I asked, looking from the painting to my father and back again, my own heart rising to my throat, or so it felt.

"Sadly no: truth is, for a long time after that, not even art would speak to me. And now all these years later, the arrival of your letter, your arrival," he said, "like an answer to a prayer."

"HAVE YOU BEEN coming here for a long time?" I asked when he led me to a cheerful outdoor café, once a squat brick house, not far from the church, where a stout Jack Russell terrier patrolled the grounds.

"Just once," he said. "I wanted a place with no associations, but it's lovely, is it not?"

"Yes." The café was tucked into a courtyard filled with centuries' old trees. The strong twist in their branches reassured me, and the leaves provided a canopy of shade.

He ordered simply for us both: bouillabaisse, a carafe of red wine, new potatoes. There were so many questions I wanted to ask him. Was he married? Did he have children? Did he still think about my mother? Was his health better now?

Instead I ate my soup rather quietly, reminding myself there will be time—*Il sera temps*—the French phrase coming to me on its own.

"The soup is very good, isn't it?" he said.

"Yes, very." I wanted to tell him about Madame Marthurin's soup, about her restaurant.

Instead I studied his hands, recognizing the shape of his thumb nail, full and slightly squared at the top. It was the shape of my own. Did he notice these things, too? I also noticed that although my father's eyes were charcoal gray like mine, his were flecked with gold.

'With one eye, you look outward,' Modigliani said. 'With the other you look in at yourself.' Eyes were windows, gateways, doors. To the soul and to the world.

Over cappuccino, I did tell him about the Modigliani at the gallery and all I'd learned about Jeanne and the studio as well as Giovanna Modigliani's startling role in the story. "She didn't know either one of her parents," I said. "They died, Jeanne right after Modigliani, when Giovanna was three.

"And the child in the painting is her work?"

"Amazing, isn't it?"

"*Oui.*" I waited for him to ask me more, but he only stroked his chin, looking at me with what seemed a mixture of tenderness and sorrow, or maybe he just looked sad when he was mulling something over—I didn't know.

"And you?" he said, after a while. "You've told me all about Modigliani and Jeanne and their daughter, but I'd like to hear about you. *Dîtes-moi*—tell me."

His words were an invitation, and I took him through my history with art, going all the way back to those crayon drawings I'd spent hours on, relishing the deluxe box my grandmother replaced every time I wore the crayons down to nubs; the chalk sketches on my easel, the water colors; then led him along with my child self, the one who wandered those galleries at the Art Institute for hours, losing herself before Modigliani's *Girl with a Necklace* and Cassatt's *Woman Bathing Her Child*. When I mentioned my mom's presence there, his eyes seemed to flicker with understanding, but he didn't say anything.

There will be time.

"Art has always been at the very center for me," I continued. "Only lately have I begun to wonder if I wasn't trying to figure out who I was—who I am—and trying to puzzle out all the things for which I didn't have answers."

"Yes," he said. "Art is a refuge when one needs to search the soul."

"Not getting into the Art Institute of Chicago was shattering," I said finally. "It's the reason I came to France." I looked into his eyes, lured by the flecks of gold—like stars in a night sky—realizing how much I'd grown in the months I'd been here. I felt surer of myself and of the choices I had made.

What I didn't say: if I had gotten into the Art Institute, I would not have come to France this summer. We would not be sitting opposite each other now.

Did that mean there was an order to the universe? Was all of this meant to be?

"After you finish your summer with Claire and her daughter, what will you do next?" he asked at last.

The question was an opening, and soon I began telling him all about Madame Dupont, the house that once belonged to Juliette Récamier, and her extraordinary invitation to learn the art of restoration and work on the eighteenth century panels narrating the story of Psyche and Eros.

"Remarkable," my father said. "I've seen examples from the period but only in museums or in public buildings—and once," he smiled, "on the ceiling of a train station."

"You think I should accept her offer then?" I said.

"Why would you not?" he said, something in his voice, just then, reminding me of Paul Henri, a certainty and a confidence that seemed very French, with strong, deep roots.

Was he thinking what I was? that if I learned the art of restoration, he and I might one day work together? And perhaps, long before then, he himself would offer to share with me some of what he had learned.

Slow down, Julie, the voice within me said.

"And you?" I asked, once the waiter brought us each a glazed raspberry tart. "Tell me about you." And although I longed to add *père*, the French word for 'father,' I held back.

"I continue to paint, watercolors mostly," he said. "I like their delicacy, their dependence on the light. I painted the view from my farmhouse window several times. Living simply has taught me to pay attention to subtle changes: the way a field alters over the course of a day for example. The length of the shadows of the trees, or the old fence give the landscape a distinctive feel."

I leaned closer. "Are you showing your work?" I asked.

"No, no. What I paint now is rather private. I'm no longer interested in exhibiting, you see."

"Why?"

He sighed, ran his fingers through his tangle of hair. "Such a difficult question."

"You don't have to tell me," I said.

"No, no. There was a time, when your mother knew me, when I was all fire and ambition. I wanted to be like Picasso, like Sargent and Rodin. Such grandiose ideas I had, such vision! After your mother left, after she told me about you—asking me not to write, not to seek you out—I felt as if I'd fallen into a deep well. I would cry out, desperate for someone to hear me, but it was my own voice that would come back to me."

How many questions welled up within me: I wanted to pour them out as if they were so many glasses of water.

But my father's hands shook a little after that, and he ate his food slowly.

There will be time, I told myself, believing this at last. There will be time.

Thirty

AFTER WE SAID goodnight—*bonne nuit*—hugging each other so close I felt his tears on my cheeks and neck— or were the tears my own?—I walked around for a long time, still spinning with the realization—sun-kissed, sweet as the berries on the tart—I would see my father again tomorrow. *My father.* How could it be that all my life I'd lived without knowing him at all, and now here he was? After today, I'd never forget his eyes, the habit he had of running his fingertip along the lip of his glass, the gentle upsweep of his smile.

Just before we parted, he told me that he would come for me tomorrow evening and take me to dinner. "A wonderful old restaurant in the Marais that has been here for nearly half a century," he said. "This is a place I come every time I make a trip to Paris. There is a cat there, Napoleon, who is fittingly named."

"I'd love that," I said, wondering if my father had animals at home.

"Good." He took my hand in his, held it. "Afterwards, we might go and hear a concert at one of the oldest churches in Paris, St. Paul's. It's just across the river. Do you like the music of Bach?"

"I don't know it," I said. Classical music was something I didn't have much experience with. Mom preferred classic rock and folk songs—Did my father know this? Did he still remember?

"*Il sera temps*—There will be time," my father said. He reached out to touch my hair, very lightly, so that I pictured the two of us sitting side by side at a concert. Father and daughter. Us.

Hadn't art taught me, again and again, to be flexible and open when it came to composition? Hadn't life?

How long I walked before I turned onto a small street with a little park, a sort of annex joining the houses on either side, I don't know. I had no idea where I was, and for the first time I'd forgotten my map. How Genevieve would have laughed!

The park was the size of an intimate room, or a studio, and I went in. There were stone benches at all four corners. A stone path threaded flower beds filled with lavender, foxglove, and old roses, most of them overgrown and fragrant. Parisians, I'd learned again and again, loved roses. I felt sure these had names like Belle Dame, Tous les Mois, Empress Josephine, and Surpasse Tout; names I recognized from the Luxembourg Gardens where flowers and fruits and trees were all identified by name, century, and place of origin.

Inevitably I thought of that day at the Luxembourg Gardens when I spied Luc kissing that dancer. What a fool I'd been not to realize how wrong I was about him. *No, not a fool, Julie*, the voice inside me said, *just terribly naïve and in love with the possibility of a Paris romance.*

What was it about this garden that made me think of the dollhouse I'd created with Genevieve? The size? The feel of belonging to another world? Monsieur Rimbaud was right in saying she was the one person to care for it. He'd also said she was a girl, like Dorothy, looking for home. And so, I knew now, was I, minus the ruby slippers. Hadn't Giovanna Modigliani been such a girl, too? And what had she found on her journey? The current, the need, joined us.

The words of a poem I once memorized by the German poet, Rainier Maria Rilke, pierced my train of thought. *The work of the eyes now is done, go and do heart work on all the images imprisoned within you.* At last I understood that just as I had recast the meaning of the Rue de la Cherche Midi, I would recast the images locked inside of me—set them free as the white birds sailing over Notre Dame that night beside the Seine. But this time the change would be intentional, not accident—or good fortune.

My father, whose eyes were as dark as my own, but sadder, too, a sadness that spoke of a history I longed to understand, for it was mine too, had invited me to come to Provence in August. I would look out of the window at his farmhouse and see the effect of the changing light upon the field.

And after that?

Claire had told me that I could stay. Genevieve would go back to the international school after she returned from the wedding, and who knew how she would feel now that there was going to be no time together on the beach with her father, just the two of them? She would be a flower girl, alongside Margot's daughters. And in December, the baby would be born. Genevieve's half-sister or brother. She would need a friend, a sort of big sister.

How I needed to talk to Clay at this moment. How I wanted him to understand how sorry I was and how wrong I had been.

On the corner stood an old-fashioned pay phone. How many Rangers could there be in the Paris phone book? And how absurd that in all this time I hadn't learned his number?

I bit my lip, vowed not to cry.

Once I found, then dialed the number, the phone rang and rang. *Please*, I said, willing someone to pick up.

At last, someone did. It was a woman. His maverick mother, I felt sure. "Clay?" she said, talking over the barking Chihuahuas who I pictured sitting in a disorderly row at her feet. "I'm sorry, but he's still out cycling."

"Tell him Julie called," I said, hearing the catch in my voice. "Ask him to meet me at the Isle de la Cité as soon as he gets back? I'll be waiting, for as long as it takes."

"Oh, *the* Julie!" she said. "Of course I'll give him the message, but I don't expect him anytime soon. It might make more sense for him to call you. Perhaps tomorrow—"

"No, no, really," I interrupted. "I'll wait."

"Are you sure you're alright?" Barking started up in the background. "Nothing's happened?"

"Yes, I mean, I'm *fine*," I said, eager to get moving again. "I'll wait for him there. It doesn't matter how long it takes. He'll understand why."

"If you're sure," she said, the barking of the Chihuahuas growing louder. "You're really alright?"

"Yes, it's just that this is really important, okay?"

Adrenaline surged through me, and the streets blurred past, I reached the Isle of the Cité within the hour, breathless and sweaty. Absurdly, I searched the wrought iron benches, but the only other people here were a mother and a daughter, their hair that angelic pale blonde so rare in anyone over two. They were sharing triple scoops of ice cream, stain-making chocolate and what looked like pistachio—that they somehow managed to eat without making a mess.

What if he doesn't come? I asked, taunted still by the Clay of my dream, the absence, the breaking pottery like the shattering of the trust between us, Genevieve's plea.

He must come, I thought, then opened my sketchbook.

I drew the scene in front of me: the railing of the park, the Seine in the distance, and beyond that, the buildings of Paris. I put in the mother and her little girl, and then added my father and myself. The rhythm was absorbing, though it took everything I had to stay focused.

The bells of Notre Dame announced the hour. Five o'clock.

The wind ruffled the leaves on the trees, a sound so secret I stayed very still, as if there was an answer for me there. A bird flew overhead, and I gazed upward as it sliced the sky. Perhaps cycling was a little like flying. Again I thought of that evening, walking to the gallery, the birds over Notre Dame, the boundless freedom of their white flight.

What would Paris and its surrounding neighborhoods look like from the seat of a bike? Blurred with speed and the rush of air?

I pictured Clay that last night at the gallery, the fury and hurt in his face, the way his mouth twisted as he spoke, then turned away from me. I'd never wanted to be the source of such hurt; how was it I hadn't realized my actions would have consequences?

The mother and her daughter finished their cones and stood, and then the little girl shouted "Papa!" before running into the arms of a man carrying a briefcase. He scooped her into his arms, then joined the woman, and kissed her.

Beyond the wrought iron railing that surrounded this small island garden with its neat plantings of roses, the Seine was crowded by two barges chugging away from Notre Dame, sending forth muffled groans rather like freight trains' whistles. Seagulls soared through the air with the usual sound effects; and on the left side of the river, there was a carnival going on, its bells and chimes and drumbeats, as well as peals of laughter, floating across the Seine to where I sat taking in the distant glint of lights.

The woman gathered up her things, and then she and her husband and daughter walked away. I watched them go, followed their dwindling presence until they reached the mainland and stepped off the bridge.

I even let myself imagine that it was my own alternate life that I was watching, that other Julie in the parallel universe that one of my childhood friends believed in.

No, another voice cut in. *All we have is now.*

"Hey!"

I turned, my heart lifting, to find Clay still wearing his biking gear. "Your mother said you'd be gone for hours. Did you cut your ride short?"

"That's one way of looking at it." The tips of his ears crimsoned. "I blew out a tire on the Boulevard Haussmann before I was even out of the city, so I had to go home."

"I'm sorry," I said. "You're not hurt are you?"

"No." He sat down on the bench.

"I'm sorry," I said again, "not just about the bike."

His eyes held my own. "Sorry, huh?"

"Yes, about what happened at the gallery—all of it. I wish I could undo it."

He didn't say anything, just tip-tapped his heels together.

"Come on, Clay," I said. "Talk to me."

"I'm not sure I can or if I even want to."

"But you came," I said.

"I did," he said, as if the fact of his coming surprised him.

"Well then?" I said, hearing the hope in my voice.

"I want to be able to trust you, Julie," he said, with a seriousness I hadn't heard before, the kind of seriousness it would take to bicycle across France.

"You can trust me."

"Can I?" he said, his voice catching.

"Yes," I said, putting all I had into that single word. "You were right to call me self-absorbed. I was."

"I'd have to agree," he said.

I wanted to laugh, wanted to go back to how it usually was with us, but Clay's face stayed grave.

"Tell me this: that day at the Sorbonne when we kissed, and all those other times, holding hands at the Louvre, was that, was any of it real?"

"Yes," I said. "All of that was completely real. I don't know why I didn't hold onto that—I should have."

"You're right," he said, and at last he smiled. "You should have." He stared out at the water and perhaps beyond at the glinting lights of the carnival. My heart pummeled away, and I knew I was holding my breath, my eyes riveted on his face.

He turned to me, his freckles re-arranging themselves as he smiled. "Okay."

"Really?"

"Let's just say I believe in second chances."

I smiled back so hard my lips felt like they would crack, and we sat there staring at each other, until I said, "That drawing, the one of the Hotel de Ville?"

"What about it?"

"Where'd you hang it in your room? Or did you tear it down?"

"Above my desk," Clay said, "and no, I didn't tear it down. I couldn't do that—not to a work of art."

"Thanks," I said, reaching for his hand. The breath poured out of my lungs and then I drank it back in again. "I hoped you'd say that, especially now that I'm going to be here for another year."

"Madame Dupont?"

"Yeah, I'm going to work for her, learn art restoration; but I'll continue to live with Claire and Genevieve. They want me to stay. Claire asked me this morning. And Genevieve needs me, and I, well, I need her."

"I'm glad you figured that out."

"Me too."

"Well then," Clay said, "as I see it, there's only one thing to do."

"Really? What?"

"We'll have to get you a bike."

"I would absolutely love that."

He squeezed my hand, and I began to mentally draw him—the high, freckled stretch of his forehead, the sunny warmth of his cheeks, the upturned edges of his eyes.

When Luc kissed me, it had been like being submerged deep beneath the surface where I could hear the heartbeat of the ocean, a thrilling thing yes, though it carried with it the threat of drowning.

Now as Clay placed his hands on my shoulders, I breathed in the clean, soapy smell of him. American clean, boy after the bath clean. But it wasn't just a boyish cleanness. There was something pungent about the way he smelled, something earthy and delicious, and as his lips met mine, my passion startled me.

We continued to kiss, and I leaned into him, not the least bit surprised at how strong he was. I knew, then, that we would spend a lot of time kissing like this o   n park benches, in doorways, beneath historic archways while beyond us it rained; and yes, after tucking our bikes under a leafy horse chestnut tree or along the railing beside the Seine. We would have a whole year!

"Look," I heard someone say, as she passed. "Lovers."

"This is the City of Love," her companion said wistfully.

Carried back to that day at the flea market with Paul Henri, to the way the tourists had mistaken us for just that, this incredible lightness swept over me. I tried to think of something clever to say; but the only thing that came was either a cliché or far too obscure to make sense.

"How about that ice cream?" was all I could come up with.

"I thought you'd never ask." Keeping hold of my hand, Clay stood and pulled me to my feet.

"And afterwards I have something important I want to tell you. It's about my father."

Clay's face opened, his eyes expectant, bright. "You met him today, didn't you?"

"Yes," I said, my heart overflowing with all that I wanted to share.

"I had a feeling something had happened while I was out biking, an odd knowing, that I had to get back, and then the tire—"

Marie France's *serendipity* came flooding back—maybe this was fate.

"Julie," Clay said. "You alright?"

"Yes," I said, "I am, I really am. At last."

He reached out, stroked my cheek.

"There's something more I need to tell you: after I left my father, it was you I wanted to talk to."

I thought back to the story of Eros and Psyche... Had my search led me to this place—to this person—with whom I began my stay here? Serendipity is all about discovering something absolutely necessary, something you didn't even know you were searching for, a sort of unplanned or unknown quest—

"Oh, Julie," Clay whispered into my hair, holding me close.

"I was so worried you wouldn't come," I said, my arms encircling his waist.

"I'm here," he said, kissing me again, very gently. "And I hope you've figured out by now, I'm a pretty good listener."

About the Author

Jacqueline Kolosov's young adult novels include *Along the Way, The Red Queen's Daughter, A Sweet Disorder* and *Grace from China*. She has written several books of poetry, including *Modigliani's Muse* and *Memory of Blue*. An art lover and traveler, she has spent a great deal of time in the City of Light. Originally from Chicago, Jacqueline now lives in windy west Texas with her family and a menagerie of animals, including a Spanish mare, three incorrigible dogs, a tuxedo cat, two guinea pigs, and a very fluffy rabbit. Visit her at www.jacquelinekolosovreads.com.